BLOOD

&

HUNGER

THE VANESSA KENSLEY SERIES

STEPHANIE MARKS

RED DAGGER

Copyright © 2015 by Stephanie Marks
All rights reserved.
ISBN: 978-0-9940667-0-1

This is a work of fiction. Names, characters, places, and incidents are the product of the author's imagination or are used fictitiously. Any resemblance to actual persons, living or dead, events, or locales is entirely coincidental.

OTHER BOOKS BY STEPHANIE MARKS

SILVERLAKE CITY STORIES

HIDDEN FALLS
HUNTING CRIMSON

THE CLAN MACGREGOR SERIES

CLAIMED BY THE HIGHLAND WOLF
TAKEN BY THE HIGHLAND WOLF
CRAVED BY THE HIGHLAND WOLF

For my mom.

ACKNOWLEDGEMENTS

Thank you to my fabulous editor, Teri, and to all of my friends and family for their unwavering support.

"No power in the 'verse can stop me."
- River Tam, *Firefly*

CHAPTER ONE

I stretched and poured my second cup of coffee. It's not that I even really like coffee that much, but at 7 o'clock in the morning, after only four hours of sleep, I pretty much needed to find a way to get it pumped into my bloodstream intravenously. I paused with my croissant sandwich halfway to my mouth, listening intently for any sound of life coming from my bedroom. Apparently, my guest didn't understand the socially acceptable response for, "I have an early meeting tomorrow," is to get the hell out, not to roll over and *pass out*. Setting down my mug, I wrapped the sash on my red silk kimono robe more tightly before heading down the hall.

"Phil... Paul... ummm, Peter?"
"Eric," he corrected me groggily before rolling over. He pulled the pillow over his face to block out the morning. Right, as if my blackout blinds allowed any light through.

Hmmm, maybe he was trying to block out my voice?

"Right, Eric," Really, *Eric?* I wasn't even at the right end of the alphabet with this one, "Look, you've got to go."

Sliding his shaggy brown head out from under the pillow he flashed a sly smile at me before his eyes landed on the swell of my breasts beneath my robe. His gaze trailed down my body as he admired my long, tan legs.

"Or you could always just come back to bed and join me," he replied, while patting the empty spot on the bed beside him. He sat up and the blankets fell away to reveal a nice, smooth six-pack. Firm and hairless, it was the feel of those abs the night before that made my choice to bring him home so easy.

"As much fun as it was to tear up the Egyptian cotton with you last night, I just don't have any time right now. I have people to meet, and... well, you know, places to be." I walked over to the bed and threw back the rest of the covers. The light from my hall poured into the bedroom, giving me a full view of him and revealing how much he preferred his idea to mine, but I had my fill last night, and really didn't feel like any leftovers this morning. "Out," I announced, pointing towards the door before walking around the room and collecting whatever articles of clothing I could find for him. "Shirt, boxers, socks. There we are; good to go," I grabbed his pants off the corner of my dresser and pushed him, using both hands on his back, towards the front door.

"Thanks for the great time, Kyle."

"It's Eric."

"That's what I said. Have a great day, I'll catch you later," I finished, giving him a final shove before slamming the door. I leaned my forehead against it with a sigh.

"Ummm..." Eric called back through the door, "my pants?"

I looked down at the pair of jeans I still held in my hand. *Crap*. Opening the door, I threw them at him before quickly retreating inside.

No matter how many times it happened, I still hated the morning after a one-night-stand. Just because it was a necessity didn't make it any easier either. It was either sex or starvation, and what sane woman would actually choose to starve herself to death? So what if I have to keep working on my *morning after* routine? I'd have to do it later though, because I still hadn't finished my coffee and had to get my ass to work. Ah, the glamorous life of a succubus, where the fun just keeps on coming.

"Oh, my God! Did you see the paper this morning?" Karen hissed over the top of our shared beige cubicle wall. Her giant, flaming mass of curly hair was held up off her neck in a banana clip, as barely restrained as her excitement.

"Nope, didn't get a chance, why?"

"What do you mean, 'why'?" she whisper-shrieked. She began looking around for our supervisor, Mr. Mooney, lest he bust us for the grievous offence of wasting company time, *again*.

"Why do you think? Another body was found last night!

Just like the others, with no head! Silverlake has its very own deranged serial killer. And they still have no clue who he might be. He could be anywhere. He could be anyone!"

"He could be Mr. Mooney," I said. We craned our necks to look down the hall at his closed office door for a few moments, in complete silence, before breaking out into peals of laughter.

"Oh, my God, Vanessa, could you even imagine? Mr. Mooney, a psycho killer! How could he even manage to hold onto a weapon, his hands are always so damp!"

We snickered at the idea of our supervisor trying to grasp a knife long enough to properly hack and slash when I saw the door to his office open. "Red alert, red alert," I mumbled, frantically waving my hand to tell Karen to get back in her seat.

Opening up a random file in my email inbox, I started banging away blindly at the keys while keeping my head down and my eyes fastened on the screen. If I had to hear one more lecture on the "perils of mismanaging company time," I might have to introduce him to the perils of the pointy end of my ballpoint pen.

A presence hovered at the corner of my cubicle for a moment before clearing its throat. Continuing to hammer away at my keyboard, I pretended to be working so intently that I didn't notice. *If I can't see it, it can't see me. Or is that just for the boogeyman?* My eyes surreptitiously slid down to my left to see a pair of sad, nondescript, brown loafers that were polished within an inch of their life. *Close enough.*

"Ms. Kensley?" my skin crawled at the sound of Mr. Mooney's nasally voice and I repressed a shudder.

"Yes, Mr. Mooney?" I looked up sweetly, my eyes trailing from his sad loafers to his ill-fitting, tan pants that were a disturbingly similar color to the depressing office carpet. I wished he would hurry up and get on with whatever he wanted to say so that I could get back to my work without fear of contracting a fatal case of the cooties. Was unsexiness catching? If so, I was screwed.

"I'm still waiting for a copy of that Mitchley report I asked you for yesterday. Is it ready yet?"

"Almost, Mr. Mooney, I'm just returning an email marked urgent. I'll have the report to you before lunch," I shot him a bright smile, although it may have come off more as a grimace. Succubus or not, I've always had a problem wasting my charm on people that are prone to inducing nausea.

"Hmmm," he replied, pursing his lips and not-so-subtly glancing down my top. "I'll expect it by one o'clock then. And, Vanessa?"

"Yes, Mr. Mooney?"

"Do try to better manage your time," he replied, looking down his long, slim nose at me over his glasses.

Biting the inside of my bottom lip, I nodded and returned to my computer screen, while he continued his rounds as dungeon torture master.

My phone rang the moment he got around the corner.

"Thank you for calling Shuster Bramble and Brown, this is Vanessa."

"Sooo the girls and I are going to the Roxy tonight to get this weekend started right," came Karen's voice on the other end of the line. I looked at the screenful of gibberish I had just written, and then at the computer clock, which read 9:30 AM, before putting my head down on my desk and closing my eyes.

"I'm so in."

The Roxy was one of those great clubs that knew exactly what it was: dark, loud and filled with people trying to get laid. It was well known for its cheap shots and laid back atmosphere. I would have lived there if I could.

Swaying my denim-clad hips, I made my way to the front of the line. I pressed my hand lightly on the chest of the bouncer at the door. Looking him in the eye without blinking, I gave him a small smile before walking past him and into the club without paying. I completely ignored the angry protests of the people waiting in line that had been standing out there for over half an hour to get in. On my *Top 5* list of succu-perks, I would definitely have to include line-jumping and free drinks. Not that I abused my power or anything, what little of it I had, but with the high cost of rent these days, who had extra cash to waste on Jager-bombs?

The smell of stale beer and sweat assaulted my nostrils

as I entered. I found the girls off to one side of the dance floor. They were crammed into a booth and scanning the crowd. Waving to them, I wound my way through the mass of half naked, gyrating flesh and counted backwards from fifty under my breath. The first few minutes for me in places like this was always a bit of a head rush. All the tension and sexual energy pulsing through the air was like knocking back three shots of tequila in a row. A total rush with a side effect: it hurt like a swift kick to the gut. I kept walking and counting, trying to stay focused on making it to our table, instead of sticking my tongue in the mouth of the next person who happened to brush against me. There would be more than enough time for that later.

"Weekend!" I yelled when I got to the table.

"Whoo!" They all cheered back, raising their glasses in the air.

"I ordered you a Crown and ginger," Karen yelled over the booming bass. She slid my drink to the end of the table towards me.

"Thanks, Kare."

"I heard about your theory on Mooney," said Colleen, a short, pert blonde. Colleen was everyone's friend, and you just had to love her. I was pretty sure there was a law written about it somewhere. She was the sweetest person I knew and I loved her like a sister.

"Is it wrong that I can see him as the killer? Like, really, really see it?" She leaned in closer to us, the dim illumination accentuating the red flush of her cheeks. "I mean, he's always so cranky and rigid. He never talks about anything, but work, and no one knows anything about him. I wouldn't be surprised at all if it really did turn out to be him."

"Umm, Colleen, how many drinks have you had?" I asked.

Colleen looked down, momentarily puzzled at her empty drink glass. "Two, I think, no, three."

We all laughed. "God, you are such a lightweight," I giggled.

"Oh, please," Sophia drawled, tossing her long, sleek, black hair over her shoulder. "Mooney a killer? I think you've been wearing your ponytail too tight, Colleen."

"Sophia, don't be mean!" Karen jabbed her in the side.

"I'm not! Seriously though, how can she really believe that dickless wonder would have the balls to kill one person, let alone, go on a murderous rampage for weeks?"

"I don't know," I said. "Maybe it's from all those bitches calling him things like 'dickless wonder' all his life? Maybe he finally snapped."

Sophia twisted in her seat to glare at me. "Did you just call me a bitch?" she asked, her eyes flashing.

"What? Moi? Call you a bitch?" I opened my eyes wide and pointed at my chest dramatically. "Never! I believe the proper term to address one such as yourself is 'Her High and Mighty Queen Bitchcakes'."

She sniffed and turned back to her drink. "And don't you forget it. May all you lesser bitches bow before me."

"Come on, you guys," Karen cajoled as we laughed, "enough about creepy murderers and crappy bosses; I wanna dance!"

On the dance floor, I let the music and the crowd's energy wash over me in waves. Raising my arms in the air, I rolled my hips and undulated with the rhythm, letting my head fall back as my cares from the day floated away. Slender arms wrapped around me as a flat chest pressed against my back. Looking down at the arms, I saw a tattoo of an eagle's head on the right forearm above the words, *Live Free*.

"Hey there," my dance partner yelled in my ear. Ignoring him, I kept dancing although I didn't move from his arms.

"You're really hot. What's your name?" he tried again. I just smiled and shrugged, pretending that I couldn't hear him over the music.

"I'm Jason!"

Turning in his arms, I put my hands in his hair and pulled his head down so that my mouth was close to his ear. "Jason, less talking, more dancing," I yelled over the music before pushing his head away. I went back to swinging my hips to the music. A shocked hiss escaped me as he grabbed my upper arm too tightly. His fingers dug into my flesh when he pulled me back around to face him.

"Look, I'm just trying to get to know you better. Isn't that what you chicks always want? To talk and shit?" he sneered.

I looked down at the hand gripping my arm, then up at

him. "That's great, Jason, but I really don't want to get to know you. Now let go of my arm."

"Why are you being such a bitch? You think you're all kinds of hot shit, huh?"

Grabbing the front of his shirt with my free hand, I pulled him towards me and stared into his eyes. "Leave me the hell alone!" I yelled before shoving him backwards as hard as I could.

Losing his footing, he toppled into the people behind him, landing on the dance floor with an audible thud. His face twisted in a sneer as everyone around us stared and scoffed at his dramatic and very public rejection. Lifting my middle finger toward him, I turned on my heels and walked away.

A few hours later, I was well into my sixth drink and back at the table. I started doing shots with the girls.

"To us," Colleen toasted. "May we always have crappy jobs to keep our friendship alive!" Downing the shot, we grabbed the next glass.

"To the girls," yelled Karen. "May we always have crappy love lives to keep the others entertained!" Throwing back that shot, we swiftly moved on to the next.

"To you losers," joked Sophia. "May you always make me look this good!"

"Boo!" we jeered, throwing our cocktail napkins at her. She held up her hands in surrender before trying to duck under the table.

"Okay, okay. May you always be around to put up with me. God knows, nobody else will."

"Here, here!" I agreed. "And to my ladies," I said, picking up the last glass, "may we always... oh, crap!" Slapping a hand over my mouth, I ran towards the bathrooms, and the sound of their laughter followed me. It wasn't until I saw the urinals that I realized I was in the wrong one.

Slamming into one of the stalls, I looked down to find a headless body on the floor. It was wrapped around the toilet. One arm was flung out with an eagle head tattoo above the words *Live Free*. I froze, feeling completely paralyzed before throwing up all over the stall.

CHAPTER TWO

Staring down at the glass of ice water in my hand, I watched a water droplet slide down the condensation on the side of the glass. The manager's office at the Roxy seemed eerily quiet after all the confusion. The club was cleared of stragglers after the police showed up; and now, the only people left were the few witnesses still needing to be interviewed.

The first half hour remained a complete blur. Whether it was from shock, or due to the alcohol still coursing through my system was a complete toss-up at this point. After nearly stumbling over the body, I rushed to my purse to find my cell phone and called 911. I remember the girls asking me what was wrong, but I couldn't get any words out. Then suddenly, there was screaming, so much screaming. Someone else must have come across the body in the bathroom. After that, it was just chaos with people running around, desperate to get out of the building, and no one could believe it. The serial killer had been right there, mixing in with everyone, and no one had a clue. It's amazing how quickly a freaky story on the TV, or featured in the news, can suddenly become so... real.

Ms. Kensley?" said a handsome, blonde man that entered the office, closing the door behind him. A few inches over six feet tall, and broad through the shoulders, he looked like he hadn't slept in days. His large, gray eyes were dull and had dark circles around them. He rubbed his stubble-covered jaw before introducing himself.

"I'm Detective Hache. I understand you've had quite a night."

I looked at him and nodded, my throat too dry to talk. I hastily took sip of water and it went down the wrong way so I started coughing and sputtering. Alarmed, Detective Hache rushed over and pounded me repeatedly on the back.

"I'm okay," I coughed, waving him away, "I'm okay."

"Are you sure?"

"Yeah," I coughed again and wiped a tear from my eye. "Sorry, what was your name?"

"I'm Detective Hache, I just want to ask you a few questions about what happened tonight."

"I don't really know anything," I replied while swaying in my seat. "I just found him there." I shuddered visibly at the memory and wrapped my arms around myself.

"Why don't you just walk me through what happened to the best of your memory?"

I looked down at my shoes and the room swirled, so I took a few deep breaths, trying not to slur my words. *Crap, were those drinks doubles or triples?*

"It all happened really quickly. The girls and I were drinking, taking shots and making toasts. I had a lot to drink and not enough to eat today, so I, ummm, I got sick." I glanced at him, but looked away quickly, totally embarrassed. "So I ran to the bathroom. When I opened a stall, he was there on the floor."

"Did you mean to go into the men's washroom?"

"No! I just ran through the first door I saw. I didn't even know it was the wrong one until I got inside."

"Did you know the victim?"

"No."

He raised his eyebrows at me and looked down at his notes. "Apparently, you were observed earlier and said to be fighting with the victim, is that right?"

"Oh, well, yeah, I did," I nodded. Closing my eyes to block out the swirling room, I breathed deeply through my nose. I really needed to hold my head still.

"But you didn't know him?" he asked, sounding skeptical.

"Well, no, I didn't *know* him. I mean, sure, I danced with him, until he turned into a total asshole and grabbed me, so..."

"He grabbed you?" Hache frowned as he jotted down a note.

"Yeah, he grabbed my arm really hard and wouldn't let

me go, so I shoved him. He fell over and I walked away." I shrugged.

"So you had some problems with this guy?"

"Yeah, but it was no big deal." I shrugged again and took a sip of water.

"No big deal? Wouldn't most women consider having a strange man get a bit rough with them a big deal? Not to mention, a bit scary?"

"Maybe they would, but I'm not most women. I can take care of myself, and I knew I could handle him."

"Is that what you did then, Vanessa?" Detective Hache walked over to me and looked me straight in the eye. "Did you *handle* him?"

I sat there, blinking at him for a few minutes before answering, "Are you serious?" I tried to focus on his face, but it was all blurry around the edges. "You really think I did that? Right! And I just stashed his head inside my purse?" I shook my head and laughed. It wasn't funny, and I knew it; what happened was horrible, but I was still really drunk. This guy had to be joking.

"No, I know it wasn't you, but I have to ask," he admitted before backing away from me and leaning against the wall. He crossed his arms over his chest. I followed the movement, enjoying the way it emphasized his biceps. Oh, God! I couldn't be getting hungry now! I was too drunk and too freaked out to feed.

"Is there anything else about tonight that you remember or can think of? Anyone that looked suspicious, or out of place?"

"No, sorry. I came. I drank. I tripped over a dead guy."

Banging his hand against the wall, he jabbed a finger at me, saying, "You know, you seem pretty cavalier about all of this. A man is dead. Whoever killed him took his head; and by tomorrow, his family will know, and their world will be ripped into tiny pieces. You could at least show a little respect," he snapped.

I looked at the wall above his head, avoiding his gaze. He was right, of course, and I was making a complete ass of myself, but he didn't have to be such a jerk about it.

"Look, I'm drunk. Like, *really drunk*, I just want to go home and pass out, okay? This whole thing seems pretty damn surreal to me and freaky as hell. So excuse me if I crack a joke or two, instead of throwing myself, weeping, into your arms." I hopped to my feet, only stumbling a little when the room actually tilted and I had to grab for the desk.

"Shit!" Detective Hache appeared and put a hand under my elbow, helping me straighten up. "You really are drunk," he remarked.

"Didn't I just say that!?" I snarled. "What did you think? I just go throwing up in men's bathrooms for the fun of it?" I pulled my arm out of his firm grip, and took a couple of shaky steps towards the door. "What an idiot," I mumbled.

"What was that, Ms. Kensley?"

"I asked if we were done here? I really want to go to bed and I don't have anything else to tell you."

Frowning, he reached into his wallet and pulled out a business card, saying, "If you remember anything else when you sober up, please give me a call?"

Taking his card, I managed a little salute before leaving the office to find my friends.

As the last person to be dropped off in the cab, I was grateful for the few minutes of silence. The girls badgered me during the entire ride for all the juicy details of what happened with Detective Hache. It was not something I really wanted to dwell on, so I relished finally having a few minutes of peace.

After paying the cabby, I stepped out onto the sidewalk in front of my condo building and searched through my small purse for my keys. All of a sudden, I felt a prickling on the back of my neck. Looking up from my bag, I spun around and scanned the street behind me. I couldn't see anyone in either direction, but the uneasy feeling of being watched remained with me. I dug through my purse again until I found my keys and ran up the front steps. Hurrying to let myself into the building, I made sure to pull the door tightly closed behind me before rushing for the elevator.

Getting off on my floor, I walked as quickly down the hall as I could without breaking into a full-on run. I entered my apartment and flipped the deadbolt behind me before looking out the spyhole, but of course, no one was there.

Stretching my arms above my head, I cracked one of my eyes open before slamming it shut again. The morning sun's rays streamed into my room, practically searing a layer off my cornea.

"Damn it!" I forgot to close my blackout blinds last night.

I rolled over in bed and pulled the blankets above my head, effectively blocking out the morning sun. Unfortunately, it did nothing to muffle the irritatingly incessant chirping of the stupid bird outside my window. If it didn't shut up immediately, I would hunt it down and break its neck! The thought of broken necks reminded me of the night before, and I rolled over, groaning into my pillow. *What a terrible way to end a great night out.* Pulling the covers back slowly, I gingerly opened my eyes and let them adjust to the light. *Oh God! No drink in the world was worth this kind of pain! What the hell was I thinking?* Throwing on an oversized t-shirt, I zombie-shuffled my way into the kitchen, searching for something to wash the cotton balls out of my mouth with. All I wanted to do was put the last twenty-four hours far behind me.

I opened up my windows to let some fresh air into the apartment. The heat outside was still pleasant, not yet high enough to be oppressive, and I wanted to enjoy it. It wouldn't be long before I had to lock myself inside with the air conditioning cranked up to freezing. I pulled a large glass tumbler down from the cupboard and grabbed the pitcher of apple juice from the fridge just as I heard a scream that came from the hallway.

"Oh, what the bloody hell is it now?" Running to the front door, I threw it open and rushed outside. At least, I tried to rush outside. Actually, I took two steps before I tripped over the body that was lying across my doorway.

"No no no no no no no!" I moaned, closing my eyes and counting to five before glancing back to see if it were still there. "Oh God, oh God, oh God!" This time, I closed my eyes and counted to ten. *Please, oh please, let this be some sort of post traumatic hallucination.* But when I reopened my eyes, the body lay there still, right in front of my door. Her brown eyes were wide open as she stared at nothing. The blood from a wide gash in her throat had formed a large puddle on the floor.

Jumping onto my feet, I ignored the growing crowd in the hall as I ran back inside to grab my purse. Upending it on the counter, I searched frantically through the contents until I found Detective Hache's crumpled card. I smoothed it out with shaking hands and took a deep breath before dialing his number.

"Hache here."

"Detective Hache? It's Vanessa, I need your help!" I yelled into the phone.

"Vanessa?"

"Vanessa Kensley! From last night? Seriously!"

"Of course, Vanessa, what's wrong?"

"There's a body!"

"What body?"

"Get your ass over here. There's a body in my doorway!"

"Shit. Call 911. What's your address? I'll be right there."

The cops were everywhere, swarming the halls and knocking on doors, trying to get some leads, but after hearing their frustrated whispers, they obviously hadn't gotten very far.

"I made you some tea," Detective Hache said softly. I accepted the steaming mug he passed to me and gave him a grateful smile. He looked even rougher than he did last night. The ends of his hair were sticking up all over the place like he constantly kept running his hands through it. He was also a lot hotter than I remembered. Okay, so some parts of last night were a bit blurry, but you'd think I would have remembered someone that looked like him. *Hmmm, maybe I should have thrown my weeping self into his arms.*

"Thank you; why don't you have a seat?" I offered, pushing one of the chairs away from the table with my foot.

"Thanks," he turned to look at me, and his stormy gray eyes were full of sympathy. I felt my stomach clench. *Whoa! Down, girl!* Shaking my head, I looked away, I had to refocus my thoughts. *Now was so not the time for a snack.*

"Look, Vanessa, you've had a really brutal couple of days, but I need you to work with me here. Can you think of anyone that might want to hurt you?"

"No."

"Are you sure? Ex-boyfriends, ex-bosses, anyone that might be holding a grudge?"

"No, I can't think of anyone. I've had the same job for years, and I don't date."

He paused, looking me over from head to toe. After calling the police, I threw on a pair of jeans and a tank top to avoid getting stuck without my pants when they showed up. This day was turning out bad enough without getting trapped in my condo with a bunch of cops and being interrogated in my underwear.

"You don't date, at all?" he asked skeptically.

"No, I don't." I glared at him. "Is that a problem?"

"I just find it hard to believe; that's all."

"And why is that?"

"Well, I mean, come on," he coughed and shrugged, "you look like a girl that does her fair share of dating."

I crossed my arms and legs, leaning back in my chair slowly, and raised my eyebrow at his comment. I just waited.

"No, I mean, you're attractive, so you probably, I mean, you wouldn't have a problem finding…" He stopped and tried again. "It wouldn't be hard for you to… shit." He closed his eyes and groaned.

"Yeah, you should probably just shut up now. No, I don't date, so you can cross ex-boyfriends-with-a-grudge off your list." *One-night-stands, on the other hand, would have filled three of his notebooks; but what were the chances it was really one of them?*

"Right."

"I was wondering if it was maybe, the same guy from last night. At the club?"

"What would make you think that?" he asked slowly.

"Maybe because I found that body last night, then I talked to you, and then, when I got home, I felt like I was being watched, Now, this morning, I find a body left at my door!"

"Wait, you were being watched last night?"

"Yes. Well, no, I don't know, it was all super creepy and I was probably just drunk and still freaking out from finding that guy in the club. But when I got dropped off last night, I swear, I could feel someone watching me." I shuddered at the memory and took another sip of tea.

"Why didn't you mention that before?"

"Maybe because I forgot about it in all the trauma of tripping over another dead body this morning?" I snapped, "I forgot, okay? It wasn't really the foremost thing on my mind."

"Right, I'm sorry," he said as he tapped his pen on the table and looked around the room. "This one isn't like the others though. It seems a lot more personal. The victim was left right in front of your door."

"Like a cat leaves dead mice for its master," I whispered.

"Besides the placement, she still has her head attached. It's a completely different MO, so it's probably not the same guy. Look, Vanessa, I'm not trying to scare you, but I want you to be extra careful for a little while, okay? You know, don't go anywhere alone at night, carry pepper spray—"

"Don't take candy from strangers?" I interrupted wryly, but he just frowned at me. "Sorry, reflex; but don't worry, I'm taking this seriously. I'll be careful, I promise."

"And if you feel like someone is watching you, or following you, be sure to find a safe place that's filled with lots of people and call me right away. It doesn't matter if you think it's nothing, or just your imagination, you call me, understand?"

"I promise I'll call you."

Another officer from the CSI crew came over and tapped Detective Hache on the shoulder. "Hey Hache, we're finishing up here."

"Thanks, I'll see you in a bit," he nodded.

The other officer left and Detective Hache turned back to me. "Do you have someone that you can call? It might help to spend a little time with a friend instead of staying here alone tonight."

"Yeah, I can call someone." I lifted my mug to take a sip, but put it back down quickly when my hand started to shake. Closing my eyes, I let out a breath, and said, "This was all a coincidence, you know, and has nothing to do with me."

I felt a warm, comforting pressure as the detective took my hand. "You're probably right, but I still want you to be careful, okay?"

I bit my lip and nodded, "Okay."

Waking up from my nap, I saw that the sun had already gone down. After the police left, I worked myself to exhaustion. I scrubbed every square inch of my apartment in an attempt to keep my mind busy. The volume on my stereo was still turned up loud enough for it to blast through every room just to drown out the emptiness. I grabbed the remote and turned the volume down as I picked up my phone. I scrolled through the numbers until I found Colleen's; I knew that she would offer a sympathetic ear. I started to type a text message to invite her over when I felt the familiar prickling on the back of my neck.

Dropping the phone on the counter, I spun around to face the empty kitchen window. Rushing over, I looked outside, but there was no one there. *Of course, there's no one there, you idiot, you're four floors up.* Hitting pause on the stereo, I went back to grab my phone. It was definitely time to call Colleen; I was starting to go crazy.

CHAPTER THREE

Two weeks after discovering the two dead bodies, my life, thankfully, returned to normal, with nothing more exciting than an occasional dive behind a cubicle partition to avoid running into Mooney at work. But while I wasn't tripping over any more dead bodies strewn around the place, the Silverlake police discovered three more victims. The reports of new killings were getting more frequent, and the police department didn't seem any closer to figuring out who was behind it.

Setting down my glass of red wine on the bathroom counter, I admired myself in the full-length mirror. My hair flowed loosely over my shoulders as I adjusted the hem of my single-shouldered, black dress, the body-hugging fabric ending a good six inches above my knees. The blue of my large, almond-shaped eyes almost glowed with hunger, and I had to squeeze my eyes shut as another cramp hit me in my solar plexus, making my cravings even more intense.

STEPHANIE MARKS

Being so busy at work lately, I hadn't taken the time to feed in the past two weeks, and my absentmindedness was definitely catching up with me. The faster I found a man, the better, and the sooner I could end the pain before it got any worse.

~

Leaving the apartment, I decided to walk the three blocks to the neighbourhood bar. Going all the way downtown could just as well have been across the country at the moment; it was way too far away. The night was cool and the refreshing breeze helped me focus my energy. I couldn't fail at feeding tonight; otherwise, things would get really ugly tomorrow.

"Well, look at you, love," a lilting, British accent sang right out of the darkness.

I jumped and stumbled a bit, since the man in front of me literally came out of nowhere. The street lamp behind him cast his face in shadow, but I could make out his tall, slim frame.

"Don't you just look downright delicious?" His voice flowed over me like warm honey, and I closed my eyes, letting the sound of it caress my skin.

"I could say the same about you," I replied before stepping towards him. I tried to ignore the cramping as I focused my energy around him. All I wanted to do was get him home.

"I could smell you from blocks away," he continued as he stepped out of the shadows. I was finally able to make out his face. He was young, late twenties, with bright, emerald-green eyes and short, sandy-blonde hair. His pale skin contrasted with the black turtleneck sweater he wore. *Who in their right mind wears a turtleneck in June?*

"Why don't you give me a little taste?" he stared into my eyes while pulling me into his arms. I melted against him as he took my face in his hand, tilting it to the side.

Oh, thank God for making this so easy. The cramps were becoming unbearable, being so close to getting what I needed. Just a little taste would take the edge off the pain. Then all of a sudden, I saw a flash of fangs.

"What the fu—!" My question turned into a scream as a sharp pain pierced my neck.

"Get off, get off, get off!" I hit him repeatedly in the shoulder while trying to pull away. He reared back, sputtering, and spitting my blood out onto the cement.

Slapping my hand to my neck, I took a step back, and screamed, "What the hell!"

He shouted, "What the hell are you?"

"Me!? You want to know what I am? You just bit me!"

"Yes, well, you never would have known if you were human," he replied.

"What? So this is my fault? Look at my neck! If I bleed to death, you are so screwed!"

Before I saw him move, he was standing right in front of me. I inhaled swiftly and tried to back away, but he grabbed my shoulders and pulled me closer.

"What. Are. You?" he growled.

"You tell me first," I snapped. I couldn't believe I was arguing with the man that just attacked me, but I was so hungry and sore that my mind refused to wrap itself around what just happened. Sure, okay, I was a succubus; but I was still basically human, just a little, enhanced, that's all. But this? This was over the top.

"You know exactly what I am," he replied as he looked me up and down before leaning closer, and inhaling deeply to consume my scent. "But you? You're a mystery, aren't you? You smell almost familiar. Almost," he trailed off, letting me go and circling me while examining me from all sides, "but not quite. I know someone that would be very interested in meeting you."

Pulling my hand away from my neck, he licked his thumb and rubbed it over the two puncture marks.

"Eww!" I shrieked, pulling away.

He chuckled deeply and stepped back, saying, "It will stop the bleeding."

Lifting my hand to my neck, I gingerly touched the sore spot, although the pain was quickly fading away.

"Oh," I responded lamely.

"Now let's go."

"Oh, no way! You have got to be kidding. I'm not going anywhere with you."

"And what makes you think you have any choice in the matter?"

"What makes you think I don't?" I retorted stubbornly, crossing my arms and planting my feet. "Do you really think that I would just go who-knows-where with the psychotic man that just tried to rip my throat out?"

"If I intended to rip your throat out, you would have known it by no longer having a throat."

"Right," I drawled, "I think I will stand by my choice. I don't go anywhere with a bloodthirsty psycho." Turning around, I started heading back in the direction of my home. I would have to deal with the consequences of missing my feeding later. All of a sudden, I found myself off the ground and over his shoulder.

"What the hell do you think you're doing?" I yelled, banging my fists against his back.

"I told you: there is someone that will be very interested in meeting you."

"Well, I'm not interested in meeting anyone, so you can just PUT. ME. DOWN. Oof!"

He dropped me on the pavement beside an electric blue sports car. Then he deftly opened the door and shoved me inside, slamming the door behind me. He was around the other side and sitting in the driver seat before I even had a chance to try to get my door open again.

"I'm not going to hurt you, so why don't you relax?"

I looked at him skeptically and practically threw myself against the seat. Gunning the motor, he pulled away from the sidewalk with a loud squeal from the tires.

∽

Half an hour later, we were well beyond the city limits and following a narrow, private road. Trees surrounded the car on either side, making the inside of the small car seem even more intimate. My cramps had become harder to ignore and my head felt as if someone kept repeatedly taking a hammer to it. Sneaking a glance over at the driver's side I quickly looked out the window before sinking down lower in my seat.

A few minutes later, the narrow road opened up to a large, circular driveway, the center of which featured a huge fountain. Sitting up, I stared at the giant mansion where we just arrived. It was a sprawling, red brick manor, and the white, double door entrance was flanked by four columns and countless windows that overlooked the front courtyard. I had never come so close to such a magnificent home.

As we walked up to the front of the house, the doors opened for us and we stepped inside into a massive entrance hall, teeming with people. A few looked over, noticing us, but dismissing us just as quickly before going back to their conversations.

Taking my elbow, he led me out of the entrance hall and through a side doorway. We continued to pass through rooms until we eventually came to a large sitting area. Everyone in the room was unbelievably beautiful, yet eerily pale. A gorgeous woman with flaming red hair came towards us. She seemed to glide across the room instead of taking actual footsteps, and everyone turned to watch her graceful approach. I felt like a dirty, little urchin in her presence. It wasn't very often that any woman could make me feel so utterly inadequate just by being in the same room as I.

"William," she said, and her silky voice came out as almost a purr. "What have you brought me? A new friend? Wherever did you find her?"

William let go of my arm and inclined his head towards the woman. "I found her when I was out hunting, Elizabeth. My glamour didn't work on her. She smelled delicious, but she tasted... wrong," He shrugged, "I thought that you might know what she is."

Elizabeth looked me over and smiled, "What's your name?"

Glancing from her to William and back again, I was not sure what to do, but honesty seemed like the best approach for now. I really didn't relish the feeling of anyone else's fangs sinking into my neck at the moment.

"Vanessa." I raised my chin and looked her directly in the eye. "My name is Vanessa."

"Vanessa," Elizabeth repeated as she wrapped her arms around me in a tight embrace. Then she stepped back with a huge smile on her face and said, "Welcome, cousin."

I just stood there for a few moments, staring at Elizabeth, my mouth wide open before I managed to find my voice again, however William spoke first.

"Cousin? What do you mean, Elizabeth?" Elizabeth smiled wider and clapped her hands together.

"It's wonderful, really, and not surprising that you wouldn't have known her for what she is. In my own life, I have only met three others." Turning to me, she smiled before continuing, "Our beautiful Vanessa, here, is a succubus." Several sharp inhales from a few of the occupants in the room accompanied their looks of confusion before the others started murmuring among themselves.

"How do you know what I am? No one else knows." I narrowed my eyes at her and looked her over cautiously.

"Like I said, you're our cousin."

Exasperated, and still trying to cope with my hunger cravings, my patience was rapidly fading.

"But what does that mean?" I nearly exploded.

The whole room went silent, but I didn't care. My cramps had lessened, but now, my head was killing me, and it was getting harder for me to keep it together.

Elizabeth came closer and examined my face. "Are you all right, my dear? You don't look well."

William took a step closer to me, and I jumped back, holding up my hands in front of me. "Don't touch me."

"Don't be stupid," he said as he took another step towards me. "I'm not going to hurt you."

"No," I replied as I shook my head, "but I might hurt you."

Pausing, he turned towards Elizabeth for guidance.

"Oh, you poor thing," she cooed, "you must be hungry."

Looking at the floor, I nodded and slowly lowered my hands, but moved a step further away from William.

"I was looking for someone when William, here,

appeared out of nowhere and decided to get all fangy with me. The... umm," I paused because it felt strange to actually talk to people about that. "My cravings had already started getting pretty bad, but I've been so busy lately that I shelved it until the last minute. But my hunger has grown too strong now; I left it much too long." I was starting to get lightheaded and my breathing became labored.

"William, help her," Elizabeth commanded.

"No, I can't," I protested. I didn't care that he bit me, but I never wanted to hurt another person over my feedings again.

"Don't worry, you won't hurt him. William, what are you waiting for? Get on with it."

Shrugging, William presented himself right in front of me, but didn't touch me.

"Are you sure about this?" I asked.

The corner of his mouth went up in a half smile and he winked before replying, "Ready when you are—"

The words were barely out before I wrapped my arm around his neck and dragged his mouth down onto mine. *Finally*. Prying his mouth open with my tongue, I inhaled deeply. His hand fisted in my hair and the other one wrapped more tightly around me as I satisfied my hunger at last.

The more I took, the more I wanted, and I deepened our kiss, extricating the energy from him until I felt grounded again. Pulling my mouth from his, I shoved him away, panting temporarily. After another moment or two, the hunger finally began to subside, fully sated. Blowing out a long breath, I readjusted my dress and placed my hands on my hips.

"All right then," I said as I looked around the room and tossed my hair over my shoulder, finally feeling like myself again. "Now, why don't you tell me who the hell you guys are?"

CHAPTER FOUR

Elizabeth's laughter filled the room as she wrapped her arm around mine. "Come and sit with me, dear, and I'll explain it to you."

Even up close, Elizabeth looked flawless. Cool to the touch, her porcelain skin seemed to place her in her early forties, but after her earlier comment, I didn't even dare to guess for how long she'd been forty.

Leading me to an ornate, red velvet couch, she motioned for me to have a seat. She took one beside me, continuing to hold my hand in hers. Her hand was still cool to the touch, but the pressure was surprisingly comforting, you know, especially for someone whom, I suspected, could snap my neck before I blinked, if she wanted to.

"You know what we are," she said, tilting her head expectantly, so it obviously wasn't meant to be a question.

"I know what I think you are, but I'm still trying to wrap

my head around it. You're not supposed to exist."

"Neither are you, my dear, and yet, there you are, and here we are. Though I must admit, I'm a bit surprised that your education appears to be so lacking. How were you never told about us?"

I looked around the room and at the others gathered there, who were focused on me so intensely, I had to suppress the urge to blush, and I never blushed.

"I never had anyone to tell me, I guess. My mother died when I was eight, and my dad never really talked about her after that. I don't even know if he knew what I am. Either way, I left home when I turned nineteen, and he died in a car accident when I was twenty-one."

"Oh, you poor thing," she said as she laid her hand against my face. "So much tragedy. No wonder you don't know who we are; it's a wonder you even know who *you* are."

"All I ever really had were some stories," I admitted before closing my eyes. I was happily remembering how my mother combed my hair before bed and whispered to me.

"My mother told me stories at bedtime of beautiful, magical women, the succubi. Strong and powerful, they could be and do whatever they wanted, influencing the people around them, and making them loved and desired. She said they were our ancestors, but I always thought that was to make the story more special. To help me grow up healthy and strong, you know?" I opened my eyes and laughed, "Thinking back now, it doesn't really seem like the kind of bedtime story you'd tell a little girl. They were a bit... mature, I suppose. All my friends at school heard stories about beautiful princesses being rescued by handsome princes and later, getting whisked off to become queens."

"But not you."

"Nope, not me. In my mother's stories, the women always rescued themselves."

Elizabeth patted my hand and laughed.

"Your mother sounded like a very smart woman. It's too bad you lost her before she taught you more about us."

"Well, I haven't done too badly," *If you completely ignore twelve years ago*.

"Right, and so this thing tonight was..." she trailed off.

Pulling my hand out of hers, I turned away from her. "Tonight was a slip-up, it's not like it happens all the time," I bristled.

"Of course not," she soothed, "I didn't mean to offend you. But like us, going too long without a feeding can be just as dangerous for you as it is to the people around you. And even though we just met, I would hate for anything to happen to you. Like my own coven, you're practically family. We may live in secret, but at least, we have each other. Now you, on the other hand, have been all alone for so long, without anyone knowing who you really are. It must be so lonely for you."

With every word, my life became crappier and crappier.

She was right: none of my friends really knew who I was, and I had absolutely no one I could talk to about it. It wasn't intolerable, but it really wasn't that great either.

"You know, my dear," she placed a finger under my chin before turning me around to face her, "we could help you. From what I've heard over the years, some of your powers are very like our own. Wouldn't it be nice to have a little help every once in a while? And have someone to talk to?" Smiling slowly, she released my chin, adding, "Let us be your family now."

I looked around the room, scanning all of the people in it. More people in that one room knew what I was than all the people I've ever known for my entire life. It would be nice to fnally enjoy the company of people that understood me, and didn't fear me, or think that I was some sort of freak just because I happened to...

"Wait a minute. You eat people!"

I jumped to my feet and jabbed a finger in the direction of William, exclaiming, "He tried to eat me! I can't spend time with a bunch of fang-happy vamps that go around attacking innocent people in the middle of the night! Are you crazy?"

Not until the words left my mouth did I realize how stupid my outburst actually was. I probably shouldn't have insulted them in their own home. *Lair?* What was the proper term for the place where a bunch of vampires hung out anyway? Well, I was on their own turf, at any rate.

"I mean," I back-pedalled quickly, "I don't want to hurt

anyone, you know? I don't feel too comfortable thinking that you're out there, you know, snacking on people."

"Isn't that what you just did to me?" William asked.

"Well, okay, ya… maybe." I glared at him, but couldn't meet his eye.

"Maybe?" he snorted.

"Okay, yes, yes, that's exactly what I did; but I didn't *hurt* you, or anything. And let me tell you from recent experience: getting a couple of fangs driven into your neck really *hurts."*

"And like I told *you*, if you were human, you never would have even known what happened."

"He's right, you know," Elizabeth interrupted, "you never should have known what happened to you. Like any other creature, we must eat to survive, but we never kill the humans we feed on, and we don't even let them know what's happening. Yes, of course, long ago, our kind tended to be much more vicious and brutal, but we have evolved since those days. Now, all we want is to live our lives in peace."

"Well," I replied, "I guess that makes sense. It's not as if you could just let yourselves starve."

"Wonderful; that's settled then. William, why don't you take Vanessa home? I'm sure she's tired after such an eventful evening. And Vanessa, I'll get William to pick you up tomorrow. You can get started then; I'm sure there's much we can teach you."

Nodding my consent, I headed over to William, who,

thankfully, didn't seem overly put out after being roped into chauffeur duty.

"Oh, and Vanessa?" Elizabeth called out, "Welcome home."

As William opened the front door, the back of my neck started to tingle. I hadn't felt that particular sensation since the evening the body was found in front of my door. There was no one in the entryway, but William and me. I scanned the landing at the top of the grand staircase, but saw no one there. As I turned back to the doorway, I stopped for a moment, drawn by a blur of movement. I thought I saw a shadow moving up above, but it vanished instantly. William looked at me, somewhat puzzled, but I just shook my head and hurried outside.

I sat at my desk at work, chewing on the end of my pen, and staring off into space. I kept replaying the night before over and over again in my mind. *Vampires.* Vampires in Silverlake. How did no one ever know? Of course, that whole *glamour* thing was pretty handy, I suppose, and wiping a person's memory was a damn good way to avoid any pesky questions from being asked.

Sighing, I threw my pen on the desk and spun my chair around in a circle. Who would have thought that vampires could be so nice? *I wonder if my mother actually knew about them?* If my mother had lived, I could have grown up completely different. Who knows how many skills and abilities I might have possessed by now? Elizabeth told me that succubi and vampire powers were pretty similar, so who knows? Maybe I could glamour Mr. Mooney into raising my salary.

Getting back to work, I fired off a couple of emails before diving into the steadily growing pile in my inbox.

As an administrative assistant at a company as huge as Shuster, Bramble and Brown, I got to spend eight hours a day fielding complaint calls, and returning oh-so-heartfelt apology emails for the guys upstairs. Basically, I handled all the customer service crap they couldn't be bothered dealing with themselves. Of course, those higher-ups were way too important to deal with the minutiae of actually returning a customer's inquiry or email. Each assistant had a handful of account managers to look after, and we dutifully slapped their names on the bottoms of all the messages we sent out. If you've ever tried to contact an account manager at a major corporation just to ask a general question about their services, or make a complaint, chances are pretty high that no matter what the name at the bottom says, it's probably written by someone like me.

"Lunch time!" Karen's curly red head popped up over our petition wall. "I'm craving sushi; wanna come?"

"Oh, my God, yes! I could inhale some shrimp tempura right now; let me just grab my purse."

I bent down to dig out my bag, which I had kicked

underneath my desk, when I heard a knock on my partition wall.

"Delivery for a Ms. Vanessa Kensley," a messenger recited as he held up a long, rectangular box. "Are you Vanessa?"

"Yeah, that's me, I didn't order anything though. I wonder who it's from."

"I don't know, ma'am, I just deliver 'em. Have a great day," he replied with a jaunty salute before he left.

Karen came around to my cubicle. "You have to open it before we go, I'm curious now."

I tore off the plain, brown wrapping paper to reveal a long, glossy, white box wrapped with red satin ribbon.

"Oh, my gosh, Vanessa," Karen squealed, "that's a flower box. Open it! Open it now, or I'll open it!" Turning to me, she narrowed her eyes and asked, "You haven't started dating someone without telling me, have you? Do you have a secret boyfriend? What's his name?"

"No," I shook my head. "I have no idea who might have sent them." Untying the ribbon, I set it aside as I pulled the top off the box.

"Oh, my God!" Karen yelled.

"Fuck!" I shoved the box away from me before launching myself to the far wall of my cubicle, trying to get as far away from the box as possible. Inside, lying on top of a bouquet of dead roses was a dead cat, dried blood matting its fur and crawling with maggots. It was missing its head also.

"Holy shit, Vanessa! Who the hell would send you something like that?" Karen wrapped her arms around me and shuddered.

"I don't know, Kare," I replied before grabbing my purse. I pulled out my cell phone and searched through the contacts.

"Who are you calling? The police?" Karen looked over my shoulder at my phone.

"I'm calling Detective Hache. I was supposed to call him if anything strange happened." I nodded in the direction of the box, saying, "That is definitely strange."

Walking over to the box, I quickly put the lid back on before hitting the call button.

"Hache here," I actually forgot how deep and sexy his voice was, even though this was certainly not the time to notice that.

"Detective Hache, this is Vanessa Kensley. I've got something that I think you'll want to see."

"Vanessa?" Hearing Detective Hache's voice coming from behind me made me jump.

I told Karen to go ahead and get some lunch. She kindly offered to sit and wait with me, but I needed some time alone. Okay, I needed some time to freak out; and I didn't want anyone around to see it.

"Are you okay?"

"Yeah, but pretty wigged out. Someone sent me a

present," I said as I pointed over the partition to my cubicle. "It's on my desk."

"In the box?" Hache called from around the corner.

"Yup." A moment later, I heard the sliding sound of cardboard.

"Oh shit!" I heard the sound of cardboard again before he reappeared on my side of the wall.

"Yup."

"And nothing else has happened since the incident two weeks ago?"

I recalled last night and the undeniable feeling of being watched again, but there was no way I could explain where I was, or what I was doing there.

"Yeah, this is it."

"Well, we can definitely rule out coincidence now. There is no doubt that you are being targeted."

My stomach clenched in fear and I bit my bottom lip. "But why? What could anybody want with me?"

"I'm sorry, I just don't know yet, but whatever it is, I promise you that I'll make sure he or she never gets it."

"The cat had no head. What do you think that means? The other body, it... *She* had her head. But this time, it didn't—"

"Look," he cut me off, "let's not start speculating on this just yet, it won't do you any good. But I am going to get some security assigned to you."

"What do you mean? How much security?" I didn't know if the thought of protection twenty-four/seven comforted me, or creeped me out. Who wants to be shadowed every day? It could put a serious cramp in my feedings, which I already cut too close this week. I couldn't keep putting them off like that.

"We will have someone outside your apartment every night, and any other packages coming to you at work, or at home, will be checked by us first. You must not open them until we make sure they're safe. I also don't want you going anywhere alone; understand?"

"Yeah. The last thing I want is to give this creep any opportunity to snatch me off the street, or something." *God knows how easy that is for some people these days.* I scowled, remembering how swiftly William tossed me over his shoulder before driving off with me.

"That is *not* going to happen; do you understand? I promise to keep you safe."

"I believe you, and thanks. I feel a lot better just knowing you're watching out for me."

"I have to find this guy soon and get him behind bars before he can hurt anyone else."

I looked around the office, nodding as people started filtering back in from their lunch break.

"Crap I've got to get back to work," I said as I looked at the clock. Karen would return to her desk at any moment.

"Are you sure you want to stay for the rest of the day? I'm sure your boss would understand if you needed to take time off after something like this," he looked at me, slightly shocked.

"First of all, no, I don't want to stay here; but that doesn't magically release me from all the work I still have to do. And, no, my boss wouldn't understand me taking the rest of the day off because he is an asshole. That would also mean that I would have to tell him what was going on, and honestly, the less that little slime ball knows about my life, the better."

"Vanessa I am going to have to speak to your boss about what happened today. How do you think we plan to vet your mail?"

"I don't know, steal it? Look, Mooney already gives me enough trouble, I really don't want to give him any more ammo to use against me. That bastard just loves making everyone as miserable as he is."

"Ooooh, miserable bastards, are you talking about Mooney?" Karen dropped her purse on her desk and smiled up at Detective Hache. "Well, hello there, and who are you?" she batted her eyelashes at him. "Wow, Vanessa, no wonder you rushed me out of here so fast. I'd keep him to myself too," teased Karen.

Hache cleared his throat and looked away. "Well, Ms. Kensley I believe we're done here. I'll be sure to get in touch with you tonight. I'm just going to speak to your supervisor before I leave."

"Good luck," I snorted, "and have fun."

"Come on now, he can't seriously be as bad as all that," he scoffed with skepticism.

Karen and I looked at each other and smiled. "Have a

good afternoon, Detective Hache," I said before waving goodbye.

Hache collected the box off my desk, and with a nod, walked down the hall towards Mooney's office.

I was standing in my kitchen, finishing up my cup of coffee, when I heard a knock at my door. Walking over to open it, I plastered on a smile and fully expected to find William. I was trying not to hold a grudge, but it was hard. I kept thinking how freaked out I got when I thought I was about to become his breakfast last night.

"Hi, oh, Detective Hache! How are you?" Instead of finding William, Detective Hache was standing in my doorway. He looked downright delicious in jeans, a gray t-shirt, and a leather jacket.

"Is everything all right?" I asked, surprised to see him so late.

"Yes, I just wanted to come up and let you know that your security is all set up now. We're placing a cruiser outside your building, but tonight, I'll be on duty so that you have a familiar face out there."

"Wow, Detective Hache, that's really nice of you." Even though it was just his job, I couldn't help how touched I felt when I considered how thoughtful he seemed.

"You know, since we will be working so closely together, you can probably call me John."

"All right, John," I replied. It felt a little strange to hear his name on my lips, but also nice to be on a first name basis with the person to whom I more or less entrusted my life.

"Would you like to come in for a drink? I'm sure it will be a long night." I opened the door wider to let him in.

"No, that's all right; I'm all set up downstairs. I just wanted to come up and make sure that you—"

"Evening, love, who's this then?" William suddenly appeared beside John, cutting him off.

I turned to introduce them to one another. "Oh, William, this is—"

"I'm John," the detective interrupted, holding his hand out to William, "nice to meet you, and you are?"

William ignored John's outstretched hand, and turned to me. "Running late; are you ready to go?"

"Are you going somewhere?" John looked at me, surprised. I completely forgot about my former plans the moment I opened the door and found him standing there.

"Oh, yeah, sorry. I'm actually on my way out," I explained.

"I thought you told me you didn't date?" He frowned, looking back and forth between us.

"Trust me, this isn't a date. I was telling the truth."

"Are you sure you want to do that tonight?" John asked.

"Look, mate, you're outta luck. Vanessa, here, has plans tonight, you're just going to have to try again some other night. Now, aren't you going to invite me in, love?" William asked with a slight more emphasis. I was really tempted to say *no* when I saw how unbelievably irritating he could be.

"John, I shouldn't be gone long, I have work in the morning."

John glared at William and then turned to me. "Just be sure to check back in soon," he finished.

"I promise," I agreed, hoping I would actually remember to do something so mundane after the night I had in store for me.

"Don't worry, Dad. I'll have her back before dawn, I promise," William joked.

"Right," John sneered. "Good night, Vanessa," he said as he turned and walked towards the elevators.

"Good night," I called after him.

"So... who's that guy?" William asked once John was well out of earshot.

"That's really none of your business, and why did you have to be such a jerk?" I grabbed my purse off the kitchen counter.

"I have no idea what you're talking about! He loved me! Come on, let's go."

CHAPTER FIVE

"So, I trust you've fed. Am I right?" William glanced over at me from the driver's seat as we sped out of town towards Elizabeth's manor.

"Why? Are you volunteering?" I shot him a smile. "Enjoyed yourself, did you?"

He scowled at me and focused back on the road. "I just don't want you losing it with me tonight, that's all."

"Oh? Do you plan to help too? I thought it would just be Elizabeth..." I wasn't thrilled with the idea of William sticking around to watch me screw up in training. "Do you even know what she intends to start teaching me?"

He shrugged and continued to watch the road. "Beats me, love, self-control most likely, and how to avoid long time lapses between feedings. If I were human last night, I'd hate to think of the state you'd have left me in," he said, raking his eyes over me. "Especially if we hadn't been in a room full of people."

Rolling my eyes, I watched the trees whipping past the window. "Oh, please! I had everything perfectly under control.

"Of course, you did, love," he reached over to pat my leg and sent a shiver through me. *He's dead, his hands are cold, and that's it*. Resisting the urge to squirm in my seat, I stared intensely at the scenery. *That's it*.

"Vanessa! Welcome back, my dear," Elizabeth greeted me upon entering the quiet study. William and I had been sitting there for the past five minutes, looking at everything but each other. Once again, she seemed immaculate. This time, she wore cream linen pants and a moss-green, silk blouse that complimented her hair. Kissing me on both cheeks, she settled herself into a plush armchair.

"Thank you for having me, Elizabeth," I replied with a nervous smile as I sat back down.

"Of course, darling, of course. So tell me, what is it you would like to learn most of all? Like I told you last night, I only possess a limited knowledge of your kind, but I'm sure I can provide you with the basics. Why don't you tell me what you can already do?"

"Well, I don't know if I really can *do* anything. I just kind of..." I looked around the room, suddenly lost for words, and lamely finished with "am.".

"Meaning...?" she pressed.

"Well, I can do a few glamours," I began as I shot a glare

at William, "but I can't make people forget that I was ever there, or anything. I guess it's more like hypnosis. God, I can't even explain it, since I've never had to tell anyone before. I just have no problem influencing people, and making them want whatever I decide they should want, I guess. I don't use it very often though, because it seems a bit wrong."

"So you're totally wasting it," William commented before rolling his eyes at me and adding, "big surprise."

"I'm not wasting it," I snapped. "I'm just maybe not using it to its greatest potential," I mumbled. God, he was really getting on my nerves. Didn't he have somewhere better to be?

"I bet you don't let yourself have any fun with it at all. Afraid you'll end up hurting someone's feelings, love? You're a succubus, for crying out loud!" he exclaimed as he turned to Elizabeth. "She's a lost cause, Elizabeth. I say we put her right back where we found her."

Flying off the couch, I stormed over to him and slapped my hand against his chest. "First of all, how about you stop talking about me like I'm not standing right here? And second, who the hell are you to call me *a lost cause*? I'm not some goddamn charity case that you picked up off the streets. And while we're talking about the streets, who the hell straight-up *abducted* me and dragged my ass out into the middle of nowhere? I'm pretty sure that I remember telling him to piss off, too. Oh, yeah, now I remember… that was you," I shouted as I smacked his chest again. "I was doing just fine before you came along! Thanks, and you know what? I'm pretty sure I don't need your help after all." Turning my back on him, I took one step before he grabbed me and yanked me against his chest. His arm wrapped around me and felt like an iron manacle, but I continued struggling to free myself.

Pulling my hair back, he nuzzled his face into the side of my neck. "Oh, yeah?" he growled, "prove it."

"Get off me."

"Make me."

Feeling the pressure of his fangs against my neck, I tried not to panic. "Why are you such an asshole?"

"Why are you so weak?" Unexpectedly, he let me go with a shove.

Swinging around, I punched him with a right hook to the face. Unfortunately, my hand took most of the impact and the pain started there and ran right through to my shoulder, "Oh, goddamn sonofabitch!" I cursed while pressing my injured hand between my legs.

"Well, I didn't expect that one," he rubbed his face and smiled. "You hit a lot harder than you look like you could."

"Oh? Why thank you, Sir Jerks-a-lot, and may I add you are much too gracious with your praise," I sneered. Standing up, I took a moment to examine my hand, which had already started to swell. There was no way I could get out of this without some serious bruising.

"Well, now," Elizabeth said as she looked back and forth between us, "there's an idea. William, I want you to train

Elizabeth in how to defend herself."

"Umm," I replied while glancing over at William who seemed to like the idea of smacking me around just a little too much. "Are you sure that's a good idea?"

"Of course, who else? Don't worry, Vanessa, I'm sure that our William, here, won't go any harder on you than necessary. Will you, William?"

"No, of course not. No harder than necessary to get the job done," he replied sweetly. I was *so* screwed.

"So have you taken any self-defence courses at all?" William asked as he circled me. We had been at it for a few hours. I was already covered in bruises, short of breath, and had yet to land a solid hit.

"Of course, I have. What do you think? I'm an idiot?" I held up my hand when he started to open his mouth. "Don't answer that," I added before turning slowly and following his movements.

We were outside the manor, on one of the soft, grassy patches dedicated for training. I felt sure that every inch of me would be covered in dirt and grass stains by the time we finally finished.

"I took kickboxing and some krav maga. I can hold my own when I have to."

"Like you did earlier?"

"Yeah, well, you cheated. You have super creepy vamp strength." I stuck my tongue out at him and waited for him to make his move.

"Oh? So I'm creepy now?"

"Don't kid yourself, you were always creepy. Now are you going to attack me, or not?" I took a couple of jabs while dancing around as if I were in a boxing ring. In a blink, he had me by the throat, holding me away at arm's length.

"You're going to have to do a bit better than that if you want to survive, love," he teased, releasing me.

"Okay, fine," I replied. Taking two left jabs at him, I followed with a right hook. It was so annoying when he easily managed to block or dodge my punches.

"Good, keep going," he encouraged me, "you're not bad, you know."

"I know." I continued my attack on him as we moved around the lawn. "I took my training pretty seriously, but I never expected to defend myself against someone I couldn't see. Let's just hope that my super stalker is human."

"What?" Temporarily losing his focus, I managed to surprise him with a front kick directly into his chest. "Oof!"

"Ha!" I jumped around with my hands in the air, clowning for my imaginary crowd.

Taking both of my arms, he held me still. "What stalker, Vanessa?"

"Shit. Maybe I wasn't supposed to tell you."

"That you have a stalker? That's probably something I should know."

"Why? I really don't see how it's any of your business," I replied before pushing his hands off me. I stretched and took a moment to catch my breath, and added, "Or why you would even care since you don't even like me."

"What do you mean, I don't like you?"

"Oh, come on," I snorted. "You're always such a jerk."

"Do you really think I would be out here with you if I didn't like you?"

"I don't know. Elizabeth ordered you to help me," I said as I looked at him curiously, "and I didn't really get the impression that you were in any position to refuse."

"I'm out here because I *want* to be, pet, not because Elizabeth told me to."

"Oh." I wasn't quite sure what to say to that, but I began to feel a bit awkward. I was so determined not to like him… then I thought about the way he treated John. Yup, he was still a jerk.

"Do you know who this guy is?" he asked.

"Well, no, but…"

"What?" he stared so intensely into my eyes that I had to look away. I was starting to feel a familiar tug in my solar plexus, which I ignored because I did *not* want to need or desire him.

"You're going to think it's stupid." I looked at him, but he stayed silent, "I think it might be the Silverlake serial killer. The one that keeps taking people's heads off," I blurted out.

William froze, and did not say anything for a moment.

"What makes you think it might be him?" he asked slowly.

"I don't know, it's just a feeling I get. My stalker left me a headless cat. *Headless*. Who else goes around beheading things these days?"

"Did he do anything else?"

Wrapping my arms around myself to ward off the chill, I looked up at all the stars that shone in the sky. It was so much easier to see them out here than in the city, and they seemed so much brighter too.

"He left a woman's body outside the door to my apartment. Her throat was cut and blood was everywhere. I... I tripped over her when I rushed out the door. I heard screaming outside and..." I looked at him before noticing the trees surrounding the manor. It suddenly seemed so much darker outside. "I was there the night before, when the body was found at the Roxy. I was actually the one that found it. I spoke to the police, and then there she was, right in front of my door the next day. Who else could it be?" I whispered.

William wrapped his arms around me and held me close. I closed my eyes and accepted the comfort he offered, while listening to the night sounds around us.

"I don't hear your heartbeat," I whispered into his chest.

"That's because I don't have one, love," he whispered back.

I looked up at him and said, "Because you're a vampire," but it wasn't a question.

He nodded and tucked my head back under his chin,

saying, "Because I'm a vampire."

"Maybe if I were a vampire, this stalker guy wouldn't be so scary." The tension began to leave my shoulders as I let my body slowly mold against his. For a jerk, he was surprisingly comforting.

"Don't worry about the stalker, I'll help you find him."

"You will?" I pulled back, momentarily loosening myself from his embrace, but not stepping away completely. "Why?"

William laughed, shaking his head. "Maybe because you're being stalked by a psychopath that has no problem taking lives and leaving their bodies for you as gifts. I know you're not overly fond of me, love, but I hope you believe me when I say that I don't want to see you being terrorized, or killed." He stepped forward, tightening his arms around me again. "Besides, if someone is following you, the whole coven could be in jeopardy of exposure."

"You know, if you really want me to feel safe, you could always get me a gun," I suggested.

"Do you even know how to fire a gun?"

"Yes, there are some serious crazies out there, you know. I like going to the gun range, and I'm even a decent shot. I just never got around to buying myself one."

"So you can fire a gun, but don't own one," he replied as his shoulders shook silently.

"Look, I never thought I would actually *need* a gun, okay? I just thought that it would be a good skill to know in case the time ever arrived when I really needed one. And right now, I'm thinking that the time is most seriously nigh."

"Fine," he sighed into my hair, "if you really want a gun, I'll get you a gun."

"I can't believe how non-jerktastic you're being about all of this. You know, maybe you could help John," I teased.

"Who?"

"John. From earlier tonight? Okay, seriously, you can't have forgotten him already, you were so rude to him." I don't know why I was so caught off guard when John didn't know who I was talking about. It's not as if he acknowledged John's existence for anything except to mock him.

"Oh, right, that guy. Why would I help him?"

"Because he's the detective working my case." I no longer saw any point in keeping that a secret. If William intended to help me find my stalker, he might as well know that someone else was investigating it too.

"No."

"I was just kidding. But you should probably know that he's working on it. Crap! What time is it? I should get back before he starts wondering where I am."

CHAPER SIX

Silverlake City is on high alert, the tension almost palpable when you walk down the street. Over the last three weeks, the police have recovered the bodies of ten more victims. It appears the killer is no longer satisfied with simple decapitation. The most recent bodies have been horribly mutilated as well, with hacked off limbs, or strips of flesh, torn away from their bones. The police refuse to comment on whether or not they have any suspects yet, but my sources say—"

"Jesus, Karen, I can't believe you read that blog," I said before reaching over and closing the web browser on the laptop. I tucked my feet under my legs on the couch, adding, "It's such fear-mongering trash."

"Oh, come on, Nessa, you, of all people, can't honestly tell me that you're not afraid these days."

"Well, sure I am, but I have a *reason* to be afraid."

"Oh, right, sure," Sophia called from the kitchen.

"Because you're so special, and those of us without personal stalkers to call our very own shouldn't be afraid of the insane-o running around town on the murderous rampage? Hey, where's your salt?"

"In the cupboard, beside the stove." I headed towards the kitchen to help prepare the margaritas. The girls were over for margarita and movie night. We chose to indulge in an all-night, slasher-flick marathon, thinking, what better way to forget about your own troubles than to scream at a blonde bimbo not to go up the stairs? Or outside? Or say that she would be *right back?* "I'm not saying that people shouldn't be scared, everyone is already pretty much pissing their pants, but that blogger is such a little leech."

"Hey, don't hate *The Informant*; at least, he gives us information, unlike the *Silverlake Daily*. They didn't even mention the mutilations, they just said that more bodies had been found."

"Maybe that's so the whole city won't panic and accidentally shoot their neighbours in the middle of the night, when they see them going outside for a smoke?" I suggested.

"So where is this guy even getting his information from?" asked Sophia.

"Maybe he's making it all up," I suggested. "You know Kare, you can't believe everything you read."

"He has a source inside the police station," Karen retorted. "Apparently, they even gave him crime scene photos too, but he decided they were too gory to post."

"Oh, so he refrained from posting them for the sake of decency, did he? Nice to know this guy has some sort of journalistic integrity," I snickered.

Sophia looked at me and frowned. "Journalists have integrity? Since when?"

"Ummm," I thought for a moment. "I think they probably have integrity if they aren't paparazzi. Or if they are willing to jump out of helicopters in order to report on wars in Bosnia and all those other countries with chronic unrest."

Sophia paused and looked over at my computer. "What are the chances that *The Informant* is jumping out of helicopters into war-torn countries?"

"About as much chance that he's *not* some pimply, sixteen-year-old, holed up in his mom's basement," I laughed.

"You guys can joke all you want," Karen stated solemnly, "but I'd rather be prepared for the worst even if it *is* exaggerated. I mean, isn't that why we're here tonight? To forget what's happening out there" she gestured towards my windows, "by getting ourselves freaked out about what's going on in there?" She waved her hand towards the TV.

I flpped the switch on the blender to mix the margaritas. "Sorry, Karen, what was that?" I hollered, "I can't hear you." I lifted my hand to my ear.

Karen stuck her tongue out at me before flopping back on the couch. Sophia took pity on her and smacked a kiss on the top of her head before joining her on the couch. Once I finished blending the drinks, I made sure to pour Karen an extra full glass, if only to help take the sting out of our teasing.

"Way to abandon me in the kitchen, Soph."

"I'm sure you'll manage," she replied.

Walking back to the living room, I very slowly carried the three fishbowl glasses in my hands. Hey, if you're doing girl's night, you might as well do it right.

"See?" Sophia said, taking a glass, "I knew you would be fine."

"Here, Kare," I said as I held out a glass to her.

"Ooh, thank you."

"Hey, how come mine isn't that full?" Sophia pouted.

"Maybe because you weren't the one that spent the last ten minutes getting teased? Now move over," I sat in my spot on the end of the couch. "It's too bad Colleen couldn't make it tonight."

Sophia took a long drink of her strawberry margarita and smacked her lips together. "I know, but she said her mom was really freaking out. She's afraid that she or Colleen could be offed at any minute."

"Aww, poor Mrs. Baker," Karen said as she started pulling DVDs out of her large overnight bag, "she's really sweet."

"And makes the best chocolate fudge brownies on the planet," Sophia groaned.

"God... don't talk to me about her brownies. I dream

about her brownies, and her apple pie. Oh, God, can we please have a moment of silence for that pie?"

We all bowed our heads, trying to suppress our laughter, when a knock came at the door.

"Are you expecting someone else?" Sophia asked.

"Nope, just you guys."

"Ooh, maybe it's the hunky Detective Hache," Karen said before faking a swoon.

"Okay, seriously, how have I not met this guy yet? Karen won't shut up about him, and if she hadn't spilled the beans about your twisted valentine, I doubt I'd even know he existed. I'm starting to think you guys just made him up," Sophia said.

Making sure to check the peephole first, I opened the door. "Detective Hache! Come on in!"

"John," he corrected me.

"Right, John. We were actually just talking about you."

"We?"

"Hi," Karen and Sophia chimed in unison from the living room.

"John, I'm sure you remember Karen." I gestured for him to take a seat, adding, "and this is my friend, Sophia."

"Nice to meet you, Sophia."

She looked him up and down before giving him a sly smile. "Nice to meet you too, Detective. Karen was right, you *are* cute." Winking at him, she took another sip of her drink.

Clearing his throat, John looked away, embarrassed, but

replied, "Thank you," albeit gruffly.

"So John, what brings you up here? I feel like I haven't seen you in ages. Thought you might have forgotten about me. Even though there's always a car outside, you're never the one inside it." It came out a little sharper than I intended. Okay, so I was feeling a touch sulky about the whole thing, but one minute he was there, and the next, he seemed to be foisting me off on someone else.

"And I wanted to apologize for that, but with this last group of killings, the homicide department is going insane. I've been trying to find the serial killer, as well as your stalker."

"So you don't think he's the same guy?" Sophie interjected.

"I don't think it would be a good idea to talk about this with anyone who was not central to the investigation," John replied, shooting her down.

"Well, I'm central to the investigation! And I'm asking you the same question. Do you still really not think that my stalker and the killer are the same person? I thought that was because the MO changed. Are you saying that nothing has changed in the method with which these victims were killed?"

John was silent for a moment before responding carefully. "The method of the killings is not exactly the same as it was before. There is a chance that our suspect could be changing his patterns. But that doesn't automatically suggest he is the same guy who's targeting you."

"You know, I don't know if you're trying to make me feel better, or just think I'm stupid."

"I think he's trying to make you feel better," Karen offered kindly.

"I don't think you're stupid, Vanessa; but so far, we just don't have enough to go on to tie them together. I don't want to cause you unnecessary panic or distress."

"Oh, right, because knowing there are actually *two* homicidal killers running around out there is so much more comforting."

"I didn't come up here to fight with you."

"Well, then, what did you come up here for?" I yelled, "Obviously, not to give me good news. Do you have any clues at all as to who this guy is?"

He clenched his jaw tightly, "No."

"And do you have any idea when he might strike again?"

"No."

"And do you have any idea what it's like just waiting day after day, week after week to see if he's going to leave another body for me to find? Or jump out of the bushes to hack me to pieces? Or perhaps, he's gotten bored playing his sick games with me and chosen to leave me hanging, consumed with fear for the rest of my life?"

John opened his mouth to say something, but I cut him off. "No, you don't. You don't know anything about it." Picking up my drink, I downed a few swallows before slamming my glass on the coffee table.

John rose from his chair and strode heavily to the front hall before turning around and storming back. "I'm sorry!" he yelled. "I'm sorry that you're scared; and I'm sorry that this is happening to you. I'm sorry that I've been working day in and day out, following every shitty, dead end lead just hoping, no, praying, that it will be the one that finally catches this guy for you. I'm sorry for lying awake at night, thinking about you, and praying that I won't get a call the next day saying that something else happened to you because I was too damn slow!" He grabbed me by the shoulders and continued to yell. "I'm trying to find him, Vanessa, I'm trying, but bodies just keep showing up! Innocent people keep getting killed and we aren't getting anywhere. I've never felt so useless in my life." Letting me go, his arms dropped to his sides and he hung his head. "I'm sorry. That was unprofessional of me. I haven't been sleeping lately and... I'm just sorry."

The entire apartment went silent apart from the sound of his ragged breathing. "I..." I began, but my mind went completely blank.

Holding up his hand, John shook his head and walked out of the apartment with only the sound of the front door closing quietly behind him.

"What the hell just happened?" Sophia blurted out as soon as the door shut.

I turned to look at them with my mouth still hanging open, shaking my head in confusion. "I have no idea."

"You have no idea?" she asked skeptically. "The man had

all of that just bubbling away, brewing inside of him, and you're telling me that you never saw it coming?"

"I barely ever saw him. How was I supposed to know he was that close to losing it?"

"Can you blame him? I can't even imagine what the police department is going through right now. They must really have no leads at all," Karen said as she shuddered and wrapped her arms around herself.

"Maybe go a little easier on him next time," Sophia mumbled into her glass.

I shot her a glare, but jerked my head in a nod.

Standing at the top of the stairs outside my apartment building, I did a few quick stretches to prepare for a run. The unmarked police car was still parked across the street so I waved as I trotted by, and the two officers in the car waved back. I was a bit relieved that neither of them were John. I still felt bad about snapping at him last night. I never meant to push him so hard.

The evening air was cool against my face as I jogged around the block, and the gathering gray clouds promised a welcome shower of rain. It was getting too hot in the city, and the water coming off the lake ramped up the humidity to an uncomfortable degree. On my third pass of the squad car, I waved again. Running was part of my new training. William thought it would help increase my stamina during our bouts. Since the officers were ordered to keep an eye on me at all times, I simply did a few laps around the block where I lived. That way, they didn't have to worry about me being gone too long.

By my fifth lap, I decided it was more than enough for the night. Resting my hands on my knees, I took a few deep breaths before heading over to the squad car, just to let them know I was finished for the evening. As I walked up to the vehicle, I started to feel a tight tingling on the back of my neck and I slowed down as I approached. The cement around the driver's side of the car was sparkly under the street lamp, and as I approached, I realized it was shattered glass glittering on the ground.

Moving slowly along the side of the vehicle, I could see the two officers still sitting inside, but the fear churning my gut didn't abate. Looking into the window, I let loose a blood-curdling scream. The two officers' throats were ripped wide open. They sat there, staring ahead but not seeing, with empty sockets, their eyes torn out. The spurting blood from their necks had sprayed everywhere, coating the inside of the patrol car in blood red.

The tingling on the back of my neck exploded into a burning pain. I spun around to face my attacker. His twisted visage snarled at me, and the officers' blood still dripped from his mouth. He clamped a hand around my throat and lifted me high into the air. His fangs glinted in the yellow light from the street lamp as he licked the blood from his lips. Kicking wildly, I lashed out at him, but the edges of my vision started to dim as he applied more pressure, cutting off my breath.

"No," I croaked feebly.

Lowering me, he slammed me hard against the side of the car before dropping me on the pavement. Tears burned my eyes as he gathered my hair in his fist and hauled me off the ground, jerking my head to the side. His eyes were shiny and black, reflecting an endless pit of pain and sorrow. Desperate and hungry to feed on the suffering of others, in those horrid eyes, I saw myself die.

Fear and hunger crashed into me like a wave. Screaming with rage, I reached up and raked my nails down his face, clawing his skin. He let go of my hair in surprise, his hand instantly covering his wound before lunging at me again. Moving on instinct, I lashed out, slamming him in the chest with the flat of my palm, and focusing all of my rising energy into the blow. The impact knocked him a good ten feet and he landed on his back.

"My turn," I smiled viciously, walking towards him with cold, determined intent. I could feel the hunger clawing at me from the inside, desperate to get out, like a living thing. All I wanted was to kill this creature. He intended to hurt me and now he had to pay for it. He moved in a flash, coming at me again, but my calm was like the eye of a tornado. I could sense his movements, and feel him coming. At the last moment, I spun to the left, shooting my arm out, and clothes-lined him, once more knocking him off his feet.

Kneeling above him, I grabbed the front of his shirt, and

pulled his face towards mine. My vision was tinged with red as I sneered down at him.

"Let's see how you like being lunch," I hissed as I closed my mouth over his.

My whole body screamed as I ripped the energy from him. I could feel him fading away, no less than the monster deserved.

"Vanessa!" William's voice penetrated my feeding haze just before I got shoved off my attacker.

"Don't let him get away," I snarled.

William held the other vampire down and looked me over, "Are you all right, love?"

"I'll be a lot better after I kill that murderous fucker," I spat out angrily.

"I can't let you do that," William shook his head, "I'm sorry."

"Why the hell not?" I ground out through clenched teeth. The red tinge at the edges of my vision were starting to fade, and my violent hunger slowly began to subside.

"Because I need him. He might have some answers for me. Answers about your stalker, among other things."

"You mean that's not him? But he killed the policemen who were watching me. And then he tried to eat me!" My voice became increasingly higher in pitch. Whatever power I'd drawn on before was leaving me just as quickly.

"And you took him out," William said, looking puzzled, "how did you manage that?"

"Do we really have to get into that right now? What the

hell is going on around here? Why did he attack me? I thought the Silverlake Coven was all about living in peace with humans?"

"We are. Well, most of us anyway. It appears that a renegade faction are rebelling, and have been for some time now. They've just been covering their tracks really well."

"What do you mean?"

"I don't think any human has been killing all of those people. I think it has to be vampires."

CHAPTER SEVEN

After lifting the other vampire up, William headed down a side street. Refusing to be left behind, I hurried after them. I quickly scanned the windows above us to see if anyone was watching, but they were all empty. The narrow street was dark as William dropped my attacker beside a large dumpster before crouching down in front of him. The vampire tried to push himself away, but was too weak to do anything except prop himself up.

"It looks like you've done a real number on him here," William said as he looked over at me and frowned. "I don't know how much we'll be able to get out of him."

"But you think he's involved with all the killings?"

William ignored me and grabbed the vampire's face, forcing him to look him in the eye. The vampire's eyes rolled up in his head and he started to twitch violently, while foam trickled from the corner of his mouth.

"Shit," William moved back as the spasms continued.

I watched in horror when black veining started to spread over the vampire's exposed skin. His body turned a sickly shade of gray before lying completely still. William reached out and kicked the body gently with his foot, then withdrew it quickly as the corpse was reduced to a pile of ash. Turning to look at me, he said nothing, but grabbed my hand before walking me out of the alley and down the street.

When we got to his car, I quickly busied myself with buckling my seatbelt and trying to avoid eye contact. *What the hell had I done back there? I killed. I'm a killer.* My stomach roiled and churned and I had to concentrate pretty hard on keeping my dinner down.

"I have to get you the hell out of here. You won't be able to come back here tonight. Do you understand?" William drove right through an amber light and kept going. I nodded and kept my head down. "You can't report the officers being dead. The last time you saw them, they were alive and well. You lucked out. You just happened to not be at home when they were attacked. Do you understand me, Vanessa? You. Lucked. Out."

"I understand," I whispered. All I wanted now was to fall asleep and wait for this nightmare to end.

"Where are we?" I asked quietly as we made our way to the elevators in the underground parking lot of a giant, high-rise apartment building.

Inside the elevator, William pulled out a key card and swiped it before punching the button marked PH, "My place," he answered.

William unlocked the door to a gigantic penthouse apartment. The entire level overlooked the city with floor-to-ceiling, wraparound windows, offering amazing glimpses of the other glass-encased, high-rise buildings in the area. Expansive, white granite counters were only one of the elaborate appointments the kitchen boasted. They extended out into a breakfast bar, which accented the deep, rich grain of the dark mahogany cabinets. Off to the side, a staircase led to a second level. "This place is amazing," I commented as I wandered around, taking it all in.

"I've always enjoyed it. Can I get you a drink?"

"I don't think so. I'm not particularly partial to O positive."

Chuckling, he held up a bottle of wine. "I was thinking of something more along the lines of a Shiraz."

"Thanks, I could really use a glass of wine right now."

"I'd be willing to bet you could really use an entire bottle of wine right now."

"That bet could make you a very rich man," I said softly, walking over to look out the window at the city below.

William stood behind me and offered me a glass. "Are you ready to talk about what happened back there?"

Shaking my head, I took a sip of wine. It was rich and velvety with a hint of something smoky. Closing my eyes, I took a bigger swallow before admitting, "I don't know if I'll ever be ready."

"You took out a vampire, Vanessa, without weapons; we have to know how."

"I don't *know* how. One minute, his hands were on me and I knew I was about to die, I just knew it." I placed my hand against my throat where I could still feel him squeezing the life out of me, "And the next thing I knew, I was killing him."

"But *how*?" he pressed.

"I *don't know*," I cried, turning to face him. "I don't know how I did it. My anger just came over me, crashing into me, pushing me forward, and making me stronger. I was so pissed, so *damn pissed*, that he would dare raise a hand to me. It was like the need to feed, except so much stronger. I didn't *need* his energy, but I knew that I could take it, take it all, and leave him with nothing. Just a broken, empty shell. I didn't feel like myself; I felt, God I don't know... stronger, better, worse, powerful, out of control, in perfect control, absolutely perfect." I pressed myself against William and held his gaze. "I felt like perfection. And I've never been so afraid of myself in my life."

Wrapping his arms around my waist, William slowly lowered his face towards me, hesitating only a moment before pressing his lips on mine. My hunger roared up inside me and I started to panic before pressing it back down again. I didn't want to take anything from him; I just wanted to enjoy the feeling of his mouth on mine.

His tongue slid across my lips and I opened my mouth to allow him entry, sighing when his hands slid down my back to grab my ass. He released my mouth and trailed kisses along my jaw towards my ear, flicking my earlobe with his tongue. I tensed as his face nuzzled my neck, remembering the painful sting of his bite; but instead of sinking his fangs, he placed a gentle kiss there and held me closer. A sigh escaped my lips as his mouth discovered my shoulder.

"You should get some sleep, love," he mumbled into my hair.

"I don't want to sleep," I murmured.

Chuckling, he released me and tilted my chin up. "I know you don't, but you've had a very long night, and you'll soon need your rest."

"And what are you going to do while I'm sleeping?" I asked, my body still buzzing from his touch.

"I'm going to see if I can find out who attacked you tonight, since he wasn't familiar to me." He kissed me softly and ran his thumb over my lips, adding, "I need to know if the vampires from the Silverlake Coven are committing these killings, or if new vampires are hiding out in town."

"What happens when you find out?"

"Well, if they're ours, Elizabeth will be the one to decide what happens to them. Most likely, they will quickly be executed."

I looked up at him in shock. "Elizabeth would kill them, just like that?"

"Vampire law is very strict, love. If they are from our coven, they will have broken the very laws our coven was established to uphold, not to mention the risk of exposing us all. Elizabeth cannot and will not allow that. If they aren't from our coven, and we find them, they will most surely die. They entered our territory and started a killing rampage in a very public way. We can't allow it to continue; we have to eliminate the threat."

I nodded, fully understanding. While I didn't like the idea of more killing, I could see that they didn't have much of a choice.

"Just be careful, okay?"

"What's this now? Was that a hint of concern? Careful there, or I might think you're actually starting to like me."

Sighing, I pulled away and swallowed the last of my wine, "Don't worry, I'm not."

Frowning, he headed towards the elevator. "Feel free to make yourself at home, the bedrooms are upstairs. I'll be back before dawn."

"Don't get staked," I called as the front door closed.

"Ugh," I groaned while rolling over in the pitch-black bedroom. My whole body felt pummelled and bruised. The screen on my cell phone lit up when it vibrated on the bedside table. Checking the call display, I saw that it was John. "Hello," I replied, my voice still groggy from sleep.

"Thank fucking God, Vanessa, where the hell have you

been?" John barked at me. "I've been calling you all morning. Are you all right?"

Sitting up slowly, I adjusted the grip on my phone and cleared my throat. "Of course, I'm okay, I was just sleeping."

"Where are you?"

"I'm at a friend's house," I replied. Taking a deep breath, I tried to sound more light-hearted when I asked, "Why? What's going on?"

"Something happened at your apartment, and when we couldn't find you, we got worried."

"My apartment? Is everything okay?"

"The two officers assigned to watch over you were attacked last night."

"Oh, my God!" I shrieked, instantly wincing at the pitch of my own voice. "Are they okay?" I asked, trying to dial it back a bit.

"I'm sorry, Vanessa, but they're dead."

A tear ran down my cheek and I hastily wiped it away. If I allowed myself to start crying, I would completely fall apart. The horrors of the previous evening became real again. And I just wasn't ready for that yet.

"Look, Vanessa, if you can stay right where you are for a few days, then do it. I'm calling into work for you, don't go in. Don't go anywhere alone. I'll be in touch with you as soon as I can."

"Okay," I whispered.

"Stay safe; we're going to catch this bastard," John added as he hung up. I sat there in a daze, staring at my phone screen.

~

Throwing on one of William's shirts that I found the night before, I went downstairs in search of food. After John's phone call, I was suddenly starving. Even though the chances of my finding anything edible in the apartment were pretty slim, I decided to check out his fridge.

To my happy surprise, the fridge was stocked with all kinds of food: fruit, chicken, and various sandwich ingredients. *Hmmm, maybe I'm not the only human he hosts here.* Taking an apple out of the fridge and pouring myself a generous glass of milk, I made myself comfortable on the couch before turning on the giant, flat screen TV. I had no idea how old William was, but he was definitely not stuck in the past! Both his TV and stereo system were clearly brand new and top end.

The sun was still fairly high in the sky as it reflected off the surrounding buildings, making their windows sparkle. Turning the volume on the TV to low, I admired William's view again. This time, I could appreciate the long stretch of the lake, and the vista encompassed by being so high up. The lake was quite deep, and there were still some places in which the depth was still unknown. We were all raised on tales of the water monster that lived in the deepest depths of the lake, and I still found myself imagining what it would be like to catch a glimpse of it one day. All of the kids swore they knew someone who knew someone who swore they actually saw it moving beneath the surface while boating. It was so innocent and exciting then, monsters in Silver Lake. Who could have guessed that real monsters existed in Silverlake City? They could have been face-to-face with one at any time and never even known it.

Sighing, I turned my back on the window. Although I didn't consider the Silverlake Coven to be monsters, exactly, the truth was: the peaceful existence they set up wasn't in their nature. No. Rather, it was their choice to do so. Their real nature, I'm sure, was probably just as violent as any other wild animal. They still fed on unsuspecting people even if their victims couldn't remember it afterwards. I paced the room, trying to make sense of it all. What really mattered? Nature or choice? Desire or action? William annoyed me pretty much constantly, and yet, I found some comfort in him, but that didn't matter.

Lifting my hand to my neck, I ran my fingers along the smooth skin, remembering the first time we met. What really mattered now was: could I actually trust him?

CHAPTER EIGHT

"Wake up, love," William's voice pulled me gently from sleep as I caught the scent of something delicious and spicy. "I've made you something to eat."

I sat up on the couch and rubbed my eyes, looking over towards the kitchen. "You cooked for me?" Even with the delicious aroma for evidence, I couldn't help wondering why he would go to the effort.

"Well, I couldn't let you starve. That would defeat the purpose of keeping you safe, don't you think? I made you jambalaya."

"Really?" Walking over to the dining table, I looked down at the plate he set out for me. The meal looked amazing: a hearty blend of prawns, sausage, and chicken with vegetables and rice. "I didn't know you could cook."

"There's a lot about me you don't know," he said before motioning for me to sit. He took a seat near me. "I spent quite some time in New Orleans."

"Where you learned to cook even though you don't need to eat?" I asked skeptically.

"No, where I learned to cook this particular dish, and I wasn't making it for myself." The corner of his mouth went up in a half smile, and a pang of envy shot through me that I quickly squelched.

I made a noise of polite interest and took a bite. The savory meal was delicious and offered an assortment of rich flavors with just the perfect amount of bite. "It's amazing," I sighed before taking another bite. "So who did you learn to make it for?" I had to remind myself that I didn't really care. I mean, why shouldn't I be curious? Besides, he was the one that brought it up.

"No one important, just a woman I knew," he said, swiftly dismissing the topic with a careless wave of his hand.

"A lover?" I probed. I had no idea why I wanted to know the details so badly, although it was starting to piss me off.

"For a time."

"What happened to her?" *Shut up, Vanessa. Shut up. Shut up.*

"Why don't I leave you now and let you eat in peace?" he said as he started to get up from the table.

"No, wait," I held out my hand to stop him. "I'm sorry for asking. It's none of my business. Thank you for dinner."

Sitting back down, he sat there in silence while I finished my meal. I couldn't stifle my curiosity as to who this woman was though. She must have meant a great deal to him if he didn't want to talk about her. Why did that frustrate me so much? Glancing up, I saw William watching me, and our eyes locked while my stomach clenched. I glanced back down at my plate and only realized then I had already finished.

"Would you like some more?"

"No, that was perfect; thank you." Setting my fork down on the plate, I moved to get up.

"I've got it," he said, taking the dishes from me. After putting them in the dishwasher, he came back to join me at the table.

"You know," I cleared my throat, "you're not as, umm…" I was searching for the right word. "As irritating as I first thought."

"High praise coming from you indeed. Nice to know that you think I'm not all bad," he replied with a wink as he sat back down in his chair. "So how was your day today?"

"Oh! I completely forgot! John called me today. They found the dead officers this morning. He said he was really worried when he couldn't find me."

William made a dismissive noise. "And how is the intrepid Detective Hache? Getting any further in his investigation? He's not doing the best job of keeping you out of danger, is he?"

"Don't be a jerk, William; he's doing the best he can."

"Then his best is seriously deficient."

"Well, I highly doubt the suggestion that the murders were committed by something that isn't human is not an option the Silverlake Police Department would just stumble onto," I snapped. "And speaking of investigations, how did *yours* go last night? Do you have any idea what the hell is going on around here?" I asked sweetly. I hated how often he snuck in little jabs at John.

"It's starting to look more like the killings were done by members of our own coven. There have been some loud whispers."

"What loud whispers?"

"I heard a rumor that a tiny faction of our vampires have formed a group that intends to revive the old ways."

"Did the old ways require high profile, killing rampages? Because I feel like this is something pretty hard to conceal or cover up."

"Traditionally, vampires killed their victims after feeding on them, by draining them dry. But what's happening in Silverlake? Well, it could be the perfect cover. No one would ever suspect vampires because they don't look like vampire kills. It would be another thing entirely if people were dropping dead with two puncture wounds in their necks. But these decapitations, and the publicity they draw, make it look like a typical, bloodthirsty, human serial killer. It also means that the vampire community won't suspect it's being executed by their own people for quite a while."

"So how do you figure it's vampires?"

"So many unsolved killings and still the police have no clues to work with at all? It's very unlikely that a human could manage to be so high profile, and kill so many people in such a public way without slipping up a single time. Or leaving absolutely no traces behind. But vampires? We've been hiding amongst humans for thousands of years."

"So what you're telling me is: right now a group of vampires are stalking humans because they are determined to remain the top of the food chain?"

"Exactly."

"We are so screwed," I whispered.

"Which is why you're staying here."

"Excuse me?"

"Vanessa, you can't go back to your apartment right now. It's too easy for them to get to you there. Between your stalker and the attack last night, you're much better off staying with me."

"Do I even get a vote in this?"

"Do you have a better idea?"

"No, but that's not really the point." I sighed, feeling more than just a little frustrated. "You and John have both decided that I'm supposed to just sit here and twiddle my thumbs all day while you two go out and protect me from the big, bad evildoers. Well, maybe I'm tired of sitting around. I hate feeling scared and not knowing what's happening! I want to help. I want to fight. I want to *do* something! I refuse to sit around helplessly waiting to be attacked again. Look, when I thought it was just a crazy stalker, that was one thing; but whoever is after me is not just a killer, William, he's a *vampire*. No matter how badly John wants to catch this guy, he never will. And there's no way in hell I'm letting you handle it alone."

"Look, pet," William replied, holding up both hands. "I know you're feeling a wee bit frustrated here, but let's be reasonable. If you go out there, looking for this guy, you're only going to get yourself killed."

"Damn it, William, I'm not your pet! And I'm not your love. We've been training like crazy and last night, I proved that I'm not as helpless as you seem to think I am."

"So you think you've got it all figured out, do you? After taking out a single vampire, on pure luck, and now you're ready to take on God knows how many others, while trying to track this guy down?"

"Yes."

"And what makes you so sure that your stalker is a vampire as well?"

"I know he is," I replied, remembering the night at the Roxy, and the feeling of being watched. "Whenever he's near, my neck tingles."

"Your neck... tingles?"

"Yes, William, my neck tingles. The hair on the back of my neck stands up and I just *know* I'm being watched. It happened the night I found the first body, and on the day of the second body. My neck was practically on fire last night, right before I was attacked, and then even..."

"Even what?" William asked.

"Oh, my God! Even on the first night you took me to Elizabeth's!"

"What?" William exploded.

I got up from the dining table and paced the length of his living room, then stopped to stare at him. "I completely forgot," I mumbled. "I felt it when we were leaving, but I couldn't see anyone except for this, this shadow that was only visible for a second."

"It was a house full of vampires, Vanessa, it could have been anyone's shadow."

"Don't, William, just don't. Whoever it was wanted to hurt me. I know he did. The only time my neck tingles like that is when vampires are around, trying to fuck up my day. No one in that place should have known who I was; and yet, someone wanted to hurt me. He was in the house."

William was silent as he rose and walked up the stairs. He returned a couple of minutes later with a black case. Setting it on the coffee table, he looked at me and said, "Open it."

I arched an eyebrow at him before unlatching the case. Inside, I found a matching pair of black, semi-automatic pistols with cherrywood grips. I ran my finger along the wood inlay and let out a long whistle.

"Sig Sauer p220, .45 caliber. I thought they would suit you," he smiled.

"They are absolutely gorgeous," I replied before picking one up. I tested the weight and felt the grip in my hand, then I tested the sight. After making sure the chamber was empty, I pulled a few dry fires. I could practically hear the angels singing behind me. "I can't believe that these are the ones you found for me! This is my ultimate dream gun!" I gushed, still grinning from one ear to the other. "Holy crap! You can't read minds, or can you? Is that a vamp thing? Is that how you knew?"

He laughed as he watched me strike a few *Charlie's Angels* poses. "They took a little longer to customize than expected. They've been modified to fire some special rounds."

"Oh, my God! Please tell me they're some sort of UV bullets," I squealed.

He frowned and shook his head, "No, what kind of movies have you been watching lately, love?"

I shrugged, laughing, and replied, "Oh, well, a girl can always dream! What kind of rounds do they take?"

"Silver."

"Silver? Silver bullets in a semi-automatic?"

"Well, it's more like they're silver-plated..." he waved his hand, indicating he did not want to get lost in the technicalities. "The point is: although they won't kill a vampire, they will surely slow one down, and they burn like hell."

"Hopefully, that would give me enough time to get up close and send them there permanently."

"You know, you're a little scary with a gun in your hand. Maybe I should take them back," he said before reaching out, but I quickly danced beyond his reach.

"Don't even think about it! They're mine, all mine," I said before laughing maniacally.

"Do you want your other gift now? Or are you good for

the night?" he teased.

"Ooh, there's more? Gimme! Gimme! Gimme!"

"Lift up the bottom tray in the case," he replied. Grinning, he appeared to be having just as much fun as I. I didn't know what it was, but feeling a weapon finally in my hand gave me a renewed sense of confidence and I believed I had a good chance of coming out of this thing alive.

Lifting the cushioned tray from the case revealed a second level. Lying beneath it was a gorgeous hunting knife. The blade was about nine inches long and curved on one side with vicious-looking ridges along the other. The center of the blade was etched with scrollwork that extended on both sides.

"And you weren't expecting me to come with you?" I asked skeptically.

"I just wanted to make sure you had proper protection if you needed it. The flat of the blade is silver except for the edges. That wiring around the hilt is also silver, so if any vampire tries to use your knife against you, it will really hurt, at the very least. When I realized what we were dealing with, I didn't think I was overdoing it."

I couldn't believe how much thought he invested into this for me. "So silver really works against you guys huh? That's not just a werewolf thing? Holy crap! Do werewolves exist too? No, don't tell me, I don't want to know. But what about garlic? Does garlic mess you up?"

"Yes, silver repels vampires. No, garlic doesn't. Yes, to sunlight and decapitation, but good luck getting anywhere near one of us if you plan to take the stake in the heart thing for a test drive."

"And now me." I whispered.

"So it would seem," William replied although he wouldn't look me directly in the eye. "But your power won't do you any good if you can't control it."

"I'll control it, just give me some time."

CHAPTER NINE

I sat on the mat in the gym of the condominium and worked through my floor exercise, finishing my set of crunches. As I neared the end of my two hundred-crunch goal, the door opened and a man walked in. He looked about in his mid forties, and the short hair curling around his ears was starting to gray at the temples. His body, however, was trim and lean, a living testament to what must have been regular workouts. As he walked over to the treadmill, I could see him watching me out of the corner of my eye. The sudden urge to feed reared up. I ignored the impulse, and continued to move swiftly through the rest of my routine, watching him as he switched from cardio to weights.

After my routine was over, I stood and stretched in front of the mirror, looking at him in the reflection. He sat on the bench of the universal weight machine. I smiled when our eyes met, thinking it was the perfect time for a feeding.

I walked over to the weight area and stood in front of him.

"Hello." His voice was strained from the effort of lifting weights.

"Hi there." Putting a hand on the back of his neck, I straddled him.

"What—?" I pressed my mouth against his, swiftly cutting him off. Frozen in shock, he released the handle of the weights, causing them to crash back into place. The blood roared in my ears as I drained his energy from him. I had never taken so much so quickly before, and it was so easy. I pulled away and climbed off him, my breathing ragged. I felt lightheaded and had to take a moment to catch my breath. He was slumped over and looked up at me with glazed eyes. I tried to ignore the niggling guilt and worry that I may have taken too much. Grabbing my towel off the wall hook, I wrapped it around my shoulders and walked out of the gym without a backwards glance.

It was only my second day in William's apartment, but I already felt sulky and cooped up. Just knowing that I couldn't go outside made it seem so much worse. I passed by one of the large windows on the amenity floor, and stopped to close my eyes. How I relished the feeling of warm sunshine on my face. *Oh, my God.* I was such an idiot. The sun was up, meaning, it was perfectly safe for me to go outside. No vampire ventured out in the middle of the day without risk of being fried to a crisp. No vampire would go so far just for the off chance of nailing me. I did a little victory dance as I rushed to the bank of elevators.

Today was a beautiful day to play hooky.

I sat in the cab, parked a little way down the street from my apartment building, and scanned the road for signs of a police car. I saw a few cars parked on the street, but I was too far away to see if any of them were occupied. I decided to play it safe, and tugged the baseball cap down further over my eyes. "Wait here for me," I told the cab driver before hopping out of the car. With my head down, I walked briskly up to my building while trying not to draw any attention. I opened the front door, and rushed for the elevator, breathing a sigh of relief when I realized I made it inside without being stopped.

Opening the door of my apartment, I cautiously looked around. It felt as if I'd been gone for two weeks instead of just two days. Going to my hall closet, I pulled out my duffel bag and headed towards my bedroom. There was just no way I could endure an extended sleepover at William's without a few essentials.

Preferring not to spend a second longer in my apartment than necessary, and also to avoid being caught, I didn't bother folding any of my clothes. I yanked them off their hangers and shoved them into the bag, along with my cosmetic case and my wallet. Thankfully, I had some emergency cash hidden in my cell phone case, enough to get me over here, but I wasn't going very far without my bankcards and ID.

Zipping up the bag, I threw it over my shoulder, and hurried out again after locking the door behind me. When I got downstairs, I looked up and down the street, but didn't see anyone watching the building. Readjusting my hat, I ducked my head down as I raced back to the cab before my luck ran out.

"Do you carry colloidal silver?"

"Sure do! Just head down the aisle there behind you, to your left. It'll be on the bottom shelf," the girl replied cheerfully. She was working the counter in the health food store, and politely pointed me in the right direction before going back to playing on her phone.

I found the colloidal silver exactly where she said I would, but I was ill-prepared for the price tag. "Holy crap! That's expensive," I mumbled, "this had seriously better work." Scooping ten bottles into my arms, I carefully took them up to the counter.

"Just that for you?"

"Yeah, thanks."

"That'll be $267.34 please."

I cringed, but obediently handed over my debit card, chanting, *This is for a good cause. This is for a good cause. This is for a good cause.*

"What do you mean, you left the apartment building?" William exploded when I told him about my little trip downtown today. He didn't take it as well as I thought he would.

"I was fine, William. You didn't even notice I was gone. You know why? Because the sun was up. I figured it would kind of put a kink in any vampire's plans to off me."

"Maybe, but you went by your place. Don't you think it might be a little strange to be seen there when detective what's-his-face told you not to go anywhere near it? Don't you think they might wonder why you don't seem too worried about saving your own skin?"

"Of course, I'm worried, and I made sure I wasn't seen or recognized. My face wasn't visible, and there was no one around."

"That you could see! Do you really think they would just assign more officers out front again after what happened? Use your head, Vanessa! You're not coming with me tonight."

"The hell I'm not! If you think I'll let you just leave me here like a good, little dog, waiting for you to come home, you can just trash that idea right now, buddy, because it ain't gonna happen."

"I can't trust you. I'm afraid you'll do something stupid, since you aren't taking this seriously enough."

"Not taking this seriously enough? I'm holed up here with you, aren't I? I left today in order to get things I *needed*, not to have a picnic in the park!"

"I could have gone to your apartment for you, and picked up whatever you needed; you didn't have to go alone."

"Oh? And could you have grabbed me the vamp mace too? How could you have pulled that one off without getting fried? The only store that carries it closed long before the sun went down."

"Vamp mace?"

"Colloidal silver, genius." I rolled my eyes. "There will be times when I can't walk around, packing handguns and a big-ass hunting knife. It might look just the teeniest bit suspicious. But colloidal silver? No one will question that if they see it; and it will blind any fangy fuckers that try to take a bite out of me."

"Huh, not bad," he admitted begrudgingly.

"I know." Okay, so I wasn't as gracious as I could have been, but he was really starting to piss me off again. I abhorred all that high-handed, macho crap. "Looks like you didn't think of everything after all."

"It doesn't matter, love, you're still not coming with me tonight."

Without blinking, I whipped the knife out of the scabbard on my hip and pointed it at him. "Call me *love* one more time," I said slowly.

William vanished swiftly before reappearing in front of me. He allowed the tip of my knife to barely graze the fabric on the front of his silk shirt. Looking down at the blade, and then back up at me, he cocked his head to the side, and said, "Feeling a little feisty, are we... *love*?"

"Arg!" I cried out in frustration Dropping the knife, I

lashed out and cracked him straight in the jaw with my fist. I returned the knife to the scabbard and started breathing harder. My shoulders rose and fell as I took large, gasping breaths while centering all of my energy on my anger and frustration.

"Don't even think about it, Vanessa," he cautioned.

As I stared at him, the edges of my vision started to redden, and my solar plexus began to burn. "You want me to prove that I can do it? I'll show you I can."

"Don't, Vanessa, you can't control it yet!"

"Don't tell me what I can't do," I snarled. Yes, I was aching for a fight. I knew I could do it, I had it in me; and I wanted to prove it to him, once and for all. "What's the matter, Will? Afraid I might hurt you?" I taunted.

With an unexpected lunge, William shoved me against the living room wall. I brought my hands around his arms and down, loosening his grip on me, before grabbing his shoulders. Slamming my knee up into his stomach, I used enough force to make him grunt. When he bent over, I shoved him backwards and brought the heel of my hand underneath his jaw, snapping his head back.

"Vanessa, stop!" he demanded.

"No, not until you admit that I can do it." I advanced on him as he straightened up.

"You're not ready," he insisted.

He moved so quickly, he became a blur, but I could still barely see him. My powers weren't as strong as the other night, but they could handle this. I felt him coming up behind me so I jabbed an elbow backward with as much force as I could muster. A sharp pain jolted through my arm at the impact, and I cried out, cradling my elbow as I turned around. Okay, so I wasn't anywhere near as strong as I was the night before. William clutched his stomach and dropped to his knees, glaring up at me.

"Have I made my point?" I gasped, holding my arm tightly to my chest. I hoped my expression did not indicate just how much it hurt.

"Point made," William said as he stood up and grabbed my face in his hand. "But don't get overconfident. You got a couple of solid shots in, I admit, but if I wanted you dead, believe me, you would have been dead. You're nowhere near as strong as you were the other night. You can't depend on your powers to keep you alive, love, so don't pretend like you can." Loosening his grip, he held my face gently and added, "You do have more control over it than I thought, so you might just stay alive a little longer after all. Get whatever you need; it's time to go."

CHAPTER TEN

"Where are we going?" I asked William as we sped through downtown.

"Hunting," he said simply.

"Can you give me a little more than that?"

"We're also going drinking," he replied less than eagerly. He'd been short with me ever since the apartment. I didn't care. The whole situation could have been avoided if he had only put a little faith in me. *I just hope I'll be stronger than I was tonight when the time comes.*

"So we're going drinking and hunting. Oh, God," I said, suddenly worried. "I don't have to watch you eat, do I?" The thought made my stomach roil with disgust.

"You wanted to come along, remember? If you're feeling delicate about it, love, feel free to shut your eyes."

I decided to let the *love* slide as we sat in silence for a few minutes.

"There are a few clubs in town that offer pretty good

hunting. Big, loud, and packed. I've been checking them out, trying to get a feel for the vampires there. Seeing if any of them seem, you know, off. It seems pretty easy for these renegades to snatch their victims from there. No one notices them leaving together, and even if they did, it wouldn't be seen as suspicious."

"Just another club night hook-up," I nodded, fully understanding. It was all feeling a little too familiar, since it was how I hunted at the clubs. At least, my meals woke up alive and happy the next morning. Hell, they were often happier than they were when their evening started the night before. "So where are we going tonight?"

"Crimson."

"Crimson? Really?" he had to be kidding, "Is that some sort of inside vamp joke?"

"The humor of it was acknowledged, yes."

I tried not to roll my eyes. The idea of finding vampires who were seeking blood meals at the name of a place, which described the color of said blood was too coincidental.

"If I knew we were going to Crimson, I would have changed," I lamented as I looked down at my black jeans and combat boots. My guns were hidden under my red leather jacket in their shoulder holsters. "I would have also probably left the girls at home." William's eyes went directly to my cleavage. "Not *those* girls," I said, turning his face back toward the road, "I meant *these* girls," I emphasized while patting where my weapons were concealed.

"Don't worry about security; it won't be a problem."

"Glamour the bouncer?"

He nodded, "Glamour the bouncer."

"I really have to learn how to do that. It could save me a lot of pain with Mr. Mooney."

"Mr. Mooney?"

"He's my boss, and a complete dick. Honestly, I think the best part of all this is not having to go to work for the next whatever. You know, I haven't said anything to my friends yet about getting the call from John, and Karen's probably been wondering where I am." I looked down at my lap, feeling guilty. "I haven't even been checking my phone because I don't want to think up another lie, or half truth, or whatever, to explain my absence."

"Why don't you just tell them that Detective Whatever forbade you from going in?"

"Will you stop that?"

"Stop what?"

"Stop pretending that you don't know his name. His name is John. Or call him Detective Hache, but stop acting like you can never remember him. He's the other person trying to keep me alive."

"I can't be bothered to remember his name," he shrugged.

"Why the hell not?"

"Because it doesn't matter to me. He might be trying to solve a case, but he's never going to. He means nothing to me. And if, by some random fluke, he does happen to blunder his way in, and stumble upon the killers, he'll be dead so fast, it won't even matter anyway."

"That's extremely harsh."

"Maybe, but it's still true."

I started to argue with him, but stopped. Just because I didn't like it didn't make it any less true.

"Should we split up?" I shouted over the deep, throbbing bass blasting out of the speakers. Crimson was in full swing, and one of the hottest places to be on a Saturday night. A gorgeous blonde model swished by me before her gaze fell on William. She winked at him before sashaying off. "You know what? Maybe we should stick together," I suggested while pushing him deeper into the crowd. It also happened to be the complete opposite direction from which the blonde was headed. "I mean, what if I can't pick the other guys out? You should probably stick around, you know, just to give me a heads up." William laughed at me. I guess he wasn't buying it.

The crowd became intoxicating. I hadn't been to a bar since that night at the Roxy, over two months ago, and the energy ran up and down my skin like an electric current.

"Vanessa, focus; and keep looking," William said, getting visibly irritated with me.

"Everyone looks the same to me," I groaned, frustrated. I could barely keep my eyes from glazing over, as I moved my hips lightly to the music.

"Are you all right?" he asked with a worried look on his face.

"I'm fine. I'm fine," I giggled as I grinned up at him.

"You don't look fine, you look... really drunk."

"I'm not drunk, how could I be drunk? I haven't swallowed a single sip of booze! You've been with me all night; don't be crazy." Turning my back to him, I slipped and fell against him. I raised my arms and wrapped them around his neck, saying, "Silly William."

"Okay, you are seriously not well, pet." William tried to pull my arms from his neck, but I held on tightly.

"Love! Pet! Why do you hardly ever call me by my name? It's Vanessa. Go on, try it, it's easy. Va-nes-sa." I pronounced it slowly, drawing out the syllables.

"Vanessa, we don't have time for this," he replied in a wavering voice.

"Come dance with me." I grabbed his hand and dragged him onto the dance floor. I knew we had a job to do, but I didn't care anymore. I felt amazing. Everything there seemed foggy and primal, as the bodies gyrated around me, pulsing in unison. Stopping in the middle of the dance floor, I pressed myself against William before undulating in time with the rhythm. I closed my eyes and let my mind reach out to the crowd, feeling the group's pulsating energy of sex and desire. It caressed me like a blanket. As I stretched my arms out wide, my hand collided with another dancer. I smiled and wrapped my arms around her, ignoring William and allowing her to grind up against me.

Wrapping my arms around her waist, I pulled her in closer and kissed her. I fed off all the extra energy that rolled off her like waves. Eventually releasing her to her former dance partner, I turned around to find William staring at me, apparently at a loss for words.

I reached out to draw him toward me when I suddenly felt something was wrong. I spun around in a circle, searching the crowd. Over in a corner, across from the main bar, I spotted the back of a man. His head was dipped down as if he were speaking to someone, but the other person was out of sight. I starting to move in that direction until William's hand on my arm stopped me.

"What is it?" he asked.

"I'm not sure. That guy there," I turned to point where the man was standing, but the corner was now empty. "He was right there," I indicated the spot where I saw him, "over in the corner. I had this undeniable feeling that he was, *wrong*. I think he may be the one we're looking for, but he's gone now."

"Come on! Maybe we can catch him if we hurry," William said before yanking my hand and cutting a path through the crowd. He was heading towards the spot where I last saw the guy.

When we got there, I looked around to see which direction he might have gone. Suddenly, I spotted him beside the front door. "Over there! And he's got someone with him."

Working our way around the edge of the dance floor, we

got to the front door and rushed outside. We both looked up and down the busy street, frantically trying to spot the pair.

Lifting his face towards the sky, William inhaled deeply before heading to the left. "This way," he said.

"How do you know?" I hurried to keep up with him, my boots pounding loudly on the pavement as we ran down the street.

"I can sense him, as well as her fear."

"Why couldn't you sense him in there?"

"I don't know. It's strange; even now, it's still very faint."

We slowed down when we came to a side alley, and William held out his arm to stop me from entering. It was hard to see anything in the darkness. The light from the street lamps didn't illuminate much, being that far off the main street. There were no windows either that might have cast some light into the area to brighten our way. Moving slowly and quietly, we entered the alley, and William went ahead of me to make sure it was safe.

"Dammit! They're already gone!" William swore.

"Are you sure they came this way?"

"Yes, I can smell the blood. Follow me."

Going further down the narrow street, I watched William inspecting the ground as we walked. Finding what he was looking for, he crouched down and touched a spot on the pavement. He held his hand up to me and I saw a dark smudge on his fingers. I knew it was blood.

"There's a lot down here," he said, standing up.

"Do you think he killed her right here?"

"Maybe, and even if he didn't, she will, no doubt, be dead soon. The guy wouldn't have made such a mess if he had planned to let her go."

"Dammit!" I kicked the cement wall of the building in frustration. "We were so close. We could have stopped it if we hadn't been so slow. You could have moved much faster without me."

"Don't, Vanessa, don't blame yourself for this. I didn't even sense his presence, and that doesn't make any sense. Vampires can sense one another and the crowd in there wasn't big enough to block his presence from me for as long as he did. Yet I had no idea he was there. You sensed him, not I. If you hadn't been with me tonight, I might have never even known one of them was here."

"Yeah, but what good does that do us? Another person will get killed. What do you want to bet that her body will show up in a few days, if not tomorrow? And what do we have to show for this little outing tonight? Nothing! That's what. Just another dead body."

"We also learned that you can sense us after all, even when a vampire fails to detect another. That's useful, Vanessa, and that can help us."

"Well, hopefully, it will help us move faster next time."

"Come on, let's get out of here; there's nothing else we can do."

I was still steaming when we walked out of the alley. The street seemed garish and bright as we emerged from the shadows. I stepped onto the sidewalk and someone ran into me. "Watch it," I warned, ready to curse the jerk for his clumsiness. I was in no mood for stupid people's bullshit, not after what just happened.

"Sorry," the guy replied as he turned around to apologize and froze. "Vanessa? What are you doing here?"

I looked up at the shocked expression of Detective John Hache and racked my brain for any excuse. "I'm just..."

"You can't seriously be out partying! Didn't I tell you to lie low? Do you have a death wish?"

My eyes darted towards the alley and back again. I was still trying to come up with a reply. When did I become such a crap liar? "I'm just out getting a little fresh air. I felt a little cooped up."

"Cooped up? After what? Three days? Give me a break, Vanessa. And you came out alone? That's way beyond stupid."

"I'm not alone, I'm with..." As my words trailed off, I looked around for William. I had no idea where he went.

"She's with me," William said as he came out of nowhere. He wrapped his arm around my shoulders protectively.

Detective Hache looked puzzled for a moment before glaring at William. "I remember you; we met at Vanessa's."

"Did we?" William asked innocently, "I'm afraid I don't remember."

Adjusting myself slightly, I jabbed William in the ribs as subtly as I could, before grinning stupidly at John. "William offered to take me out tonight just to get out of the house," I explained quickly.

"Oh, I see. So none of the girls wanted to join you tonight?"

"Oh, well, they were all busy; and I didn't want to beg, so… you know."

"Right," John sounded skeptical, "I never did ask which one you're staying with. I'll also need her address in case I, or any of the other officers, need to come by and check on you."

"Ummm… which one of the girls am I staying with?" Our conversation was getting more awkward by the second.

"She's not," William answered. He might as well have thrown a live grenade.

"She's not… what? Exactly?" John looked back and forth between us.

"She's not staying with one of the girls, mate," William replied smugly. I had to repress the urge to wipe the look off his face with the bottom of my boot.

"Uh-huh… where is she staying then?"

"With me, of course," William answered oh-so-unhelpfully.

"Of course," John nodded as he crossed his arms, and his face went blank.

"Well, then, I suppose it's your address I need to have on record."

"I suppose you do," William said. He was all but

grinning now.

John reached into his pocket and pulled out his cell phone. "Would you mind just putting it in here then?" John asked coldly as he passed the phone to William, but William didn't take it.

"Actually, I do mind. I don't like the thought of you swinging by my place whenever you feel like it."

"William," I snapped, moving away from him, but with the smallest gesture, he clamped his arm down on me like a vise without John noticing anything. I growled under my breath, knowing that William could hear me loud and clear.

"Look, mister..."

"Just call me William," he replied affably.

"William." The way John said his name made it sound like a foul swear word. "I must assume that you know why Vanessa is staying with you."

"Because she can't get enough of my good looks and stellar personality?"

"Hardly," I muttered. Feeling William's squeeze, I stifled an "Oof!"

"Because the Silverlake Police Department believes she is in serious danger. We think it is best for her to remain somewhere that the perpetrator won't be able to find her easily."

"Well, see? It's a good thing no one knows where she's staying then, isn't it? I agree with you completely, Officer."

"Detective," Hache corrected him.

"Sorry, of course, I meant, Detective. So we both agree that it's best if no one knows where Vanessa is staying for the time being."

"Everyone except the police, of course," Hache amended.

"And please explain to me why that is now?"

John looked at William like he was talking to a half-witted twit. "We have to know where she is in case we need to get to her quickly. If we think she's in danger, how can we find her to warn her?" he explained slowly.

"Nasty business with those officers in front of her building the other day," William tossed out casually.

John seemed startled, momentarily caught off guard by his abrupt change of topic. "Yes, it was. There are no words for it."

"Amazing how that guy managed to take out two of Silverlake's finest," William continued aimlessly.

"What are you getting at?"

"Well, I imagine that someone who has no problems killing a cop or two probably wouldn't feel squeamish while torturing one. Especially one that he blamed for getting in the way of what he wanted." William's steely eyes held John's gaze. "So tell me, Detective, how long do you think you could hold out before this guy tortured Vanessa's location from you? An hour? Two hours? It doesn't really matter how long, does it? Eventually, you would give her up." William smiled softly. "So no, I don't think I will provide you with my address, and I'm sure you'll agree that it's for the best. Now if you'll excuse us, I must be getting Vanessa back home, where it's safe." Turning around, William directed us back towards the car, leaving Detective Hache standing there, staring blankly after us.

"I'm surprised you didn't even try to defend your poor, well-meaning Detective John Hache," William said as he opened the car door for me.

"I wanted to," I replied. It was the truth, but would have led to another pointless argument. "Your attitude was overly high-handed! You tried to rile him up on purpose. But you also made a good point. His knowing where I am could do more harm than good. If this guy comes after me, and I can't handle him, there's probably very little that John could do. But I don't doubt for a second that whoever this guy is, he would have no problem torturing John. Especially if he thought it would lead to me, and I couldn't live with the knowledge that I let that happen."

CHAPTER ELEVEN

Standing in William's kitchen, I was making myself lunch when my phone started to vibrate on the counter. Pressing the grilled cheese sandwich down with the metal spatula, I put the lid on the pan and snatched my phone, checking the call display. No matter how guilty I felt, I was still ducking the girls, only returning their calls with vague text messages about police-ordered seclusion. I promised to fill them in on everything as soon as I could. So far, it was working, but I doubted it would keep them satisfied for long. I needn't have worried though, as the call display guaranteed a much worse call: Detective John Hache.

"Hello, Detective Hache, how are you?"

"Vanessa," he said, and his voice was curt and professional. *Hmmm, he must still be upset about the whole William thing.*

"That's me, what's up?"

"I'm going to ask you something, and I need you to be

completely honest with me; do you understand? I need the absolute truth."

No conversation in the history of the world could go well if it started with an opener like that. "Of course, what is it?"

"What were you doing out last Saturday night?"

"What? I told you, I was getting some fresh air. Why?"

"See? That's what I told the chief when he asked me the same question, but unfortunately, he doesn't seem quite so ready to believe that." His voice was cold as stone.

"I don't understand, what's going on?"

"What's going on, Ms. Kensley, is another body was found Sunday morning."

Oh shit. "That's horrible, but what does that have to do with my being out? You even said my situation wasn't related to any of that."

"Well, that's what we thought, except this time, the killer wasn't quite as smart."

"Really? That's wonderful, did he leave some kind of clue behind?" I racked my brain, trying to remember if my fingerprints could have been found anywhere near the blood left behind in the alley, but I couldn't remember touching anything.

"Yes, actually, they gave us a pretty good lead. Turns out the victim had a club stamp on her inside wrist. The killer apparently failed to notice it and left it behind. Can you guess where the stamp was from?"

"No, why don't you tell me since you're so obviously

dying to?"

"Don't get smart with me, Vanessa," he snapped. "The stamp was from Crimson. The exact same bar you were so keen on hanging around that night."

"Oh, my God! Are you saying another person was killed in the same bar where I was?" I asked, trying to imbue some fear into my voice. It wasn't that hard.

"Something like that, except the body wasn't found at the club."

"Where was it found?"

"Now here is where things get *really* interesting. It was found in an alley."

"An alley?" My stomach felt like it was lodged in my throat and I couldn't breathe. I knew exactly what was coming next, but I had to ask anyway. "Where?"

"The same goddamn alley you were coming out of when I bumped into you on Saturday night!" he shouted on the line.

I winced and clenched the phone so tightly, the palm of my hand hurt, "Oh, my God," I whispered.

"Yes, Vanessa, *oh, my God* pretty much sums it up, don't you think? How the hell does a goddamn body end up in the same alley where I found you less than twenty-four hours ago? What the hell were you doing in that alley, Vanessa?" He kept yelling at me, but his voice only grew more faint as a buzzing filled my ears, blocking him out.

"I can't believe it," I choked.

"You'd better believe it, Vanessa, because I have another

body and a mountain of paperwork to prove it. Now, answer the damn question! What the hell were you doing in that alley? It doesn't seem like the sort of place any woman would be skulking around, especially when she knows a psychopath has got her in his sights, now does it?"

"I wasn't skulking, I just needed to get away from the crowd for a quick moment. I was starting to feel claustrophobic."

"Is that right? And you thought the best place to catch a little fresh air was a pitch-black alley?"

"Look, Detective, I don't know what you're trying to say, so why don't you just come out and say it, okay?" My head was starting to spin.

"You want me to be straight with you? Fine? I'm starting to think that your stalker and my killer are the same person after all, but now, I'm also suspicious that you might know more about this than your letting on."

"What the hell are you talking about? Do you think I'm in on this, or something?" I hissed.

"I don't think you're killing people, but I think you may have an idea about who might be doing these things; and if you do, you had better open your goddamn mouth and tell me what you know! Do you understand me? People keep showing up dead, Vanessa, and a lot of them seem to happen around you! Why is that? Why is it never you?"

"Holy shit, John!" I couldn't believe what I was hearing. "Are you saying that you *want* this guy to get me?"

"No, of course not. But things aren't looking too good

for you here, Vanessa. Between this last killing and your *friend* refusing to disclose where you are; well, it's making you look uncooperative now."

"I've cooperated the whole time! That is completely ridiculous."

"So, then, tell me where you are, Vanessa. It's just you and me now, so why don't you just tell me where you are?"

"I... I can't."

"Why not, Vanessa? Because William doesn't want you to tell me? What does he have to hide? Why doesn't he want us to know where he lives?"

"He doesn't have anything to hide; are you crazy?" John was starting to ask too many questions. "He told you his reasons last night, he thinks having less people know my whereabouts makes me safer."

"And do you believe that, Vanessa? Do you believe you're safer there with him than you would be somewhere else? I'm sorry, but he seems pretty damn overconfident to me. Does he understand the kind of danger you're in? Or is he just taking this like a game? An exciting opportunity for him to act like the big hero?"

"I'm safe here, John, I'm sure of it. I know that William can be a bit... okay, extremely irritating, but he knows this isn't a game. He's taking this seriously and fully understands how dangerous it is," *more than you would ever be able to*.

"Fine, I hope that you know what you're doing, Vanessa, because if your stubbornness gets you killed, I would really hate to be the one who says, 'I told you so' at your funeral. Stay the hell inside! Do you understand me? Promise me that you won't give this guy another chance to get close to you."

"I promise to keep myself safe." It was as much as I could honestly say without it being a flat-out lie. Didn't my guns count towards my active participation on ensuring my safety?

"Don't do anything stupid, Vanessa. I can only do so much to keep you alive if you don't cooperate."

"I understand." I hung up the phone and stood up to see smoke coming out from under the lid on the pan on the stove. Cursing, I opened it before waving my hands to clear a giant cloud of smoke, which billowed out. I waved my hands again and looked down at my sandwich. Flipping it over, the underside was burned completely black. Sighing, I dumped the sandwich in the garbage can and started over again.

William and I sat in his living room. I filled him in on the call from Detective Hache while William kept my wine glass filled for me. I was starting to enjoy a nice buzz.

"You know what this means, don't you?" I looked at William and frowned. He was much too attractive in a cream, v-neck sweater and dark, stonewashed jeans.

"It means the killer knew we were there. He's mocking us," he summarized. Leaning forward, he grabbed the wine bottle off the table, and topped off my glass again.

"That's what I thought too. What was the point of taking the body out of the alley just to put it back there again? It must have been a message for us," I said as I shook my head. "As if he's saying, 'you are good, but not nearly good enough!' The cruel bastard."

"That means he knows we're looking for him. So by now, the others will know as well. Although I don't know who they are, they most likely know me."

"They do?" Well, that was no good.

"The Silverlake Coven isn't particularly large, it couldn't possibly be if we wanted to continue operating in secret. The more vampires in an area, the more feedings they need, so naturally, the easier they are to be seen and exposed. Every vampire in the coven has been to Elizabeth's place at some point; and most of us spend quite a lot of time there. These renegade vampires are bound to know who I am."

"What does Elizabeth think about all of this? She's the coven leader, right? She must be furious that this is all happening on her turf."

"She is. I brought my suspicions to her, but she refuses to believe that it could be our people doing this. She's convinced it must be nomads."

I took a sip of wine and nodded. I could see how Elizabeth wouldn't want to believe that any of her own could break her laws, but denying it could happen was making her blind to the possibility, and that was dangerous. It could sneak up and bite her on the ass. "Does she have some sort of plan for how to handle this? It's been going on so long now that I can't see her just sitting back and letting it continue. What were you telling me before about swift justice?"

"You're right; she has been working on something. That's actually where we're going tonight. Elizabeth is hosting a gathering at the manor tonight."

"Wait. I'm coming with you!? Without a fight, or an argument? Just like that, I get to join the cool kids club?"

He shook his head, saying, "Not that I would have tried to stop you, but Elizabeth specifically told me to bring you along."

"Oh, well, at least, you wouldn't ditch me here again."

"No, I'm learning how completely pointless that is. Besides, I think it's important for you to know whatever the plan is. You being targeted means you have as much interest in this as the rest of us, even if you aren't exactly one of us."

"Looks like I'm close enough to skate by on a technicality."

"Looks like it, love, looks like it."

It didn't matter how many times I saw Elizabeth's place, it took my breath away every single time. There were a few other vehicles parked outside as we pulled up.

"Do you know who else was invited?" I asked, looking

around the courtyard, but the vehicles were all unoccupied.

"No, she wouldn't tell me anyone else's name."

"Gotta love a little espionage," I joked. Laughing, William put his hand on my back and guided me into the house.

We were all gathered in the same lounge I entered the first night I was introduced to Elizabeth. I had yet to see very much of her house, as most of my training took place outside, in the sprawling grounds behind the manor. I was curious as to what I might find tucked away behind the dozens of doors scattered throughout her home.

"William, Vanessa, thank you for coming tonight," Elizabeth said as she enveloped me in a hug and kissed William on both cheeks. "As you both know, we have something very serious to discuss. I would like to introduce you to a new task force that I have recently put together." She turned towards the open door before three militant-looking vampires walked in. All three were dressed from head-to-toe in black. The two men wore matching black, turtleneck sweaters, black jeans and combat books. The woman opted for a deep, v-neck sweater and leather pants.

"Vanessa, William, I would like to introduce you to the new Vampire Regulation Task Force. This situation with the renegades has gone on for far too long. I cannot and I will not allow it to continue any longer. I have chosen these three because I believe in and trust them."

"So you three are going to take down the renegades?

How?" I asked. Sure, they were an impressive-looking bunch, but I found it a bit hard to believe that three lone vampires would suddenly just waltz into some hidden vamp den, knock them around for a bit, and then later pat themselves on the back for a job well done. If it were that easy, it would have been done already, right?

"That's exactly what we're going to do! Don't you worry your pretty, little head about that, sweet cheeks." I placed my hands on my hips and cocked my head to the side, examining the ass hat of a vampire who spoke. He wasn't tall, roughly the same height as my five-foot-seven, but he stood there, all puffed out like a man who was used to being in charge. If asked, I'm sure he would swear up, down, and sideways that he topped six-foot-one.

Pulling the cigarette that was tucked behind his ear out, he placed it in his mouth. A soft cough came from Elizabeth's direction, and his eyes flickered towards her before quickly returning the cigarette back to his ear.

"Did you seriously just call me 'sweet cheeks'?" I had more than half a dozen redneck insults on the tip of my tongue.

"Yeah, I did, and just to be clear, I wasn't talkin' 'bout the cheeks on your face neither," he added, as his eyes skimmed over my body before coming to rest on my hips.

I took a step forward with my fists clenched. This jerk deserved to be laid flat on his ass. But before I could reach him, the woman stepped forward and pulled him back. Then she inserted herself between us.

She was gorgeous, which was no surprise; supermodel-caliber good looks seemed to be a requirement for all the women around here. I had yet to see a single overweight, or homely female vampire in the coven, but this one was truly something else.

Her sharply defined European features were quite striking: high cheekbones set off by wide, almond-shaped eyes the color of storm clouds. The dark gray lightened around her pupils. Her blonde hair was shockingly pure: icy platinum that fell in a heavy, straight curtain, ending at her waist. She was taller than me, maybe five-foot-ten, with a lithe, willowy figure and small, pert breasts. She moved with the confidence of someone who never experienced a single second of self-doubt.

Had she been in my class at school, I would have hated her on sight. But I was an adult now, and above such petty things. I resolved not to hate her until she proved what a complete bitch she probably was.

"Thatcher, don't be rude," she chided. I was right; her thick accent was distinctly European, but I couldn't place it. It sounded like a mix of French and something I couldn't quite put my finger on. "Not everyone wants to listen to your crude jokes."

She held out her hand toward me and I shook it, instantly noticing the long, manicured nails that were painted a shocking, electric-green. I couldn't restrain my smile; the color was hot.

"I'm Vanessa," I offered politely, trying not to cringe

when her receptive smile revealed a set of the most perfect teeth I ever saw in my life. *Who the hell has teeth so perfect?* Freaks, that's who.

"I am Anastasia, and that," she said while indicating redneck Joe, "is Thatcher. Please try not to be too offended by his remarks. I think he simply enjoys rubbing people the wrong way. He really doesn't mean any of it."

"I'll have to take your word for that, I suppose," I replied while glaring at Thatcher. He just smiled and winked at me. Rolling my eyes, I ignored him and walked over to the other member of the team. I never had to tilt my head so far back just to look someone in the eye before.

"I'm Bull." A truer nickname was never given. Not only tall at easily seven feet, he dwarfed us in height, as well as mass. The circumference of his thighs looked like they were the same size as my waist. I would have bet good money the only way he managed to get his biceps so large was by bench pressing small vehicles.

Hard to believe that behind all his immense size, he also had the advantage of supernatural vampire skills. Some guys had all the luck.

His sleeveless shirt revealed two full sleeves of tattoos on both arms. They ended at his wrists, and were partially covered by his shirt. His smooth, bald head shone under the light from the sconces hanging around the room. I tried not to stare at the long scar that ran down the side of his face from his left eye to his collarbone.

Oh, please, God! Never let me get on this guy's bad side.

"Nice to meet you, Bull," I straightened up to my full height and looked him right in the eye. Never show anyone your fear.

"You too," his voice was gruff, but not altogether unfriendly.

After meeting everyone, I turned back to Elizabeth and William.

"So, this is the dream team."

"Yes," Elizabeth replied, scanning the room and taking them all in. "I felt that you deserved to know what actions were being taken by those of us in the vampire community, since your stalker is obviously one of our own. You're deeply invested in this." She turned to William, "And as to you, I am hoping that you will choose to join the Task Force as well. I trust you, William, and your judgment, as I always have. Will you help us?"

"Of course, I will, Elizabeth. I'll do everything that I can."

Satisfied, Elizabeth sat down again, saying, "Well, then, it looks like we are all set. Everyone, welcome to--"

"Sorry," I cleared my throat as I raised my hand, "hate to interrupt, but aren't we forgetting something?"

"Are we?" Elizabeth looked puzzled, "What is that?"

"Me?" I pointed down at the top of my head.

"You?" she repeated.

"Yes, me. What about me joining this Task Force business? My life is in danger and if you think I'm just going to sit back and rely on other people to take care of this problem for me, well, it's never going to happen; just ask William. No, if you've assembled a task force to deal with this problem, then I want to be on it. I want to fight, I want to help."

"You?" Thatcher laughed, "You're not even a vampire! What the hell could you do to help? All you'll do is slow us down and get us killed!"

"Excuse me? No, I'm not a vampire; I'm a succubus. Do you know what that means?" I started ticking off my points on my fingers, saying, "It means that I can walk in daylight, touch silver, oh, yeah, and kill vampires just by sucking the energy out of them. In other words, I'm totally badass. Just ask William! He's seen me do it. And while I may not have a complete handle on my powers just yet, I'm getting better every day. So how about you just shut your big mouth until you actually know what you're talking about, yeah?"

"Well," Elizabeth clapped her hands together, "I suppose that settles it then. Vanessa, welcome to the Vampire Regulation Task Force. Everyone, get to work! We have a job to do."

CHAPTER TWELVE

"All right, people, we're almost there so listen up," Thatcher barked at us as we sat in the back of the van. We were heading towards one of the renegade safe houses. "This is going to be a simple sweep and clean. We've been monitoring this location for the past week, and it's definitely what we're looking for."

"How did we find this place?" I asked.

Thatcher frowned at me. "We caught one just over a week ago. It took some persuasion, but he eventually told us about this place." His subsequent grin made my skin crawl. I swallowed and nodded, checking my weapons again.

"Are you ready for this?" William leaned over and whispered. I nodded, but didn't look at him. I was trying to calm my nerves as well as build up my energy. I wanted to be as strong as possible when I went in there. The last thing I desired was William engraving *I told you so* on my tombstone.

"Anastasia and Bull will take the back of the house. Vanessa, William, and I will go through the front. And it's showtime."

The van came to a stop and Thatcher gave us a quick nod before jumping out the back. The rest of us filed out behind him and followed him down the street. Crouching low, we hurried down the sidewalk, using the bushes for cover while scanning the area for any signs of activity. Once we were sure the coast was clear, we split up to cover the front and back of the house, thereby blocking the main exits.

We made our way carefully up the path to the front door and took our positions. I stood to the right while William took the spot on the left. Thatcher gave us a quick nod before he kicked the front door in.

My heart was hammering in my throat as I rushed through the door after them, my Sig Sauer out in front of me. I scanned the front hall.

A hand shot out from around the corner and wrapped around my wrist. With a sharp jerk, my attacker pulled me forward and I lost my balance.

"Oof!" the air came out of me in a whoosh as a knee rammed me hard in the stomach.

He smashed my hand back into the wall, and I instantly lost the grip on my gun. Before I could get my bearings back, he grabbed me by my shirt and leg, lifting me up off the floor.

"Oh shit!" I yelled as he held me above his head. I came smashing down on the kitchen table, and the air was again knocked out of me. The table cracked with the force of the impact.

The vampire hovered over me, pressing my shoulders onto the hard wood of the table. My hands struggled, ineffectually beating his forearms as I strove in vain to get out from beneath him. A moment later, my neck began burning when his fangs grazed it.

Just as the pressure started to increase, my shoulders were suddenly freed as the vampire seemed to be ripped back from me. I rolled off the table and landed in a crouch on the floor. I was just in time to see Bull picking up my attacker and hurling him against the wall of the kitchen. Pulling my second gun from its holster, I aimed and shot the vampire twice in the chest.

"Are you all right?" Bull asked.

Lifting my hand to my stinging neck, I pulled it away and saw the blood on my fingers. "Yeah, I'm fine."

Grabbing my stake, I crossed the kitchen toward the dazed vampire. This jerk nearly took a bite out of me! With a vise-like grip on the stake, I brought it down with all of my strength and planted it into his chest.

"But I'm even better now," I said as I looked at Bull and jerked my head. "Thanks for the help."

As the sound of my racing heart calmed down in my ears, the crashing caused by all the fighting in the rest of the house started to filter back in.

"We gotta go," Bull said as he grabbed my lost gun from the kitchen floor and passed it back to me. Holstering it, I headed out of the kitchen, following behind him with a gun in one hand, and a stake in the other.

A vampire dived at me from the stairs, and I dropped

down onto the floor on one knee. Dodging him, I watched him sail over me before carefully aiming. I shot him in the back.

Bull grabbed him in a headlock and spun him towards me. Then he pulled the hapless vampire in front of his body, and ordered, "Stake him."

"With pleasure," I snarled. My rage from the close scrape I avoided was still fresh in my mind. I adjusted the grip on my stake and threw it at my target, watching it impale his chest quite efficiently.

Bull looked down at the stake and then up at me. He had an expression of shock on his face. I didn't know which one of us was more surprised, him or me. It looked like my powers had finally decided to come out and play.

"Nice throw," Bull said.

"Thanks," I grinned.

Bull let go of the vampire and dropped his body to the floor. The impact knocked the ashes out of body form and they landed in a pile on the floor.

Anastasia and Thatcher came around the corner together, shaking ash out of their clothing.

"Is that all of them?" Thatcher asked.

"I think so," Bull said.

"Then let's get out of here."

"Where's William?" I hadn't seen him since we entered the house.

"I'm here," he replied, strolling through the side door from the living room. "One was trying to escape out across the backyard, but I took care of him."

"So, that's it?" I looked around us. "We came, we killed,

we conquered?"

"For now. This is only one nest down, and there may be others."

"Okay. Maybe I'm completely out of line here, but don't you think we should have captured at least one of them for further questioning?"

"Well, shit," Thatcher cursed as he spat on the floor.

"Maybe we did get a little carried away here," Anastasia agreed, biting her lower lip.

"Okay. So where do we go now? This nest is clear, right?"

"So long as everyone in it was here; then, yes. But let's keep an eye on this place just in case anyone comes back tonight. Bull, Anastasia, I want you two to stay here for the rest of the night. If anyone else comes back, I expect you can handle it. If you manage to get any information from anyone, let me know. Everyone else, we're going back to the manor to report to Elizabeth."

"How are you feeling?" William asked as he let us into the apartment.

"All right. I'm a bit sore from the fight, but nothing a good night's sleep won't cure."

"That's good, although I can see you didn't make it out unscathed." He looked pointedly at my neck and I remembered the marks there. Mortified, I avoided his eyes as I walked away from him and started to remove my weapons.

"Okay, so things started off a little rocky, but I managed to get my shit together. I'm still here, aren't I?"

"True enough. You made it out alive; and that's the important thing."

"I'll get stronger, William, and I'll be able to control my abilities better, I know I will. I just need a little more time."

"I can't promise you that luxury, Vanessa. The renegades aren't going to just back off while you learn to get your skills under control. I doubt they would regard it in their best interest. None would be willing to allow you the time you need to learn how to kill them more efficiently."

"Look, I know things are going to be pretty damn *sink or swim* here, especially with the new task force. Don't worry, I can hold up my end."

"I don't doubt that you'll try."

"I will," I said, determined to prove to him and the rest of the team that I was born for this. There was no way in hell that I would let them all consider me the weak link. They had to trust me and know they could count on me to watch their backs when necessary.

"Come here," William said, and his voice was low and sultry. I wanted to walk over and wrap my arms around him, so I took a step farther away.

"Why?"

"So that I can heal you," he explained.

"I'm fine; it's only a scratch. It will heal on its own."

"Maybe, but I don't like seeing it on you. It reminds me how close you came to being seriously hurt tonight and I don't like that."

"So… what? You'll just make it disappear so you don't have to look at it? Too bad. Maybe I don't feel like having your vampire spit all over my neck!" I snapped as I gathered up my weapons and started to head upstairs.

"Stop being so stubborn. You're hurt, I can fix it; so just let me."

God, he was so frustrating! "Did you ever think that maybe I don't want you to fix it? Maybe I want the reminder. Maybe it will help me remember to be a little less sloppy next time. Now if you don't mind, I'm going to take a shower." As I climbed the stairs, I felt his eyes burning into me, but I didn't care. Too bad if he didn't like seeing me hurt. I wasn't ready to erase the memory of tonight just yet. Maybe I would let him heal me in the morning, but for now, I wanted to feel the sting and remember.

Dropping my weapons on top of my dresser, I pulled the elastic out of my ponytail, letting my hair free. It flowed down my back and over my shoulders. After I yanked my shirt over my head, I put my hands on the waistband of my pants, but heard a discreet cough behind me.

"Damn it, William, what the hell? Can I get like, two seconds of privacy, please?"

He didn't say anything as he walked over to me and gently placed his hands on my hips, pulling me in closer to his body.

"Seriously, I'm dying for a shower, so if you don't mind--" I lost my train of thought when his hands slipped up to my bare waist. The coolness of his skin felt good as he trailed his fingers down my spine.

"This will only take a second, love, and then you can shower in peace, I promise."

His eyes sparkled with mischief right before he kissed me. It was so soft, I barely felt his lips against mine. I closed the small gap between us, and the fabric of his shirt brushed against my bare skin.

"What was that for?" I asked when he moved his mouth away to nip my ear.

"Just had the urge, love. You're very sexy when you're upset; did you know that?"

My annoyance was slowly starting to erode, being replaced by pleasure when he moved from my ear to nuzzle my neck. I could feel the warm moisture of his mouth sliding from my neck to my shoulder. He slipped my bra strap off and let it fall down my arms.

"William," my voice wavered, "I don't think…"

"Shhh, it's all right, love, I just wanted to hold you for a minute," he explained as he replaced my bra strap and let me go.

"I just don't think it's wise for us to keep doing this." I replied. I reached for my shirt and put it back on.

"You're probably right; enjoy your shower," he answered as he turned and left the room. I noticed he left the bedroom door open behind him.

God! He was so exasperating. My skin still tingled everywhere he touched me, and I tried not to think about how good it felt.

I locked the bathroom door and leaned against it. The last thing I needed was another surprise visit once I was naked and in the shower. My skin flushed as I quickly turned the water on in the shower and got undressed. When I moved, I caught a glimpse of myself in the mirror. Where did the punctures on my neck go? Leaning in closer,

I examined my neck. I glared at the expanse of pure, soft skin. *That sneaky son of a bitch!*

"Goddamn it, William!" I yelled, slamming my fist down on the bathroom counter. The jerk had done that just so he could get to my neck! No wonder he left so fast. He guessed kissing me was the easiest way to get close enough to heal me.

Lashing out, I kicked the bathtub with my bare foot. "Ow, crap, ow!" I wailed before dropping down to the floor and grabbing my foot in both hands. The pain was my retribution for losing my temper, but I still blamed the stupid vampire for not just leaving me alone with my puncture wounds.

"I may just stake him in his sleep," I mumbled as the pain in my foot finally subsided. I eagerly stepped into the shower's relaxing spray.

The combination of heat and the pounding spray massaged my sore muscles and I let out a sigh. It felt wonderful to stand there and not have to worry that someone could jump out from the shadows and tear my throat out. It felt good to know that we made some progress today. For all we knew, perhaps we took out half the renegades tonight. After all, how many could there be? There weren't too many vampires in Silverlake in the first place. With a little luck, we could have this whole mess cleaned up, and really fast.

I leaned my shoulder against the tiles of the shower and let the hot water beat down on my scalp. My shoulders were shaking as tears streamed down my eyes. Suddenly, laughter overtook me. There was no way we could get out of this that easily.

CHAPTER THIRTEEN

The energy surrounding me was completely manic, and the frenzied mass began dissolving my concentration. The rave was in high gear; perfect hunting for any vampire. We were sure to find a few renegades hunting here tonight.

"Can you sense anything?" Bull asked as I tried to sift through the crowd's explosive energy.

"It's faint, but it's there. I just can't figure out where it's coming from yet. Give me a moment."

"Can you at least narrow it down for us, love?" William prodded.

"Nagging me won't make it happen any faster," I snapped. Closing my eyes, I mentally reached out into the seething group of bodies, trying to get a firm grasp on the renegade's location. "I think I've found it; follow me!"

Without waiting to see if they were behind me, I ran into the crowd, rushing towards the area where the faint strain of energy seemed strongest. People in the crowd pushed against me from all sides. With every new contact, I found it more difficult to hold my concentration, and my awareness of the renegade began to flicker in and out. My head swirled as my vision began to blur from the overwhelming energy now hammering me from all sides.

A sudden burning sensation on the back of my neck shocked me back to reality. I searched the crowd frantically before locking eyes with the black-eyed vampire. He smiled at me, the blood still dripping off his fangs, before turning and penetrating the gyrating throng.

"He's over there!" I yelled as I pointed. I started elbowing my way to where he was standing. I spun in a circle, trying to catch sight of him again. For a moment, there was nothing; Then I caught a glimpse of him standing perfectly still in the crowd a few feet from me before he slipped away again. He continued to lead us deeper into the rave, and every time I thought I lost him, I managed to catch his eye for a moment before he took off again. This game of Follow the Leader was starting to really piss me off.

He led us away from the main rave and deeper into the construction zone. The area was dark, and all of the equipment and building supplies could easily have been way too convenient places for him to hide behind.

"Okay, you guys, keep your eyes open," I whispered, "he's here somewhere."

"Yes, I am, sweet thing," a disembodied voice taunted me before stepping out from behind a pile of bricks. "Oh, and look! I brought some friends."

William, Bull and I circled up, keeping our backs to each other as we scanned the area and saw more vamps emerge from hiding.

"You bastards are becoming more trouble than you're worth, you know that?" he sneered.

"Oh, no," I mocked, "how rude of us. We're so sorry. Oh, wait; no, we're not." Turning, I pulled my gun from my side and fired a round into the chest of the vampire closest to me.

"You bitch!" the vampire screamed as the silver burned him from the inside, and smoke billowed out of the hole in his chest. With that, all hell broke loose and the vampires rushed us. I put another bullet in a vampire's chest as it got closer before pulling the stake from the back of my shirt.

"Oh, you think you're gonna poke me with that little stick, do you succu-bitch?" he snarled as we circled around one another.

Ignoring his taunts, I concentrated on my breathing and let my hunger take over me.

"Come and get me," he mocked.

I swung out with the stake and he dodged my attack before backhanding me across the face. My head snapped to the side and I winced in pain, but it was manageable. I could hear the screams around me, but I didn't look to see if they were coming from my guys or theirs. Taking advantage of his upper hand, the vampire planted a fist in my gut. I doubled over in pain, coughing uncontrollably as the wind was forcefully expelled from my lungs. A buzzing started in my ears, which made the sound of his laugher more muffled and far away. I inhaled deeply through my nose and the edges of my vision began to turn red.

The rage overtook me as I advanced on him again. I dropped my stake and pulled my knife from its sheath.

"Vanessa, what the hell are you doing?" William's scream sounded so faint and far away. I could see Bull holding him back from the corner of my eye as William fought to reach me.

The vampire moved towards me, but seemed as if his actions were in slow motion, and he was barely moving. This time, when he swung at me, I easily blocked his attack before spinning and planting a kick squarely in his chest. I continued to advance on him, my hunger screaming inside me to feed. His cocky expression soon turned to one of fear. Lunging, I put my hand around his neck and looked into his pitch-black eyes before plunging my blade into his gut.

"Vanessa!" a choked voice cried out, but it was not William's. Turning to look, I saw Detective Hache standing there with his gun pointed at me, All the blood was drained from his face. I shook my head and turned back to the vampire that I still held in my grip. Pulling the blade out of him, I recoiled my arm and concentrated all of my strength into the blow. Bringing it down across his neck, I effortlessly cut his head from his body in one quick move. The body crumpled to the ground before turning to ash and further collapsing into an indistinguishable pile of dust.

"Vanessa, don't you move! Don't any of you fucking move!" John yelled while aiming his gun at the three of us. I looked around to see the other three piles of ash at our feet. "You're all under arrest. Now drop your weapons and put your hands in the air. Do it now!"

In a flash, Bull was in front of the detective, baring his fangs before ripping the gun from his hands. John's eyes were wide with fear as he looked at Bull. Taking a shaky step back, his chest kept rising and falling as he breathed in gasps.

"I'll take care of this," Bull offered.

"No, stop!" Before I realized I even moved, I had already closed the distance between us and my hand was gripping Bull's arm. "Don't hurt him." Bull looked at me in surprise, but didn't comment on my speed.

"We can't let him remember what he saw, Vanessa. He's a loose end, and we can't have any loose ends."

"You can't kill me," John warned, "I'm a police officer. Do you really want to add a cop killing to the long list of things that you're already going to jail for? Now get your hands off me, you freak."

"John, he's not going to kill you; I promise," I tried to reassure him, but only succeeded in making him angrier.

"Oh, you mean like the way you three didn't just kill those four men over there?"

"John if you just saw them die, you know they weren't

men."

"Hey!" Bull and William protested in unison.

"Not *human* men," I corrected myself.

"All I know is that you guys are a bunch of killers, and you're going to jail for what you've done. Now get on the damn ground."

"Can we please wipe his memory now, pet?" William said as he looked around the abandoned building. "Before anyone else shows up and we have to deal with more of them too?"

"You'll never get away with this," John said as he looked me in the eye and swore. "I will make sure that you are all incarcerated. That's where you murderers belong."

"I'm sorry, John, but the boys are right. We can't allow you to remember this and risk exposing everyone." I looked at Bull and nodded before saying, "Do it."

Suddenly, another vampire emerged from nowhere and attacked Bull, causing him to lose his grip on John. The vampire lashed out widely at all three of us, and his attack had no organization or finesse. It didn't take long for us to kill him, but we still lost precious moments. When we turned back to deal with John, he had already gotten away.

"Shit!" I yelled, pounding on one of the metal construction beams. "Shit, shit, shit! Does anyone else feel like were just set the fuck up?"

"This is definitely smelling like a goddamn setup to me."

"We have to hunt him down before he can form a lynch mob and pursue us, pet."

"I know; let's move."

We caught up with John right before he reached the rave, and snatched him back into the darkness. He struggled against Bull's grip, but it was useless, there was no chance he could get free this time.

"Is there no other way?" I asked. I couldn't stand the way he was looking at us. I knew that glamouring him would be safer for us all around, but I still hated it.

"There's no other way, love, he can't keep those memories."

"You guys are crazy, fucking crazy! And you're all going down for this."

"No, John, we're not. We were set up tonight, but..." I trailed off. "William, wait!"

"Vanessa, we can't—" he started.

"No, really, just wait," I said as I held up my hand to stop him, "just think for a second. We were set up, right? So what do you want to bet there is at least one other renegade around here who's making sure this all goes as planned?" I lowered my voice and my head. "If we wipe his memory out and they decide to go after him, he will have no idea that an attack is coming. If we do that, he's as good as dead. He won't stand a chance because he'll never see them coming."

"See who coming?" John asked skeptically.

"The group that is responsible for all of these murders, John. They know who you are, and they played you tonight, just like they played us all."

"And you expect me to take your word for it? Are you nuts? One minute, you are just an innocent victim; and the next, you know who's behind it all and are taking justice into your own hands? I saw you kill a man, Vanessa. You stabbed him before cutting off his goddamn head! And you, bastard," he said, turning to William. "I knew there was something wrong with you from the first moment we met. Vanessa may have fooled me, but I knew instantly you were no good."

William looked at me as he rolled his eyes. "He's a touch dramatic, this one, isn't he?"

"William, now is so not the time," I scolded him. "John, you know that you saw more than just that tonight. What happened to the bodies, John? Tell me what happened to the bodies."

All of the blood drained from his face and he shook his head. "I don't know what I saw, and I'm not going to let you confuse me."

"John, I know how scary and confusing this is, but I need you to focus, okay? I need you to focus and trust me because I'm trying really hard to save your life here."

"Vanessa, if you know who's doing these killings, then you should have told the police. We would have taken care of it."

"The way you've taken care of it so far?" I shook my head, "The Silverlake Police Department doesn't stand a chance. You're out of your league here and there's nothing you can do about it."

"But you, you three, can deal with, whatever it is? What makes you so special all of a sudden?"

"I was always special, I just didn't know how much. And as for these two, well... Why don't you show him, William?"

"That is a terrible idea, love."

"Just do it. Please."

William sighed and pulled himself to his full height before taking hold of John's face.

"Let go of me," John demanded.

"Just look at me," said William before his eyes turned black and his fangs descended.

John started yelling and thrashing in fear, trying to break away, so I had to slap my hand over his mouth in order to muffle his cries. William released his face and stepped back before his eyes returned to normal.

"John? John? Please, just breathe, okay? You need to calm down and take deep breaths for me. Can you do that?" His eyes darted to me as he nodded his head.

"Okay, I'm going to take my hand away from your mouth now. Please don't scream. I know this is scary, but we aren't going to hurt you, okay?" I bit my lip while waiting for him to respond, but he finally nodded. Very slowly, I took my hand away from his mouth. I was preparing to slap it back if John changed his mind, or decided he would rather have a good, old-fashioned meltdown instead.

"What the hell is going on around here?" he asked us

quietly, "and what the hell are you?"

"We'll answer all of your questions, but not here. We might not be alone yet. William, where can we go?"

"Probably best if we use your apartment for this, love. If we happen to be followed, we won't lead them to any place they don't already know about.

Spinning John around, Bull kept a good grip on him as we all headed back to the van as quickly as we could.

My apartment seemed even more foreign to me this time than it did the last time I stopped by. I hardly noticed how William's place felt more and more like home to me, but it became glaringly obvious as I moved through my living room. Especially to poor Detective Hache. I poured him a generous amount of whiskey to calm his nerves.

He picked up the glass and downed his drink in two swallows, coughing at the burn, then holding out his glass again for me to refill it. Topping it up with a generous three fingers' worth, I gave him a shy smile and set the bottle down in front of him. He would probably need quite a bit before this ordeal was over.

"First things first," John said as he gripped his glass, "what are you people?"

"Bull and I are vampires," William answered, getting straight to it. "So were there the men that attacked us tonight. The ones that you saw us kill."

"And I'm just supposed to believe that vampires really

exist?"

"Well, if you still need more proof, I can always oblige you, Detective," William goaded him.

"Stop it," I snapped.

"And you?" John asked, "are you a vampire too?"

"No, I'm something altogether different."

"Altogether different?"

I inhaled deeply before exhaling in a long stream. I couldn't believe I was about to tell someone my secret. No, the vampires knowing didn't count, "I'm a succubus. I, uh, feed off sexual energy."

"You feed off..."

"Sexual energy, yes."

"Right," he replied, drawing the word out as he looked around at us, "and the others that were there tonight?"

"They're vampires as well," said Bull, "only they ain't nearly as cute and cuddly as we are."

I looked at the scar that ran from the corner of Bull's left eye and down his neck. It was a painful-looking reminder of his former life before he was turned. His entire upper body was covered in tattoos. Even without vampire strength, his massive hands looked like they could break any one of us in two without much effort. It was a bit hard to attribute *cute and cuddly* to his description.

"Like we said earlier, they're the ones behind these murders," I explained, "it's not just one killer. There are a group of vampires in Silverlake that decided they want to feed off people again! The murders are just a way to cover up their actions. The deaths look explainable, and it keeps both humans and other vampires from becoming too suspicious."

William leaned back in his seat and put his feet up on the table, saying, "It took us a while, but we finally started tracking them down so they could be dealt with."

"'Dealt with'? Do you mean..."

"Killed," Bull explained, "like you saw tonight. We can't have vampires killing humans all over the city."

"But you have no problem killing your own kind?"

Bull shrugged and went back to looking out the window.

"We would all prefer to not have this problem in the first place, Detective. But we can't just give these renegades a slap on the wrist, or send them to bed without supper. There is only one way to deal with them, and that's by making sure they don't get a chance to do it again," William told him.

"John, I have to ask: how did you know we would be there tonight?" I put my hand on his. Flinching, he pulled his hand away from me and refused to meet my eyes.

"I got an anonymous tip there would be an attack tonight," he admitted.

"And you just believed it, mate?"

"Of course, I believed it!. After everything else that's going on, we take every single tip we get completely seriously."

"So seriously that you came alone?" William challenged.

"Seriously enough for someone to at least, check it out."

"So they called you with a fake tip and set us up to make sure we would take the fall," I summarized while shaking my head. "But how could they explain the way the vampires died? You know, the whole turning to ash thing?" I asked William.

"Glamouring, love. It makes sense. The good detective here needed to see us killing people. After that, all they had to do was erase his memory of the bodies turning to ash. They probably planned to dump other bodies there as well, just to make sure the story really stuck."

"Right," I bit my thumbnail, thinking it all over. "But now, we have John, so that plan has gone to crap for them."

"It may have bought us a little time, love, but not much. This means, they know who John is and his connection to you. He's probably in more danger now than he was before."

I saw John blanch and shook my head. "You really know how to take the fun out of a job well done, don't you? Come on, guys, we took out more renegades tonight! Woo-hoo!" I held up my hand for a high five, but they all just stared at me. "Way to leave me hanging," I grumbled while lowering my hand and coughing uncomfortably. "So what's next?"

"Well, now, that's up to Detective Hache here," William said as he nodded towards him.

"Me? Why would it be up to me?"

"Because what we do next depends on whether you're with us or against us," William replied before he picked a non-existent piece of lint off his sweater.

"And if I'm against you?" John lifted his head and jutted out his chin. From the corner of my eye, I saw Bull stand up and take a step towards us.

"Well, you see now, John, if you decide that you're against us, I'm just going to have to remove some of those inconvenient memories from that mind of yours, drop you off somewhere, and leave you with my heartfelt wishes that the renegades don't decide to take out their frustrations from their failed plan on you."

John looked at me with alarm, but I just shrugged. If he were so stupid as to go against us in all of this, there was really very little we could do for him.

"And if I'm with you?"

"Well, now, if you're with us, then I promise to try my very best to keep you from being gruesomely killed anytime soon."

"John, you can trust us, I promise you can. The police simply can't deal with this. Even if they did believe that vamps were running around Silverlake, no matter what they tried to stop them, they would be mercilessly slaughtered." I shook my head. "It's better if you just let us deal with this quietly."

"It's not like I can just call off the investigation, Vanessa."

"I know you can't; and I don't expect you to. Just accept why you guys aren't getting anywhere; it's for a damn good reason. You never stood a chance at solving the case."

"What about your stalker?" John asked. "Have you found

out who he is too?"

"No, not yet, but I feel sure he's a vampire, and a renegade. We could have taken him out tonight for all I know, but I seriously doubt that I'd be that lucky. Thankfully, he hasn't found me since I've been staying with William."

John nodded and looked me in the eye for the first time since we got to my apartment. "I'm glad. I really am," he said softly.

With a shy smile, I looked away, grateful that after everything he saw tonight, he could still manage to be kind. "Thank you."

John looked around at us and let out a weary sigh. "All right then, guys, I'm with you. What do we do next?"

CHAPTER FOURTEEN

"Down!" Bull roared as he dove across the room towards us and dragged me to the floor. He knocked John over backwards in his chair as my living room window exploded in a hail of glass shards and rocks the size of my fist. All of it littered my apartment floor.

"What the hell was that?" I yelled, looking around and assessing the mess.

"Looks like they found us, love," William said as he sat up and shook out his sweater. More chunks of glass fell off and landed on the floor.

"So… what? They attack by throwing rocks at us? What are they… twelve?"

"Umm, Vanessa?" John said as he tapped me on the shoulder. He placed his finger to his lips, and cocked his head to the side, saying, "Rocks don't beep."

My brow furrowed with confusion as I sat silently until I heard it, as well. "John, what the hell is that sound?" My voice wavered as I prayed it wasn't what I thought it was.

"Everyone out, now!" John screamed, grabbing my hand and running for the door.

William tore me away from John and threw me over his shoulder. I held onto him and closed my eyes against the stinging wind as he rushed me from the room. We burst out of the building and onto the street where William came to an abrupt stop. I was thrown from his arms. My vision blurred as I landed on the street with bone-jarring impact, and the wind was knocked out of my lungs once again.

Rolling onto my back, I tried to ignore the burning pain tearing through my lungs as I gasped for air. Eventually, my vision started to clear and I managed to make out a shadowy movement off to one side as the explosion rattled the air. A choked scream came from my throat when I threw my arms over my head, trying to avoid all the pieces of my apartment building that rained down on the street. A mountain of flames and smoke billowed out of the gap where my apartment once stood.

A hand clamped down on the back of my head and yanked me up roughly by my hair. I was half off the pavement, as he dragged me along the ground.

"C'mere, bitch!" Although I tried to twist around, I failed to see the face of the man who was dragging me down the street. My feet scrambled for purchase as the debris-covered ground tore the exposed flesh of my arms and ripped my shirt.

"Vanessa!" Hearing a familiar voice scream my name, I

looked up to see Colleen standing in the street. Blood poured from her nose and covered the front of her white t-shirt. Her hair was matted and more blood trailed down the side of her face from a gash in her forehead.. One of her eyes was bruised and swollen shut, and I saw more blood running down her chin from a split in her lip. She whimpered as she tried to extricate herself from the tight grip she was being held in by a pair of vampires.

"Oh, my God, Colleen," I said, trying to fight back the tears as I looked at her. Terror and pain were etched all over her face. My captor hauled me off the ground and rudely onto my feet before he shoved me forward.

"Let her go," William coughed. I turned to see him still on the ground, clutching his side. Another vampire continued to kick him repeatedly, and I could only flinch with every blow.

"Now why would we want to do that?" the vampire holding me asked with a laugh. "You guys have been a serious pain in our asses, so it's time you see what happens when you fuck with things that are none of your goddamn business."

"Fuck you, creep," I said, turning to spit in his face. With a sinister smile, he recoiled his fist and planted it in my gut. I cried out and doubled over before vomiting in the street from the excruciating pain.

"Merrick, if you lay another hand on her, I promise I will tear you to pieces," William threatened. The vampire currently beating on him pulled back to deliver another blow, but this time, Merrick held up his hand to stop him.

"You know, Will, you just ain't that scary right now," Merrick laughed. "I just can't see how you intend to get off your busted ass in time to stop me from doing this."

My face exploded in pain. Merrick smashed his fist into the side of my face, right beside my eye, with such force, I fell onto my knees.

"Merrick, I swear to God, I will tear your head off your shoulders," William roared.

"Vanessa, what's going on?" Colleen whimpered.

"Yeah, Vanessa?" Merrick taunted. "What's going on? Why don't you tell your little friend there?"

He pulled me to my feet and shoved me forward. Still uneasy from the hits I took, I stumbled, but he pulled on my arm to keep me standing.

"Colleen, I'm so sorry," I said, almost drowning in my guilt as I assessed her injuries up close. Every one was my fault, and for no other reason than that she happened to know me.

"Please, let us go," she begged, "why are you doing this?"

"Why?" Merrick chuckled, "because this little bitch just doesn't seem to know her place." He grabbed my face and turned me to look at his, digging his filthy fingers into my cheeks. "Because she dared to kill our kind," he hissed, before forcing me to look at Colleen.

"She didn't kill anyone. She would never kill anyone! You made a mistake. Please, I promise you, it was a mistake."

"A mistake, eh?" Merrick said as he reached down and pulled one of my guns from its holster. In all the confusion, I completely forgot about them, but I wouldn't have dared to reach for them. Colleen's neck could have been snapped before I even aimed it. "So she's just carrying this gun around, for what? Target practice?" He pointed it at Colleen's head. "Now, I don't need a gun to kill you, blondie, but target practice doesn't sound too bad right now. Besides, how much fun could it be to kill you with your friend's gun?" I tried not to flinch when I felt the cold steel as he pressed the muzzle of the gun to my cheek. My heart beat so loudly, I was sure they could all hear it. "Or maybe I'll just shoot you in the face instead. What do you think? Ever imagine you would be shot in the face with your own gun one day?"

"Well, no, but at least, I wouldn't have to listen to you and your bullshit anymore," I retorted with way more bravado than I possessed. I'd be damned if I let this asshole see my fear.

"Funny! That's funny. You know what else is funny?" Merrick asked. "Boys, show this stupid succu-bitch what else is funny."

The two vampires holding Colleen pulled her head back and grinned viciously at me. Their fangs elongated before plunging them into both sides of her neck.

"No!" I threw myself forward, but Merrick held me firmly in place. "Get off me, get the fuck off me! Let her go!" I protested.

Colleen's screams drowned out my cries and I could only watch the blood run down her neck as they feasted on her. Her strength gave out, and her body slumped over, but they held her upright and continued to drain her.

"I'll kill you! I swear to fucking God, I will kill you all!" I vowed. Spinning around, I punched Merrick in the throat and dove for Colleen. The vampires looked up in shock as I smashed into them, causing them to loosen their grip on her. Grabbing the other gun from its holster, I whipped it up under the first vampire's chin and pulled the trigger in one smooth move. The bullet shot clean through the top of his head. Using my other hand, I tore the stake from its spot on my back and impaled him with it as he dropped to the ground.

Colleen also fell on the ground as I advanced toward the other vampire. "Now let me show you something really funny," I snarled. I shot him twice in the stomach and he howled in pain as the silver did its job. I knocked him to the ground in a running tackle, and wrapped both of my hands around his throat before pulling all the energy from him. A moment later, the black veins started to spread across his skin as he lay frozen. I stood up and stomped my foot down into his face, and the ash flattened beneath the weight of my boot.

"Not bad."

My shoulders tightened and I turned to face Merrick. He stood there, still holding a passed-out Colleen, and the vampire that beat William was also by his side.

"Let her go," I demanded as I took a step towards him.

"Oh, I don't think so. You took mine, so now I'm taking yours. It only seems fair. I'll see you around."

"No," I tried to grab Colleen, but Merrick was already gone. The entire apartment building went up in flames and I could hear the sirens, which were not far off. Rushing over to William, I wrapped an arm around him and helped him onto his feet. "Time to go."

We stumbled down the street towards his car, and I dug into his pockets to fish out his keys. I leaned him up against the passenger side of the Mercedes and pressed the unlock button on the key fob, praying that the emergency vehicles would take a little longer to get there. "Okay, William, in you get, nice and easy, but any speed you can manage would be very much appreciated." I rushed to help him fold his long frame into the car, and tried not to worsen his injuries.

"Don't... scratch... my baby," he told me as I turned the engine over and gunned it away from the curb. Just then, the first of the fire trucks turned onto my block.

"I make no promises," I said as I glanced into the rearview mirror at the wreckage I once called my home. William coughed and groaned, drawing my attention back to him. "So you really got your ass handed to you back there, huh?"

"Haven't you ever heard the saying that it's not fair to kick a man when he's down, love?"

"I have, but that guy obviously didn't," I joked as tears

started streaming down my face.

"It will be all right," William said as he reached for me, but instantly pulled back. He was nearly hissing at the motion when it pulled on his ribs.

"It won't be all right," I frantically moaned before wiping the tears out of my eyes. Then I crashed into a tree. "It will never be all right again! I've barely spoken to any of my friends in weeks, but they found them anyway! And now Colleen's going to die. And where the hell are John and Bull? Christ! Did they even make it out of the building?"

"I don't know, love, but Bull can take care of himself. He probably gotten John to safety. We'll make them pay for all of it, Vanessa. I swear to you, we will make every one of them pay for what they did tonight."

"Yes, we will."

William lay on the couch in his living room, and I propped a pillow under his head. I removed his shirt and discovered a dark purple bruise that marred the milkiness of his pale skin, almost as if someone had upended an inkwell on his side.

"I think your ribs are broken," I told him before biting my lip. I smoothed the hair back from his face.

"I can tell you with confidence that they are definitely, without a doubt, broken, pet," William replied as he smiled up at me, thereby reopening the split in his lip.

"What can I do for you? It's not like I can take you to a

hospital. Why aren't you healing? Shouldn't you be healed by now?"

"He was stronger than he looked. Don't worry about me, I just need to feed."

"Oh, you just need to feed; no big deal then. I'll just call 1-800-Dial-a-Snack and ask them to bring someone right over then." I rubbed my forehead and paced back and forth. "Shit, shit, shit." I knelt down by the couch and gathered all of my hair up, sweeping it to one side over my shoulder before bending forward over him. "Do it."

"Vanessa, don't," William turned his head to the side to avoid looking at my neck.

"Look, just shut up, and do it. You need blood and I can't just drag someone up here off the street! That leaves us with only one option, all right? So just do it before I freak out and change my mind."

"This is a very bad idea."

"Of course, it is. When is offering a vampire your exposed neck *not* a bad idea? Now just do it already."

"I need you to come a little closer."

"Crap, crap crap!" I shuffled closer and leaned in until I could feel the softness of his lips pressing against my neck. A moment later, I felt his tongue sliding slowly up and down my skin, and the rhythmic movement excited me even as I squeezed my eyes shut in anticipation of the pain I knew was soon to follow. "Jesus Christ, William! Weren't you ever taught not to play with your food? Stop messing about and get on with it already, or I swear to God, I'll punch you in the face."

I cried out as the sharp pain penetrated my neck, and his extended fangs pierced my skin. *Oh, God, what was I thinking?* This had to be the stupidest idea I ever came up with in my whole life. I tried to focus on breathing through the pain, instead of the horrible, creepy suction I felt at my throat; but it was hard to do. I heard every time he swallowed my blood.

"So, um… any time you're finished there," I said as I moved to pull away. He wrapped his arm around me and held me closer to him, preventing my escape. "Uh, William?" I was starting to get lightheaded as he continued to drink from me. "William, I think that's enough for now." I tried to move again, but he simply held me tighter and increased the pressure on my neck. I tried not to panic when my vision began to go blurry. "Stop, William, stop!" I hit him on the leg, but from my awkward angle, I couldn't put much force behind it. "William, you have to stop," I pleaded before everything went black.

CHAPTER FIFTEEN

Opening my eyes slowly, I was staring into pitch-blackness. Memories of what happened slowly filtered back to me, and I tried to lift my hand to touch my neck, only to find it trapped between two blocks of strangely soft ice. A moment later, one of the ice blocks started to move, caressing the skin on the back of my hand. "William?" I whispered.

"I'm here, love," he squeezed my hand gently before pressing it to his lips.

"Why do you feel so cold? You're freezing."

"You've lost a lot of blood, pet. I'm so sorry, but you'll be better soon."

"It's okay. Are you okay? How are your ribs?" I turned towards the sound of his voice, and slowly made out his form as my eyes adjusted to the abysmal darkness.

"I'm much better now, thanks to you," he said as he ran a hand down my face and cupped my cheek. Sighing, I closed my eyes and turned toward the comfort of his palm.

"How long was I out for?"

"A few hours. It's daytime now, and you needed your rest."

"What about you?" I lifted my hand up to his and linked our fingers together. "Shouldn't you be sleeping?"

"I wanted to watch over you until you woke up. I couldn't leave anything to chance."

"How are you going to get back to your room now?"

"I hadn't actually thought that far ahead. I guess I'll just have to stay here with you for the rest of the day."

"So you're just going to sit here and watch me sleep all day?"

He chuckled and stood up, and I heard the sound of the chair sliding across the hardwood floor, which was followed by the rustling of fabric and the soft thump of something hitting the floor.

"Is there some other way you would prefer to pass the time, pet?" The sound of a zipper being lowered was so loud in the quiet room, he may as well have held a microphone up to his pants. A moment later, there was more shuffling, and another soft thump on the bedroom floor.

"I, umm... what are you doing?" My heart started to speed up when I felt his body stretching out over the bed across me.

"Getting into bed; what does it look like?" Once he was on the other side of me, he pulled back the sheets and slid next to me, pressing himself up against my side.

"Oh, my God! You're freezing," I hissed as he came in contact with my bare skin. Rolling over onto my side, I faced away from him and curled up into a ball, trying to put some space between us.

William nestled himself right up behind me and aligned his body to mine, spooning me snugly. His large hand was splayed wide and encompassed my whole stomach. I wriggled, trying to move away from him again, and he inhaled sharply.

"Easy there, love," he mumbled as he pressed against my stomach to hold me still. I felt his growing erection twitch against my backside. *Oh, great!* Now I was trapped in a bedroom with a horny vampire. I pressed my hands against my breasts to soothe the sharp sting in my rapidly hardening nipples. That had everything to do with me being spooned by a horny iceberg and nothing at all to do with the iceberg's hand that was now moving steadily higher up my torso and beneath my shirt. I held my breath as it came up right beneath the curve of my breast, but then stopped and slid slowly back down to my stomach, again to stop just at the top of the waistband of my underwear. We lay there silently as his hand repeated its journey, over and over again.

Finally, on the last pass, it didn't stop, but instead continued moving up before cupping my ample breast. He squeezed it gently and pinched my nipple with his two fingers. A moan escaped me and I pressed myself against him. He shifted behind me and raised himself slightly in order to leave another kiss on my exposed shoulder, then pulled me onto my back. Hovering above me for a moment, the shadowy bulk of him filled my vision as his mouth pressed hard against mine. He nibbled at my lips and continued to massage my breast before sliding his hand down my waist and grabbing the hem of my tank top.

I froze for a moment, uncertain as to whether or not this was a good idea, but my sudden ache for him far outweighed any misgivings I harbored. I lifted my arms over my head and he whipped the shirt off me. My breasts, now fully exposed, started to tingle and I knew that he was staring at them, his enhanced night vision providing him with a full and detailed view.

"You're gorgeous, love," his raspy voice floated over me in the darkness. Then, I felt his tongue sliding, warm a wet, across the nipple that he was previously squeezing.

My breath hitched when he bit down lightly on it before sucking it fully into his mouth. His tongue continued to swirl around it. My hand fisted in his hair, trying to hold him closer to me as he started to pull away. Chuckling, he licked his way across my chest before taking my other breast into his mouth.

Trailing kisses along my collarbone, he slid his hand firmly up the outside of my leg, squeezing at the top when he hit the edge of my panties. He lingered there a moment before moving his hand around to the inside of my leg. His fingertips ventured down my inner thigh, returning back up again only to stop short before reaching the juncture of my thighs.

"Tell me what you want, love," he whispered into my hair.

"You know what I want," I replied. My voice was husky and I tried to wriggle myself closer to his hands, but his fingers danced away.

"Tell me what you want," he demanded again, hooking his hand around the back of my knee and moving my legs apart.

My whole body flushed and I could feel myself growing wetter. "I want you to touch me," I whispered.

Growling, he peppered warm kisses all over my stomach and moved his hand over my underwear.

"Oh, God," I sighed before I raised my hips and he slid his thumb slowly back and forth around my center. The slow, rhythmic motion began driving me insane, and the cotton of my underwear felt too rough on my sensitive skin.

"Like that, do you? Let's see what else you like," he said as his hand felt the edge of the fabric and he pulled it to the side, exposing me to the cool air of the room. A moment later, one of his fingers wandered down between my slick folds and across my hardened nub before slipping inside me. After another moment, a second finger joined the first and he moved them with excruciating lethargy, in and out of me, as his thumb began massaging me again.

Propping himself up, he extracted his fingers fully and I

whimpered in protest.

"Easy there, love, I'm not going anywhere." Grabbing the edge of my underwear, he pulled it down slowly over my legs until they were off me.

I felt him move around toward the foot of the bed before he lifted my leg and placed it on the other side of him, nestling himself between them. Kneeling between my legs, he continued to cover my chest and stomach with his kisses. My abdominal muscles contracted when he quickly dipped his tongue into my bellybutton before continuing downwards.

"Yes," I groaned as the heat of his mouth covered me. He held my legs open and I arched against him when he pressed his tongue on me, sampling my wetness, "Oh, God, William, yes."

He moved his hands around me in order to cup my ass before lifting me closer to his mouth. I opened my legs wider as he slid two fingers back inside me and proceeded to stroke the sensitive bud between my thighs.

"Oh, Christ!" I cried out as he sucked it between his teeth, increasing his tongue's pressure and rapidly flicking it back and forth. "Oh, God! It's too much," I exclaimed as I tried to pull away. The sensitivity was almost overbearing, but he held me fast as my hands clawed the sheets.

"Christ! William, I'm going to... I'm going to..." I heard a scream that came from me as a light exploded behind my eyes. He released me and I bucked and dove for him, tumbling us both off the bed before we landed with a thump on the floor. Pressing down on him, I kissed him and the energy poured into me like a crashing tidal wave. It hammered every part of me, filling me to bursting. I flung myself back, my chest heaving as the rush began to subside.

"Feel better?" William asked from beneath me.

"Yes, actually, much better," and I did. I could see him clearly in the darkness, smirking up at me with smug satisfaction. My exhaustion was gone and he no longer felt icy to the touch, just his usual coolness. "I feel like I could run a marathon actually."

"Good, hold onto me." He sat up and I wrapped my arms around his neck. Pushing himself up off the floor, he took us back to the bed. "Time to get some sleep," he announced.

"Ummm, don't you want to, you know..." I can't believe that even after what just happened between us, I still couldn't say it.

"Another time, love," he said as he kissed me quickly before tucking the sheets in around us and repeating, "another time."

I lay my head on his chest and threw my arm over him, listening to the silence of his nonexistent heartbeat until sleep finally claimed me.

Waking up, I found myself all alone. The blackout curtains on the windows were raised, giving me a clear view of the night sky and the apartment building next door.

My stomach growled as I searched through the closet, looking for something decent to wear. After what happened earlier, I needed something good, but I didn't want to look like I was trying too hard. I also didn't want to look like I wasn't trying. Or like I was trying too hard to look like I wasn't trying when I was really trying, you know what I mean?

God! How could I have been so stupid? I slammed the closet door in disgust and went back to sit on the edge of the bed. I never should have let things go so far. And now look at me. One of my best friends was dead, and I'm worrying about looking hot for some stupid, undead guy that would laugh his ass off if he saw me like this.

Completely disgusted with myself, I went back to the closet and pulled out the first pair of jeans and a t-shirt that I found. I slipped them on and pulled my hair back into a high ponytail. I couldn't allow myself to get distracted by a little hot vampire action. Very hot vampire action. How old was William anyway? Maybe he's had a couple of hundred years to perfect that thing he does with his tongue... *Oh, my God! Vanessa! Snap out of it.*

Temporarily banishing the memories to the back of my mind, I went downstairs to find something to eat. I knew I would feel much better once I had something in my stomach.

I sat at the kitchen table, playing with my food, using

my fork to create crosshatch patterns in the pasta sauce. I tried to call John's cell six times, but there was still no answer. It went straight to voicemail. Unfortunately, I didn't have a number to call Bull, or I would have tried him too. I refused to believe that three people I cared about may have died last night and it was all because of me. Sure, William said that John and Bull were fine, but when it came right down to it, he knew just as much about their fate as I did, which was a whole lot of nothing.

I looked up from my plate at the sound of the door unlocking. William's face appeared tight as he entered the room, and I knew I wasn't going to like whatever he had to say. There was no more good news for us. We were losing this battle whether we liked it or not, and if last night proved anything, it was that any small victory we might achieve would be incredibly short-lived.

"Where were you?" I asked him as he walked over to me. He came to stand behind my chair and rested his hands on my shoulders. Leaning in closer, he deeply inhaled the scent of my hair. I sat there, frozen in uncertainty, as he took a moment to breathe in my essence.

"I went to see Elizabeth," he answered, moving away before coming to sit down beside me. "She needed a report of what happened last night. About the setup and... everything else."

I nodded and picked up my glass of wine, only to put it down again, untouched. "How did she take it?"

"About as well as can be expected, I suppose," he replied

as the deep lines formed between his brows. I fought the urge to smooth them away with my finger.

"What are you not telling me?" As far as I was concerned, Elizabeth shouldn't have been taking any of this well at all. She should have been out there fighting and bleeding and dying with the rest of us. Her people were the ones to blame here! She should have been handling it better.

"She was furious that we were almost killed, well, that *you* were almost killed. She said that I should have been watching out for you better, and that we never should have been tracked back to the apartment."

"But I was fine. I made it out of that whole mess in much better shape than you did. Didn't you tell her that?" I was so confused. Elizabeth had known William much longer than she knew me; where was her compassion for him?

"I did tell her, love, but..." he shook his head.

"But what? What is it?"

"Nothing, I think that it's all just starting to get to her. Now that it's completely out of hand. She's losing her grip on the rest of the coven. People are beginning to wonder why she allowed this mess to go on for so long. I was stopped by a few of the coven members as I was leaving, and they expressed their concern that the task force wasn't doing their job properly."

"Not doing our job properly?" I slammed my hand down on the table and looked at him with my mouth agape. He had to have been joking, "Oh, I'm sorry, but are we not getting our asses handed to us with enough flair for them? What the hell have they been doing to clean up this mess? How dare they pass judgment on us and our team? I don't see anyone else out there risking their undead asses for the rest of us."

"They're just voicing their concerns, love," he replied as he slumped in his chair.

"Well, they can take their opinions and shove them," I finished. His complacency was so unlike him, it was starting to really freak me out.

"Are you still feeling better?"

I refused to be distracted by his lame attempt to change the subject. "I'm obviously fine. Look! I'm eating and everything," I said as I waved my hand over my untouched dinner.

William eyed the plate and raised an eyebrow at my use of the term, *eating*. I sighed and dropped my napkin on top of the penne, obscuring it from his view.

"No room for seconds then?"

"Have you heard anything from Bull?" I asked. I ignored his teasing, but felt somewhat relieved to see he still had some bite to him tonight.

"No, not yet, but that doesn't mean anything."

"How the hell can that not mean anything? Do you really think that both he and John would just fail to contact either of us if they were okay?"

"There could be any number of reasons, Vanessa; don't panic."

"I'm not panicking, I'm pissed off!" I yelled. "What the hell is wrong with you? How can you just sit there like a zombie? Like none of this matters?" Shoving myself away from the table, I stormed upstairs to my bedroom and slammed the door.

I couldn't stand this anymore, none of it. I had to get out of there. I had to get out of there before I went back downstairs and staked whoever was impersonating William.

I tore my shirt off and ransacked my underwear drawer, smirking with satisfaction when I found what I was looking for. The blood-red lace was perfect. Unhooking my bra, I let it drop to the floor and replaced it with the red, over-bust bustier. I turned and admired myself in the floor-length mirror. I liked the way the top became sheer below my bra line, allowing a glimpse of creamy skin underneath.

I glanced over to the bedside table where my guns lay and considered taking them with me. Tonight, however, I wouldn't have the luxury of a vamp glamour, so I ignored them and opted for a bottle of colloidal silver instead. If the fuckers got me, they got me. But first, I would have some fun before I had to join my friends in the dirt. I grabbed my leather jacket off the back of my door and slipped it on as I rushed down the stairs. When I got to the bottom, a quick scan showed that William wasn't around, so I ran to the door and slipped out of the condo before William had a chance to stop me.

CHAPTER SIXTEEN

Standing on the street in front of William's building, I looked around for a cab, but there were none in sight. Crap! I really needed to buy a car. Why didn't I think to *borrow* William's car keys while I was making my grand escape?

A motorcyclist pulled up to the side of the street and parked, pulling off his helmet. *Desperate times and all that...* Walking up to him, I put my hand on his arm and cleared my throat. Caught off guard, the man jumped slightly as he turned to look at me, his expression softening when I flashed my most charming smile.

"Will you do me a huge favor?" I asked sweetly, leaning into him and letting the light waves of hunger flow over me.

"Sure, of course," he grinned widely. His eyes darted down to my ample cleavage before returning to my face.

"Great, because I need to borrow your bike."

"Wha—?" I cut him off with a kiss, focusing on my desire for his complacency.

When I felt the stiffness going out of him, I pulled back. His eyes were slightly glazed as they looked into mine.

"Helmet," I said, holding out my hand and he obediently handed his helmet to me. I quickly put it on, saying, "Keys." I pointed at the keys in his hand and he held them out to me. "Thanks, champ," I patted him sweetly on the cheek and straddled the bike, before kicking the engine over. With a final salute, I took off down the road.

Pulling up in front of the Roxy, I parked the bike. I didn't even know where I was going until I got there, but now it seemed so obvious. Where else would I be tonight except at the place where it all began?

Leaving the helmet on the bike seat, I shoved the keys into my pocket before heading towards the door. The bouncer looked me up and down, then gave me a nod and let me in.

No glamour necessary; this may have been my night after all! That is, so long as that guy didn't snap out of it and report his bike being stolen.

The club was as packed as always, and for once, I appreciated the crush of bodies. Hunting was always easier when I could blend into a crowd, and tonight included more than just hunting. Tonight was about making a mess.

I headed straight for the main bar, once again, ignoring the line; and flipping my middle finger at anyone that complained loud enough for me to hear.

"What can I get for you?" the bartender asked me. A lock of sandy-blonde hair fell into his green eyes and a dimple appeared in his cheek as he smiled at me. I bet this guy made a killing in tips. If I survived this ordeal, I would have to remember to come back for him some night.

"Two tequila, straight up, no salt, no lime."

"Nice. I like a girl who doesn't mess around with her drinks," he winked as he poured me the shots. "That'll be eleven dollars," he said as he cleared the glasses away.

"They're on that guy," I replied, using my thumb to point over my shoulder to whomever was in line behind me. I smiled and walked away before anyone could figure out what happened.

Standing in the middle of the dance floor, I closed my eyes and tried to sense any vampires in the crowd. There was a big difference between being a bit reckless and being completely stupid; and if any vamp were in the club, I damn well wanted to know before they managed to get the jump on me. However, the whole place was clean.

Feeling confident that no one was about to tear me to pieces in the middle of the packed dance floor, I allowed myself to enjoy the frenzied energy. A few feet away from me, dancing closely with a short brunette, was an attractive blonde man that looked about in his mid thirties. He was nicely muscled, like a guy that worked with his hands for a living, instead of exercising in the gym. He would do very nicely.

Looking away from his dance partner, he saw me staring

at them, and smiled. I winked and moved towards them, closing the distance. When I got to the couple, I laid my hand on the back of his neck and started dancing with him, while completely ignoring his current dance partner.

Turning away from her, he put his hands on my waist and began dancing with me instead, ostensibly forgetting that she was even there.

"Kevin! What the hell?" the angry brunette yelled, tugging on his arm. He turned to look at her, but I put a finger on the side of his face and turned him back towards me, without ever interrupting our rhythm.

"Kevin's a little busy right now," I said sweetly, barely sparing her a glance. "So if you don't mind..."

"He was busy dancing with me," she snapped.

"And now he's busy dancing with me. You see how this works, right?"

"But he's my boyfriend!" she shrieked, "Kevin, don't just stand there! Do something!" she demanded as she stomped her foot and smacked him on the arm.

I rolled my eyes and turned to her. "Well, he must be a pretty shitty boyfriend if he has no problem ditching you that easily. Are you sure you want him back?"

"What did you say about me?" Kevin grabbed my shoulder and turned me to face him.

"I said that you're a shitty boyfriend, oh... and probably a terrible lay."

"What the fu—?" Before he could finish, I took a swing at him and punched him in the nose. Blood exploded all over his blue shirt.

"Damn, Kevin, I think it's broken, you'd better go check that."

His girlfriend started screaming and rushing around him, whining, "What did you do to him? What did you do?"

"Well, I was *trying* to get my bar fight on, but your boyfriend here is a serious disappointment." I looked over to Kevin who had taken off his shirt and was holding it to his battered nose. "A girl can't even let off a little steam anymore," I snorted in disgust before walking away, and leaving Kevin to the ministrations of his girlfriend.

"Feel any better, love?" the low voice caressed me, sending goose bumps down my arms.

"No, actually, I don't." I turned and looked up at William, watching an amused expression flitter across his face.

"So is this how you get your kicks now? Beating up poor, helpless humans?"

"Oh, give me a break! All I wanted was a fight and a fuck! At the rate we're going, I'll probably be dead within the next two weeks; is that really so much to ask?"

"Well, if that's what you were looking for, pet, you could have just stayed home and asked." He moved in closer, pressing his body against mine and wrapping his arms around me. One hand snaked up my back and grabbed the end of my ponytail, giving it a sharp tug.

Warmth flooded my belly and I clamped my lips shut to

muffle the moan that was instantly working its way up my throat. This was the William I knew: annoyingly arrogant and wonderfully sexy.

"I didn't want to do either of those things with whoever the hell that was back in your apartment."

"You're right, I was a little distracted."

"Distracted?" I reached back and grabbed the wrist of the hand that was inching down my backside. "That wasn't distracted; that was practically catatonic. That was lobotomized."

"You exaggerate, love." He wiggled his wrist free of my grip and his hand continued the exploration southward.

"I'm not exaggerating, William, that was not you back there. At least, not the you I know."

"Oh? And do you know me so well that you feel you can honestly make that claim?"

He had me there; I didn't know him very well at all. "You're right, I don't really know you, do I? I don't even know how old you are."

"Four hundred and seven," he said simply.

"Say what now?"

"I'm four hundred and seven years old this year."

"Oh, wow, that's…" I stopped to think for a moment of something clever to say, but I had nothing. "Crap! You're old."

"Yes, I am," he laughed.

"Okay, don't hate me here for asking, but aren't vampires supposed to get stronger as they age?"

"Yes," he drew the word out, and I didn't want to insult him, but something was nagging at me.

"So how could that guy kick your ass so badly last night?"

William frowned at me, his tacit objection to my brutal description of the last night's events. I suppose I would have been embarrassed too, if I were in his position.

"I have actually been asking myself the same thing," he admitted. "Just as I have been wondering how they managed to block my sensing them and to elude Elizabeth for so long. Elizabeth is six hundred years old, you know. Everything about this is just... wrong. There is something else at work here that I fail to see."

"Come on." I took his hand and started towards the club entrance, saying, "Let's get out of here."

"I take it you've given up on your plans for the night?" William followed me through the crowd.

"Not quite," I looked back at him with a devilish smile.

We ducked outside and I went straight for the bike, pleased to see that no one had stolen the helmet. Huh! A city full of killers, but petty crime seemed to be on the descent. Who would have guessed it?

"Oh, no, I don't think so, love." William took me by the hips and steered me away from the bike towards his car.

"Well, I can't just leave it here! The guy's bound to notice it missing eventually."

"Yes, and when he does, he can report it stolen like everybody else. You've done more than enough joyriding for one night; now get into the car."

"Ah, now I see it," I said as I squinted hard at him, examining his face.

"See what?" He held a hand up to his cheek to see if something was there.

"I see your age," I replied, as I started walking away again. "You are definitely older than me, and you're suddenly starting to sound like my fa-a-a-ther." I dragged the last word out just as I swung my leg over the bike. "I promise not to go too fast."

"Vanessa, you've taken enough risks tonight. This is just stupid now, and risking your life won't bring your friends back."

I glared at him silently for a moment, then started the bike. "Just get in the car, William, before I leave you behind."

I stood beside the bank of elevators and waited for William to park the car. A few minutes later, the doors opened to reveal him standing inside, looking decidedly unimpressed.

"How did you find me anyway?" I asked before I pressed the button for the penthouse. I was leaning against the side of the elevator, staring straight ahead at the closed doors, as I waited for his answer.

"It wasn't that hard; it seemed to be the most likely place for you to go."

"Okay, that's great; now how did you really find me?" I turned to look at him with my arms crossed under my chest. William looked down at the swell of my breasts and took a step towards me before pausing.

"It was your blood."

"What do you mean?" I crossed my arms a little tighter as he took another step towards me.

"Your blood called out to me. I drank so much of it last night, it wasn't hard to find you."

"Will you always be able to find me so easily?"

He shook his head. "The connection will fade over time, unless you allow me to drink from you again."

"Hmmm… well, that's not likely to happen again any time soon."

William stopped eyeballing my cleavage and reached out to grasp my hand. With a light tug, he pulled me towards him until we were standing toe-to-toe.

"I hope you understand how truly sorry I am for that. I never meant to take so much from you. I shouldn't have endangered you so recklessly."

"I know, and I'm fine now, so don't worry about it. But that doesn't mean I'll be too anxious to offer myself up as a casual snack any time soon!"

The elevator came to a stop and the doors opened onto his floor. Covering my mouth with his, he walked me backwards slowly towards the front door without breaking off our kiss. The smooth wood of the apartment door was cool against my skin as I felt it through the lace of my top.

William almost seemed warm in comparison.

"I can think of a few other ways I might enjoy feasting on you," he whispered against my lips, "would you like me to show you?"

"I don't know," I breathed. "What's in it for me?"

"I'm sure I'll be able to come up with something suitably enjoyable for you." He reached around me and unlocked the door while continuing to kiss me as he maneuvered me inside.

Reaching down behind me, he cupped my rear end, then lifted me off the ground. Gasping, I wound my arms tightly around his neck and wrapped my legs around his waist, locking my ankles behind him.

He nipped at the top of my breast, then darted his tongue into the crevice between them as he headed towards the living room and sat on the couch.

I unlocked my ankles as I straddled him, grinding down when he reached around and undid the zipper on the side of my bustier.

"You know, this is the most delicious shade of red," he said as he peeled the top from me.

"I always thought so," my breath hitched as he took one of my now exposed nipples into his mouth.

"It's too bad you had plans to allow someone else to enjoy it tonight." Releasing my mouth from his, he suddenly flipped us over so that I was lying lengthwise on the couch.

"Well," I swallowed as I watched his hungry eyes

roaming over my body, "you know what they say about *best laid plans*."

"And what is that, love?" His fingers started to roam over the front of my jeans, the tips of them slipping just barely under the waistband before he undid the button.

I opened my mouth to answer when I felt my phone vibrating in my pocket.

"Crap! Whoever that is has some seriously bad timing." I wanted to ignore it, but I no longer had that kind of luxury.

William dipped into my pants pocket and handed me the phone. On the display screen was a number that I didn't recognize.

"Hello?"

"Vanessa, it's Bull," came his ragged voice over the line.

"Oh, my God!"

CHAPTER SEVENTEEN

"Where have you been? Are you all right? Where's John?" My words came out in a rush, I was so happy to think they were alive.

"John is fine. He took a knock, but he'll be all right. I got pretty messed up, and burned really bad. It took some time to heal. Just wanted to let you know that we're both alive."

"Thank God for that. I thought I lost the three of you last night."

"Did something happen to William?"

"No, well, yes, but he's fine. But no, I mean, I meant my friend, Colleen. They found her and..." I took a shaky breath and squeezed my eyes shut to hold back the tears. Tears couldn't help her now. Nothing could bring her back.

"I'm sorry, Vanessa," Bull replied solemnly. His normally gruff voice was soft and comforting.

"But John is okay?" That was what I needed to focus on now: the survivors.

"Yeah, but he's sleeping; otherwise I'd let you talk to him

yourself."

"That's okay, I understand. He should get whatever rest he can."

William waved a hand at me, trying to catch my attention, then mouthed for me to pass him the phone.

"One sec, William wants a word with you." I passed the phone to William and bit my thumbnail as William filled him in on what happened in the street last night. It was every bit as horrible hearing it the second time around.

When they were finished, William hung up the phone and handed it back to me. I looked at the blank screen before placing it face down on the table. I didn't want to think about it anymore. It had been a long night and all I wanted was to go to bed.

William must have sensed my overwhelming exhaustion. Taking my hand, he pulled me up from my chair and walked me upstairs to my bedroom. We didn't speak as he undid my jeans and pulled them down my legs, giving me a moment to step out of them before tossing them aside. As he undid the zipper of my top, fresh memories of the fun we were having just a few minutes before flitted through my mind. Now it seemed like hours ago and the moment was very much lost.

Once I was undressed, he pulled back the covers and helped me into bed. Thinking that he would join me, I was more than a little disappointed when he pulled the covers back up and tucked them around me. He kissed me softly and straightened up again.

"Try to get some sleep, love; you need some more rest. We can try again tomorrow."

Now that I was in bed, I was too tired to respond. I yawned widely, covering my mouth with the back of my hand and nodding silently as I closed my eyes. The last thing I heard was the bedroom door closing quietly just before I drifted off to sleep.

The morning was cold and gray, and a soft drizzle had started some time during the night. Although it didn't seem to get any stronger, it was also refusing to let up. I walked down the street a block-and-a-half from the apartment to the little, independent cafe on the corner. I saw their sign before when I was out driving with William. This was my first chance to actually go in and try them out, being determined to get out of the condo today. If I didn't get a change of scenery, I was certain my sorrow would reach up and strangle me, or hang like an anvil around my neck until I drove myself insane with self-pity.

The coffee shop was quiet, having only three other customers inside. All of them were curled up in the comfortable-looking, overstuffed, black leather chairs. Like me, none of them seemed particularly eager to head back out into the cold rain.

The screech of sirens suddenly squealed up the street, shattering the early morning calm and the serenity of being cocooned in fog and rainfall. The ambulance shot past the large front window of the coffee house and turned a corner before fading into the distance. I stared after them long after the backup of the vehicles had dispersed. My eyes stayed fixed on the spot ahead of me where they had just been seen.

"Seems like all we hear these days are sirens," one of the

patrons muttered behind me and my heart nearly froze in my chest.

Shoving back my chair, I inadvertently tipped it over, and it clattered to the floor. I backed up and tripped, my feet getting caught on the legs of the chair. With my arms flailing in a desperate attempt to regain my balance, I hit my coffee cup and sent it flying. All the contents instantly covered the floor.

Without looking back, I ran for the front door, and barely heard the shouts of the coffee shop employee as I bolted through it. I sprinted down the street as fast as I could, straining to hear any lingering sounds of the sirens. I could hear them in the distance so I headed for that direction, breathing hard as my legs galloped furiously fast.

I managed to catch up to them about two blocks away. Even without the sirens, the scene would have been impossible to miss. The crowd was massive, and it seemed like every resident from the surrounding apartment buildings came downstairs at the sound of the gruesome discovery.

The only thing audible above the screaming and crying was the collective muttering of speculation. I shoved my way to the front of the pack, my stomach and chest heaving at the thought of what I would find.

The body was propped up and bound to a cross, like a ghastly scarecrow. The blood-drenched hair fell around her face, curtaining it off and mostly blocking it from view. The few strands that weren't coated in blood were a beautiful, honey blonde.

Her white shirt was covered in blood and mud, although the incessant rain was making it transparent, and the outline of her black bra showed through. She must have been strung up there for hours in order to have gotten so wet.

I fell to the ground, expelling all the air from my lungs until I nearly choked. The corpse was wearing Colleen's clothes and had her beautiful blonde hair. It was finally real. Colleen was truly dead and no amount of wishing could bring her back.

The world tilted around me and I felt my mind slipping away. I could feel hands grabbing me as the world became all blurry. A sharp pain in my head preceded the explosion of stars in my peripheral vision just before the world went black.

Jesus, my head was killing me. I lifted my hand to the side, but stopped when I felt an uncomfortable tugging on my skin. Opening my eyes fully, I saw a tube leading from my arm to a plastic bag that slowly dripped down the line. The liquid from the IV felt uncomfortably cold.

"Oh, good; you're awake," a nurse in green scrubs said as she walked into the room with a friendly smile on her face. "How are you feeling now?"

"I'm okay, I guess," I replied as I looked around the hospital room, "but what happened?"

"You just took a little bump on the head, that's all, nothing to worry about. But you were really dehydrated so we hooked you up to a potassium drip." She walked to the end of the bed and picked up my chart, flipping through it.

"When can I leave?"

"Oh, I'm sure it won't be too long, although you were

unconscious for longer than we like to see. Now that you're awake, we want to watch you for a few hours just to make sure that you don't have a concussion, or any other head trauma. After that, you should be free to go." She put my chart back on its hook and came around the bed. I watched her check the drip on my IV before pulling the curtains back from my bed completely.

"Oh, you didn't have any ID on you when you were brought in; so I just need a few things from you before I go."

"Okay."

"Your name?"

"Vanessa Kensley. K-E-N-S-L-E-Y."

"Great. Address?"

I opened my mouth and shut it again. I didn't actually have an address anymore, "The one on my medical insurance should be 203 - 1109 Blackburne Crescent, Silverlake City."

"Oh, my God; wasn't there a huge explosion on Blackburne just a couple of days ago?"

Averting my eyes, I looked down at the blankets in my bed, and the vision of Colleen strung up in the street suddenly rushed back to me. All I could see was her begging for our lives, and the abject fear in her eyes when those bastards fed off her incessantly.

"You know, I'm actually still feeling pretty lightheaded," I mumbled. "I wouldn't mind lying back down."

"Right, of course," the nurse replied as a light blush filled her cheeks and she fumbled with the pen in her hand. "We'll be able to close your file with this. Now, get some rest." The easy smile disappeared off her face as she hurried from the room.

"Do you mind if I turn the TV up a bit, dear? I'm afraid I don't hear so well these days."

I jumped as the disembodied voice floated over from the other bed in the room. I hadn't even noticed there was someone beside me.

"No, not at all; I don't mind, go ahead."

She smiled at me and held the remote towards the television with a trembling hand. Bright blue veins crisscrossed the back of her hand and extended up her arm, easily visible through her translucent skin. Her white hair was thin and short, barely dusting the top of her ears and she looked so frail. So helpless.

I shuddered, dreading the thought of ever becoming so old. What if I could no longer defend myself, or my friends, or remember my name? I wasn't quite ready to pack it in just yet either. I had a phobia of being that vulnerable. Vampires really had it made, in some respects. They perfected the loophole of dying young and staying pretty, the dirty cheats.

"*Citizens of Silverlake are in absolute shock as another body was found early this morning. Unlike the other victims, there was no decapitation this time, but in an almost more terrifying turn of events, the body was purposely displayed and out in the open. The yet unidentified woman --*"

"I'm sorry; do you mind if we turn this off? I don't think I can listen to anymore," I asked the old woman. My heart felt as if it were being squeezed in a vise, and I was finding it hard to breathe.

"Oh, not at all, of course, dear." My roommate turned the volume completely down, but didn't change the channel.

I risked a glimpse at the TV and read the closed captioning that scrolled across the bottom of the screen. That would have to do; at least, I didn't have to hear it. I already had more details than I liked, and I didn't need to hear the rest of the city's speculations as well.

"Such horrible business," she tutted while shaking her head. "This used to be such a lovely city, and so friendly and safe. And now look at it. No one is safe these days. Such a tragedy."

I made a non-committal noise as I rolled over. I just couldn't make any small talk. I knew exactly why this one was different. Why the sudden change in pattern. It was specifically for me. They were taunting me, and mocking all of our attempts to catch them. They wanted me to know they won. We simply couldn't catch them, so why even try?

CHAPTER EIGHTEEN

The cold woke me up from a fitful sleep, and the silent shuffling I heard kept me from sitting up in my bed. I cracked my eyes open to the tiniest slits, and glimpsed the lights of the city that gently illuminated the hospital room. A large shadow obscured my view of the old woman in the other bed, and I barely caught the soft sound of repeated swallowing.

"You have *got* to be shitting me!" I spat, furious at the intrusion.

The vampire spun around and stood in front of me before I could pull the blankets back.

I sat up in the bed and tore the IV needle from my hand, its sting only fuelling my anger. "Are you seriously in *my* room, feeding off *my* roommate?"

"You know, I was only going to eat *her*, but I'm sure I could make room for the both of you," he replied as he licked a drop of blood from his lips and leaned in towards me.

"You know what? How about no?" I slapped a hand to his chest and shoved him backwards before hopping off the bed. He flew through the air and hit the wall beside the door to the hall, making me pause. I never expected to be *that* strong; I didn't even have enough time to focus my power.

The vampire looked at me with confusion and then back to the old woman as she lay, unmoving, in the bed.

"Oh, yeah? I'm going to make you pay for that one, leech." I tilted my head from one shoulder to the other, stretching out my neck.

"Right," he said before bolting out the door.

"What. The. Hell?" I stood there, staring momentarily at the empty, open doorway before taking off after him. Vampires weren't supposed to run away; where the hell was his sense of pride?

The freezing tile beneath my feet made a slapping sound that echoed down the sterile hallway. The hospital had settled into an eerie silence, with the sick and dying neatly locked away behind the countless doors that I rushed past.

How dare he use this place to try to conceal his feedings! Preying on those who were so helpless.

The sound of a pair of doors crashing open caught my attention, and I pushed myself to go faster. I refused to let the bastard get away. Slamming through the double doors only moments later, I found him barely a few feet away. With a roar, I dove for his waist, wrapping myself around him and tackling him to the ground.

"Where the hell do you think you're going?" I demanded, grabbing a handful of his hair and pulling his head backwards before slamming his face mercilessly into the floor.

"Get off me, you stupid—" I slammed his face into the floor again before he could fnish. Leaning down to whisper into his ear, I did not alleviate the pressure I was inflicting on the back of his head.

"I am having a very, very bad day. In fact, I'm not really loving the way the last few months of my life have been ticking along here, so if I were you, I would be very, *very* careful about what I said next." I released some of the pressure from his head, just enough so that he could turn his face to the side and speak.

"Bite me!" he spat.

I raised an eyebrow and looked down at him. "Isn't that supposed to be my line?"

"Screw you!"

"There is not enough booze in the world. Now shut up." I gave his head a hard jerk backwards, saying, "We're going to play a game of twenty questions, and if I like your answers, you may have a slim chance of making it out of here instead of becoming a pile of ash. Now, you don't want to become a pile of ash, do you?"

He shook his head, and his eyes darted around frantically. There was something seriously off about him, but I couldn't put my finger on it. He definitely seemed different from the other vamps somehow. I decided to begin with the question that was bothering me the most.

"Why the hell are you in here feeding off the sick and dying? That's fucking disgusting."

"I uhhh," he licked his lips rapidly, "I figured they were on their way out anyway, so what's the big deal?"

"So you thought you'd just hurry them on their way, right?"

"Hey, at least no one's going to notice a few more deaths around here. It's not like I'm stringing them up in the square, or anything."

His cavalier comment hit a nerve, and I felt obligated to slam his face into the floor again. "Watch your mouth," I warned him before taking a deep breath and trying to regain my focus. "As a member of the Silverlake Coven, you are forbidden from killing your victims. Why risk the consequences of breaking coven law?"

"The Silverlake what? Look, I don't know what you're talking about. What laws? We hunt, we feed, and that's the way."

"Don't play stupid with me! Just because I'm not a vampire doesn't mean I don't know how this works. Where are you from?"

"Here, I'm from here."

"Then why don't you know about any of this?" Just then, a thought suddenly dawned on me, and I added, "Wait, how old are you?"

"What does that matter?"

"Do you want to lose this game? Answer the question."

"Twenty-four, I'm twenty-four," he answered quickly.

"And how long have you been twenty-four, fang boy?"

"My birthday was in February."

Okay, this guy couldn't be nearly as stupid as he looked. He had to be playing me, unless... "How long have you been a vampire?" I asked slowly.

"Three months, it's been three months," he replied, his voice becoming higher and more frantic.

Someone did that to him three months ago. Turned him into this and didn't tell him the rules. They just... let him loose on the city. Elizabeth would be furious; things were even more out of control than we thought.

"Who did this to you?" I demanded.

"I don't know."

"What do you mean, you don't know? Do you remember what he or she looked like? Did they stay there after you turned?"

"I can't remember what happened, I just remember waking up. There were a lot of us. We were all in a house together. My strongest memory was thirst. I was just so thirsty all the time; we all were. The others, the ones in charge, delivered people for us to feed on."

"How many of you were there?"

"Seven, or eight maybe? I don't know. It was so hard to think through the constant hunger. There was never enough blood, and we were starving. We would drink the people dry, but we always needed more. They promised us there would be more, and said soon we would have more blood than we could ever drink. But I didn't want to wait, so I snuck out one day. I, I came here and I... I started feeding. And I've been feeding here ever since."

I couldn't believe what I was hearing! "Now, think very carefully. Do you remember any of them saying why you were there?"

"We were a family. They just kept telling us we were the children of the new family, and not to worry because they would always take care of us. And soon, we would have everything we always wanted."

"That sounds like a pretty good offer, so why didn't you stay?"

"I was just too hungry. The only thing I wanted was more blood, and they didn't seem capable of giving me that. I was tired of their promises, I just wanted to feed."

"All right, I have one last question for you, the most important one, and I promise you I will know if you're lying to me. Do you understand?"

He shook his head vigorously, "Yes."

"Where were they keeping you?"

"I don't know."

"I warned you not to lie to me. Where the hell were they keeping you?" I was rapidly running out of patience.

"I don't know! I swear, I don't know! They never let us go outside." He started whimpering. I couldn't believe this pathetic creature was actually a vampire. If his were the face of the future vampire race, they were so screwed.

"What about when you escaped? You must remember something from that."

"A bit, just a little bit. It's a blur. I ran, I just ran. I wasn't really paying attention. But there were trees, and a forest that seemed to go on forever. The house was big, but kind of run-down," his tongue darted out as he licked his lips again, saying, "Please, that's all I remember."

"Do you remember how long it took you to get to the city? Or which way you came in from?"

"It felt like I was lost out there for hours. But, but I think I came in from the east. I remember seeing a Highway 1 sign, and that's it, I swear."

It was the best lead we had so far. I looked down at him as he whimpered beneath me and said, "I believe you. Now roll over." Climbing off his back, I knelt beneath him.

He looked at me, somewhat confused, but obeyed me. "I told you everything, can I go now?"

"Look at me," I smiled at him sadly, looking deeply into his eyes. He was confused and scared as I leaned into him and kissed him deeply before holding him down and draining him completely. "I'm sorry, but no."

He stared up at me, his frightened eyes widening as final death overtook him. I stood up and looked down at his frozen form. "Too many people have already died," I whispered into the darkness.

Hearing the sound of footsteps echoing down the hallway behind the next set of double doors, I softly cursed, "Shit," before acting quickly. I took one last glance at the body and let out a sad sigh before kicking the ashes to dust and taking off at a full sprint to return to my room. I did not want to be caught out of bed; especially if it coincided with the discovery that my roommate was dead.

I rushed into my hospital room and looked toward the bed of my roommate. I hadn't even learned her name. Walking to the end of her bed, I checked her medical chart. "Margery Willis," I whispered, sending up a silent prayer to whoever or whatever might have been listening upstairs.

Moving around the edge of her bed to inspect her, I noticed the two small puncture wounds on her neck. "Oh shit! Shitty shit shit!" My hands covered my mouth in horror as the two holes seemed to stare back at me. Baby vamp hadn't healed her wounds! He might not have even known how, or that he could. How many other bodies ended up in the morgue with two holes in their necks?

I leaned over the bed and clutched the railing, breathing in through my nose and out through my mouth. If neck punctures had become a regular thing, by now someone was bound to have noticed and become suspicious. That's what post mortems were *for*, right? To determine exact cause of death? And these little love bites had WTF? written all over them.

Shaking my head, I backed away from the bed. There just wasn't anything I could do about it now. I climbed into my bed and noticed the limp IV tube hanging from the pole instead of being attached securely to my hand, as it was supposed to be. No way would I even try to stick it back in by myself. Right. Well, I had the rest of the night to come up with an excuse for that tomorrow.

Falling back onto the pillow, I closed my eyes.

I awoke to a cool hand on my face and a presence that seemed to be hovering around the head of my bed. "Oh, please God, not again," I groaned.

"Hush, love, it's only me." Relieved to hear William's voice, I smiled sleepily.

"Hi, you found me."

"Of course, I did! I got worried when I lost you," he replied and his brows furrowed, forming deep creases between them. "What happened to you?"

His concern was touching. "I'm okay, I just passed out and they brought me here. I have a lot to tell you."

"As long as you're uninjured, it can wait and you can tell me tomorrow. I don't have much time left before the sun comes up."

"They will release me from here tomorrow, they just need to watch me for a bit longer."

"Stay out of trouble," he said as he kissed me quickly and disappeared.

CHAPTER NINETEEN

After I paid the cab driver with a free ride ticket that the hospital receptionist gave me upon my discharge, I was standing outside the skyscraper that I called my temporary home. Staring up at the wall of glass before me, I must admit I was starting to actually regard this building as my home, and had done so long before the renegades blew up my apartment. I didn't like that fact at all. I had to get my own place as soon as possible. I couldn't hide out here forever. Continued cohabitation with William would surely make whatever was happening between him and me way too complicated.

I stood in the kitchen, looking down at my cell phone. Its black screen stared back at me, demanding that I pick it up. Oh, well, it's not as if it would get any easier the longer I put it off.

I scrolled through my contact list until I came to Karen's

number, and hit the call button. A moment later, her phone instantly went to voicemail.

"Karen, it's me. I'm sorry I haven't talked to you; and I know you must think I'm a terrible friend, but please call me back as soon as you get this. Please, it's really important. Please Karen, as soon as you get this, you call me." I hung up the phone and slumped against the counter. One down, one to go.

Sophia answered her phone on the second ring. "Where the hell have you been?" she demanded. Angry or not, the sound of her voice was familiar and comforting.

"I'm so sorry, Soph, I really wanted to call you."

"Uh-huh, so why didn't you? You're calling me now so you obviously didn't lose my number."

"No, I didn't lose your number, it just wouldn't have been smart for me to call you."

"Well, then… you could have texted or something."

I sighed and rubbed my temple. There was no way to avoid being yelled at. "I think the whole point was minimal communication, Soph."

"There's a difference between minimal and *none*, Vanessa. You could have been dead. First you, now Colleen. She's not answering any of my messages, and she wasn't at work today."

I bit my tongue and tried to keep from hyperventilating. Christ, of course, the girls were wondering what happened to Colleen. Sophia must have missed seeing it on the news yesterday. I opened my mouth to tell her, but nothing came out.

"So are you in the witness protection program, or what?" she continued.

"Something like that. But there's a reason I called, so I need you to listen, okay?"

"Oh, God what is it now?" she replied, and all joking vanished from her voice.

"You have to leave town. It's not safe for you here," I said. I tried to put as much authority into my voice as possible to convey my sincerity. I couldn't waver with this.

"Look, I know things haven't been the best for you lately," she replied and her voice was gentle and sympathetic, "and things here have been really freaky lately, but lots of cities have high crime rates, Nessa; it will be okay."

Oh, God! Now she must think I'm hysterical, "Sophia, you have to trust me. I'm serious. Things here are much worse than you can possibly imagine! I'm sorry, but I can't tell you how I know that. Just trust me, and get out of town. It's not safe here for my friends, Soph. I can't tell you anymore than that so please tell me that you heard what I'm saying. It's. Not. Safe." I gripped the phone tightly, focusing my will to make her understand.

"Where am I supposed to go?"

"Anywhere," I said quickly, "go anywhere that's away from here. Cash in some of your vacation pay, and travel anywhere you want for a while. You work hard, you deserve a vacation. I hear Mexico is pretty nice this time of year."

"Look, I'm not making any promises."

"Sophia—"

"But," she cut me off, "I promise to talk to Mr. Mooney about booking some time off, okay?"

"Great, that's great. Thank you."

"Okay, I have to get back to work. I'm really glad you called. Promise me that you'll take care of yourself?"

"I promise that I will, and you do the same. Oh, and if you see Karen, will you please pass on the message? I tried calling her, but it went straight to voicemail."

Sophia snorted. "That's probably because she's a little busy right now."

"Doing what?"

"More like doing *whom*, and don't ask me 'cause I don't know, but that girl has the distinct glow that screams 'secret boyfriend' about her these days. If I get any dirt, I'll be sure to let you know."

"Oh, you had better." I flicked my hair over my shoulder and giggled. "Karen having a secret lover? Now this I *have* to get all the details on. I want the *whole* scoop."

"With a cherry on top, I promise. I'll tell you everything, right down to boxers, or briefs."

"That's my girl."

I was grinning from ear-to-ear when I hung up the phone. I couldn't believe how much girly gossip I missed out on. I couldn't wait to tell Colleen.

That thought came out of nowhere and might as well

have kicked me in the stomach. Gasping, I slid down the side of the counter until I was curled up on the kitchen floor before promptly sobbing with uncontrolled tears.

"You're looking much better this evening," William said when his soft footsteps came up behind me on the balcony.

It was a beautiful night out, and a soft breeze played with the ends of my hair. "Thanks, but I feel like I've been hit by a truck. I called Karen and Sophia today. I told them to get out of town."

"Do you think they will heed your warning?"

"I honestly don't know. It's not as if I could tell them *why* they have to leave. I'm pretty sure Sophia thinks I'm just overreacting from stress. All I can do is cross my fingers and hope she'll just humor me."

"I'm sure she will."

"You don't even know her."

"Maybe not, but I know how persuasive you can be."

I laughed softly and leaned against the railing, "Yeah? Well, no one has ever made Soph do anything that she didn't want to do."

"You have to trust that your friends will be safe."

"I can't," I shook my head, "it's worse than we thought. The renegades aren't just killing people, they're turning them."

"What? How do you know that?"

"There was a vampire in the hospital last night. He killed

the lady in the bed across from mine. He ran from me, but I caught him. There was something different about him that I couldn't put my finger on. He didn't know anything about the coven, or any of the laws. He was young, William, and had only been turned a few months ago."

"Do you know how many more were turned?"

"He said there were about seven others in the house with him, but who knows how many more they turned before or after that? All the new vampires are locked inside and kept half-starved."

William paced back and forth across the length of the balcony, his face a mask of deep concentration. "They must be trying to establish a second coven. It's the only thing that makes any sense."

"But why? Wouldn't it just mean they have to kill more people in order to keep everyone fed? How can they possibly plan to remain hidden that way? How long do they think they can milk the serial killer cover-up? It's not going to work."

"No, of course, it's not going to work, and they'll end up exposing us all. If the new vampires are starving, I'm sure they don't want to bring anymore attention to themselves; but they won't be able to do that for long. Not if they don't want to drive the new turns insane with blood lust."

"We have to tell Elizabeth, she must know."

"I'll call her now," William said as he pulled his phone out of his pocket and walked back inside, closing the sliding glass door behind him.

I stood outside and listened to the sounds of the city night, while watching him in his living room on the phone to Elizabeth. He dragged his fingers through his hair and I could hear the muffled sounds of shouting through the glass.

Something was very wrong. I knew that I should have gone inside to find out what, but it seemed safer where I was.

William held up his hand and waved me towards him as he hung up the phone. I took a steadying breath and left the calmness of the balcony for whatever shit storm I was about to encounter.

"Do I even want to know what she had to say?" I asked.

"No, you don't," he growled.

"But you're going to tell me anyway..." I prompted, trailing off.

"We have to wipe them out, every last one," he spat.

Okay, now I was confused, "Wasn't that pretty much always the plan? The renegades are from your coven so we have to kill them?"

"No, Vanessa, not just the renegades; all the newly turned vampires as well.

I stood there staring at him silently. The vacant expression on my face must have been a pretty good give away as far as reflecting my non-existent level of understanding.

"When you told me about the new vamps, I thought," he raked his fingers through his hair again, causing some of the shorter strands to stick straight up. "I thought that we might be able to take in the new vampires. You know, assimilate them. None of us started out this peacefully, Vanessa, and it's not our true nature. We had to learn, and adapt. We could try to do the same for these vampires, and bring them into the main coven."

"But Elizabeth's not having it?"

"She wants them all dead. In fact, she demands it. She says they're too much of a liability now. And after suffering from starvation so early in their change, there's no telling how damaged they may be."

I looked down at the hardwood floor, my mind randomly following the patterns in the woodgrain as I thought it all through. "This second coven..."

"Yes?"

"How big would it have to be in order to challenge the position of the first coven?"

"What are you getting at?"

"Someone must be leading this coven, right? Someone had to organize this brutality for it to go on for so long and also manage to cover it up with such a simple diversionary story without getting caught. The goal was to create new vampires. That needs real organization and planning to make sure that things don't get too far beyond their control. But could it actually be Merrick? He blew up my house and ordered the death of Colleen, but he didn't kill you, or me. Why not? If we're causing him so much trouble, then why didn't he just finish us off? He had us exactly where he wanted us, so why play games? Is he just messing with us? Or is he a general dick? Who's really behind it, and what's the end game? Could this be a plan to challenge Elizabeth's position?"

"It makes sense that whoever is behind this was trying to position themselves as the new coven leader of Silverlake, but they must realize it's a suicide mission. Elizabeth is the oldest and thus, the strongest of us all in this area," he said.

"Honestly? I can't believe someone that's willing to go to such lengths would be the type of person that would stay in the background for long, can you?"

"No, you're right, I can't either."

"Exactly. How long would you agree to be hunted by people trying to preserve a way of life that you didn't believe in, and which went against everything that you represented and stood for?"

"If this keeps going on, we can pretty much guarantee a civil war."

"I wouldn't doubt it. It looks to me like they're increasing their numbers as soldiers and troops."

"It wouldn't do them much good though. Our coven is full of some very wise, not to mention, very powerful vampires."

"Yes, but if they keep turning people, couldn't they eventually overpower you with their sheer numbers?"

"The amount of vampires they would need in order to do that... Well, it would be impossible to hide them all. And beyond impossible to hide all of their feeding kills."

"That's the other thing that's been bothering me," I said as I chewed on my lip and stared into the unlit fireplace.

"What's that?"

"Something the vampire said last night about what his captors told him. A promise that soon they would have all the blood they could ever drink. I mean, they couldn't possibly..."

"Couldn't possibly what?"

"Couldn't possibly be planning to establish their dominance at the top of the food chain, or anything like that, right? It sounds a lot like announcing an all-you-can-eat buffet!"

CHAPTER TWENTY

Lying in bed with the sheets tangled around me, I rolled over again and tried to get comfortable, but my efforts failed. I couldn't shake my conversation with William out of my head. Every time I closed my eyes, I kept imagining renegade vampires swooping down on people from the shadows and dragging their victims off to a brutal death.

We had to figure out where they were keeping the new vampires. Once we found the house, I felt sure we'd find Merrick. If we took him out, we might be able to get a handle on things.

I fluffed up my pillow and pounded it with my fist before lying back down again. I needed a good night's sleep so that I was fresh to hunt again tomorrow. It was useless, however; I had too much energy running through me and I remained wide awake.

If I went downstairs, I could spend the last couple of hours before dawn with William. I could always get more sleep during the day, but I had a sneaking suspicion that if I left my bed to find him, I would just end up back in bed right away again; except, it would be his. It was probably better if I just stayed put.

At 9:30 AM, I barely started to drift off to sleep when my phone began to vibrate.

"Why do you hate me?" I asked it before answering the call. Sophia's name flashed on the screen and I held my breath, praying she had good news.

"All right, I got time off," Sophia said before I could say hello.

"You did? That's great!" Relief flooded me and I flopped back onto the pillows, thankful that she was one less person for me to worry about. Now if only Karen would return my calls. "When do you leave?"

"Soon, don't worry. I don't know what happened to get you so freaked out, but if it makes you feel better, I can get out of town for a few days. You know, hit up a spa, or something."

"Thanks, I really appreciate that. I know how vague I'm being about the whole thing, but I have no choice. Were you able to reach Karen?"

There was a long pause on the other end of the line. "I did, eventually. Sorry, babe, but she's not going anywhere."

"Shit. You couldn't convince her?"

"No, she says she's not leaving because she can't afford to

miss work."

"Oh? But she can afford to risk her life?"

"I guess so," she said simply.

I could practically hear her careless shrug over the phone. I tried to be grateful that at least one of my friends would soon be out of harm's way.

"Promise me that you'll call again and let me know when you're safely out of the city?" I asked her.

"I promise."

"Oh, hey, any word on who this mystery boyfriend of Karen's is? Do we have the goods on him yet?"

"No nothing; it's really strange. Whenever I ask her about him, she goes all quiet and tries to change the subject. I'm really not liking it. At first, it was kind of funny, but now it's just..."

"Weird," I supplied.

"Yeah, and I still haven't heard from Colleen. I even tried calling her mom, but she's not answering her phone either. I'm starting to get really freaked out."

"Maybe you just keep missing her. Don't get all panicked yet."

"I'm trying not to, but with everything that's been going on, it's hard to keep my imagination from running away with me. I know I put up a fight about it yesterday, but now I'm starting to really like the idea of getting away from here for a while."

"I'm glad; that will make it easier, and maybe you won't be so mad at me for convincing you to go."

"I'm not mad, Vanessa, just worried. I really hope that you're okay. Is Detective Hache taking good care of you?"

I thought about how he was almost blown to pieces the other night and cringed, "He's doing his best."

"Good, I'm sure you'll be safe with him. He seems like a good guy."

"He is."

"Okay, well, I've got to go and get my stuff together for this trip. I promise to call you soon. Take care of yourself, okay?"

"I will, I promise. You too."

"You know I always do."

I hung up the phone and thought about what Sophia said about Karen. It wasn't like her to keep secrets from us like this. It wasn't like her to keep secrets, period. Karen was always the first to give us the scoop. She loved to gush about guys, so why would she try so hard to convince us that this one didn't exist? When you want to hide a lover from your best friends, it's never a good thing. What was it about him that she was trying so hard to hide? *Oh, good God, please don't let him turn out to be anything that I have to shove something sharp and pointy into.*

"Okay, so we're looking at the area east of the city, someplace with a lot of trees," I said as I tapped my finger on the map we spread out on the table in one of Elizabeth's offices.

William and I decided to gather the task force together at the manor in order to start searching for the house where the new vamps were being held.

"Almost all of that area is woods. We're going to have a hell of a time trying to narrow it down."

"I know. We're just going to have to go out there and see if we can sense any of them, and keep working our way further out from the city. The house will be big and in obvious need of repair. Unfortunately, he said it felt like he was stumbling around out there for hours. Which means, we can't get a real sense of how far away he was. For all we know, he was twenty minutes away and just so delirious that he walked in a circle for five hours."

"Or he could have been five hours away and walked in a straight line here, but not realized it," Anastasia suggested, nodding her understanding.

"Exactly," I frowned at the map. "This will be slow going unless we can catch another renegade and get them to tell us where the house is."

"If we can find one, I can make 'em talk, don't you worry about that." Bull's eyes were steely. I imagined he wanted some payback after almost being blown to oblivion. I was right there with him. Right now, I had no problem with the thought of persuading a few leeches to spill their guts about their plans.

"Well, what are we waiting for then?" Thatcher grabbed the map off the table and rolled it up into a tight tube. "Let's get going!"

I walked down the front steps of the manor and started towards William's Mercedes when the back of my neck started to burn. Pulling one of my guns from its holster, I scanned the windows of the house for anyone watching us, and also peered into the trees.

"What is it?" William came up and pressed his back against mine before he started scanning the trees as well.

"I don't know, but the back of my neck is burning. I just don't know where they are. Do you see anyone?"

By now, the rest of the force had assumed their offensive stances and we had all of our backs towards one another.

"Everyone, spread out and search the trees. If you find anyone suspicious, bring them in for questioning," Thatcher barked at us before running for the trees.

I took off into the dark without bothering to find out which directions the others took, the growing tingle of awareness in my neck spurring me on.

A branch broke to my left, and the snapping sound went off like a gunshot in the silence of the trees. My heart raced as the burning on my neck intensified, and I forced myself to steady my nerves. I would not allow this asshole to get the drop on me.

There was a soft rustling of branches and I rushed towards them, but when I got to the spot, whoever had been there was gone. A soft glimmer, swaying gently at the corner of my eye, caught my attention so I approached it slowly, continuing to scan the trees as I went.

There was a small, silver, silk pouch hanging from one

of the branches. I reached out to take it, my hands trembling slightly. It was from him; I could just feel it. He was the one that was watching us.

I didn't want to take the pouch from the tree. No matter how small and unassuming it may have seemed, there were a lot of disturbing things that could still fit into a pouch that small.

I snapped the thin thread that it hung from, giving the illusion that it was dangling in thin air, simply waiting for me to see it.

I loosened the drawstring and took a deep breath before I looked down into the bag. Nestled at the bottom was a pile of chain. I held out my hand and upended the bag, emptying it, and a necklace fell into my palm.

The chain was made up of tiny, delicate links and held a heart pendant with a cluster of small sapphires that covered the face of the heart. It was about the size of my thumbnail and looked like white gold.

It was a stunning necklace, and one I could have seen myself admiring in a jeweler's glass case. I wasn't sure what disturbed me more, having this psycho present me with something that suited my taste, or the bloody smudges that were smeared all over the chain and the back of the pendant.

I repressed my crawling revulsion and dropped the necklace back into the pouch. The others would surely want to see this.

The tingling feeling disappeared from the back of my

neck, and I knew we missed our chance to catch him. He was no longer watching me and now probably long gone from the property as well.

"Vanessa?"

My heart leapt into my throat as I spun around to meet the voice, head on, with my gun aimed directly at the owner of it.

"Damn it, William! You scared me. Why the hell would you sneak up on someone holding a gun?"

"I didn't sneak up on you, you just didn't hear me coming. What's that in your hand?"

I hefted the bag a couple of times before I passed it to him.

"It's another present from my creeptastic admirer," I explained as he looked inside.

"That's who was out here watching us?"

"Looks like. I heard a branch break and then found this hanging from the trees. After I opened it, the burning sensation in my neck went away. I think he's gone for now."

"All right; we're getting you the hell out of here, come on," William said as he took my hand and led me back to the driveway where the others were waiting.

"We couldn't find anything," Anastasia remarked as she leaned against her car and examined her nails, "how about you?"

"This was waiting for Vanessa." William tossed her the bag and Anastasia shot out her hand and caught it.

Pulling the necklace from the bag, she held it up by the

chain and examined it, "Wow," she said before letting out a long whistle, "looks like your psychopath has good taste."

"Ummm, thanks?" I raised my eyebrow as I rolled my eyes. "Maybe you also noticed that it's covered in blood? I don't even want to try to guess what happened to the person that originally owned this," I said as I shuddered, rubbing my arms against the sudden chill.

"And you're sure that he's gone?" Thatcher glared at me.

"I think so; the burning on the back of my neck stopped and I couldn't feel anyone around anymore. He's fast, really fast."

"I'm taking you home. Now!" William announced as he pulled out his key fob and hit the unlock button, the car alarm beeping in response.

"William, it's over; he's gone, we can't forget the big picture. We have to look for that house tonight."

"What? And have you spending more time running around in the open when this guy obviously knows exactly where you are? Don't be stupid."

"Don't be an ass," I snapped, "Look, he's obviously had his fun for the night, so let's just move on and get back to the main job. We don't have time for this."

"And I'm telling you that I'm not about to risk it, love," he crossed his arms over his chest, pressing his mouth into a thin line.

"Bite me."

"With pleasure."

"Okay," Anastasia held up her hands as she walked

between us. "Why don't you two just take a moment to calm down? Thatcher, Bull and I can get a good start on the tracking. William, why don't you take Vanessa home?"

"What!?" I exploded, "You can't be serious? You can't expect me to just sit this out?"

"I know you don't like it," Anastasia replied as she looked at me sympathetically, "but he was here tonight. He found you. And you got away without a fight because he *let* you. He hasn't attacked you, or hurt you this whole time because he *chooses* not to. But we still don't know who he is. Why risk it? Why not just remove the temptation for tonight?"

"So you don't think I'd be able to take care of this guy, if he chose to come at me head on, instead of skulking in the shadows, is that it?" I was fuming. Hadn't I already proven to them that I was an asset to the team? How many times did I have to show them that? Even though I wasn't a vampire, I could still hold my own, and take them down too. I was sick of being looked at as "vampire lite."

"I'm not saying that you couldn't take him out," she replied as she took my hand in hers and squeezed it. "I'm just saying that none of us want to take any unnecessary risks if we don't need to. We don't want to lose you, and we don't want to needlessly give this guy another opportunity to get to you."

I sighed and looked down at the grave., "The tracking will go faster tonight if William and I come. There's so much ground to cover."

"I think we'd all prefer to lose a little time tonight rather than run the risk of losing you," she smiled at me.

"Fine." What was the point in arguing anymore? They refused to back down and that would only waste even more time.

"We'll be fine V," Bull said, thumping me on the back before the three of them headed for the truck.

"If you guys find anything, you'd better call us right away," I demanded.

"Don't worry, chicky," Thatcher winked. "We know better than to try to keep you out of the *real* fun."

I laughed and shook my head as I opened the car door, saying, "Good luck!"

Waving, they set off in Thatcher's truck down the long driveway.

"That was a smart choice," William started.

"Don't talk to me," I replied, looking away. I slid into the passenger seat and buckled my seat belt.

"Are you going to pout all the way home?" William asked as he turned the key over in the ignition and started the car.

"I'm not pouting," I ground out.

"We're just trying to look out for you."

"I'm sorry, I don't remember ever asking you to protect me from the big, scary things in the dark. I'm pretty sure my request was: let me fight this fight."

"Fighting this fight doesn't mean making reckless decisions in order to prove how tough you are," he shouted, hitting the steering wheel.

I sat there glaring at him for a moment, and then turned and looked away. Clenching my teeth tightly together, I was trying to hold back the tidal wave of unflattering things I wanted to call him.

"We know you're tough, love," William said, and his voice was softer and more soothing. "No one is doubting that you can more than hold your own. But let's not be reckless. There is enough at stake here as it is; let's just sit this one out."

"Fine! So what are we going to do tonight instead? You know, while we're sidelined?"

"I don't know," he replied, putting the car in drive and pulling away from the manor. "Why don't you think of something on the way home?"

I relaxed my fists and tried to release my anger. They were just trying to look out for me, okay, but if any one of them had been the targeted person, would they have made the same choice? As if Thatcher would have ever allowed anyone to send him home like that! What a load of crap.

"So what will it be?" William sat on the couch in the living room with one arm stretched across the back of it. He seemed perfectly content to spend the night at home instead of out in the woods with the rest of the team.

"Do you really want me to answer that?" I smiled at him sweetly.

"Are you determined to ruin the rest of this night?"

"Maybe." I batted my eyelashes at him and then walked over to join him on the couch. It's not like I really got that much free time these days, so if I had to be at home tonight, I might as well try to enjoy it.

I sat down in the middle of the couch and spun around to the side, lying down and stretching my legs across William's lap.

"Comfortable?" he asked sarcastically.

"Very, thanks," I grinned as I snuggled down into the cushions.

He looked at me, a puzzled expression on his face for a moment, before taking my legs and tucking them more tightly against his body.

"If you give me a foot rub, I'll love you forever," I said while lifting my foot and wiggling my toes in front of his face.

Laughing, he captured my foot in his hands and began rubbing it. "Well, how can I resist a deal like that?"

Sighing, I closed my eyes and tried to will the tension out of my shoulders.

"Can I ask you a question?" I opened one eye and looked at him before closing it again.

"All right."

"Why do you still feed off people?"

"Well, I don't know about you, but starving myself into insanity isn't really something that I would voluntarily choose to do."

"No, I mean, why feed off *people*. Couldn't you feed off animals, or from blood bags at the hospital or something?" I propped myself up on my elbows. "If your coven is all about living peacefully with humans, why do you continue to regard them as walking Happy Meals?"

William set down my foot and picked up the other one, rubbing his knuckles up and down the sole. "I think you may not have a clear view of what the coven is actually like. We simply don't find it necessary to kill the people we feed from, but that doesn't mean we are ready to hold hands and skip down the street with them either. You would be hard-pressed to find many vampires that considered humans their equals. The Silverlake Coven members simply don't endorse needless killing."

"And you? Do you think humans are equal to vampires?"

"No," he answered simply.

My mouth fell open in surprise. Despite the way we met, it never really occurred to me that William might consider humans beneath him.

"Do you think that about me?"

"No, I don't. You're also not human," he shrugged.

"Well, I'm closer to being human than I am to being vampire, so what makes me so deserving of your illustrious praise?"

"Possibly because I no longer think of you as food. Do you consider a cow equal to you?"

"Well, no, but then again, I don't usually have

conversations with cows. Or you know, make out with them. Perhaps that has something to do with the hierarchy structure there..."

"You have to remember that to us, a human life is fragile and fleeting. It's over in a blink of an eye and can be snuffed out just as quickly."

"So why bother keeping them alive after you feed at all? If life is so meaningless?"

"Because killing is needless and pointless. Where is the benefit in that? If you could somehow eat a hamburger without killing the cow, or causing it any pain, and allow it to live its life pretty much in peace, would you choose to continue taking its life?"

I nodded, finally understanding. "No, I wouldn't."

"Why not?" he pressed.

"Because what would be the point of that?"

"Exactly. We didn't stop killing humans because of some deep-seated love for them. We simply evolved socially to a more efficient way of feeding and coexisting."

"And now some of you just can't be bothered with the effort anymore," I sighed.

"Exactly."

I worried my bottom lip with my teeth while thinking it over. "What about covens in other cities? How many of them practice kill-free feedings?"

"A few, but more of them do kill than don't. They are just better at hiding the evidence. Of course, those are usually very small covens. They understand the need for discretion and keep the vampire populations in each town very small. The only reason our coven manages to be so large is because we don't kill. What these so-called renegades have been doing is the essence of absolute stupidity."

"I understand why we need to stop them, but..." I closed my eyes and rubbed my temples, "I never wanted to be a killer. I always tried so hard not to kill the people that I fed from. And now? Now, I kill all the time."

"You're doing it because you know it's the only way. There is no trial, or jail time for what they have done. It may not be what you wanted, but you know it's necessary."

I nodded and pulled my feet off his lap, tucking them beneath me. "I know, I just never could have guessed that killing would come so... easily."

William tugged on my hand until I moved across the couch and curled up next to him. He wrapped his arm around my shoulders and nestled the top of my head under his chin.

"I know it scares you, but the next time you wonder if you're doing the right thing, or becoming something you don't like, just think of Colleen."

"I'm doing the right thing," I said, my voice colder. I had no doubt in my mind.

"Yes, you're doing the right thing."

CHAPTER TWENTY-ONE

The warmth of the sun shone through the living room windows onto my face, waking me up way too early. I rolled onto my back and stretched my arms above my head. God, I hated falling asleep fully clothed. It was so uncomfortable; my pants felt like they were twisted halfway around me.

A robin landed on the railing of the balcony and hopped back and forth. Its bright red chest puffed out as it sang loudly. I smiled at him, barely able to hear his singing through the glass pane.

I grabbed my phone off the table and glanced at the screen. No calls, no texts, nothing. Looks like I didn't miss out on any fun last night after all. This unexpectedly peaceful moment called for a little more *me* time.

I was ready to shake off the lingering, brooding frustration from the night before. Wallowing in self-pity wouldn't help me on my next mission.

Flipping through my phone, I scrolled down the music album playlists for something upbeat, then plugged my phone into William's surround-sound stereo. A moment later, eighties rock pounded from the speakers.

Pumping my fist in the air, I surrendered to the urge to rock out with a killer air guitar solo, complete with hair swinging, and head banging as I jumped up and down on the couch. Laughter overwhelmed me and I leapt over the edge of the couch before running to the glass sliding doors, opening them and rushing onto the balcony. The sounds of Twisted Sister, telling me how they weren't "gonna take it," followed me out into the bright morning.

Closing my eyes, I opened myself up, forcing the energy up and out of my solar plexus. Then I commanding it to run through me before projecting it outwards. It came easily in my manic state, rushing up and over me almost as soon as I fully formed my intent.

I opened my eyes to the blinding sun, and the brightness shot a searing pain through my eyes. Damn! I didn't realize how my heightened powers affected my vision. There was no doubt I was meant to hunt in the dark.

I inhaled deeply though my nose and exhaled through my mouth, pushing down the shocking pain and willing my vision to dial it back to seven before I tried opening my eyes again. The sunlight was still overly bright, but bearable. Turning to the side to avoid the glaring sun, I let my hunger rise as soon as the sun was no longer in my line of vision.

My breath was coming in short gasps as I struggled to restrain my urge to feed. I had to keep it under control. It would have been so easy to take the elevator down to the ground level and grab someone as they entered the building, but I couldn't think about that now. I shook my head and tried to clear away the haze. I had to regain control over it; my powers were still too sporadic.

Adopting a sparring stance, I held both my hands up in front of me in closed fists. I centered myself before I began throwing punches. Over and over again, I threw jabs, hooks and crosses, urging myself to move faster each time. The edges of my vision were a blur of red as my hunger grew more intense, and the cramps in my abdomen screamed out for solace, but I ignored them, determined to train myself to achieve blinding speed.

A sweet chirping drew my attention. From the corner of my eye, either the robin I saw earlier was back, or our balcony had become a serious bird magnet.

It took me a moment to notice that the bird was moving strangely, as if trapped in molasses. It spread its wings and took off from the railing, but seemed to be in slow motion as it flew away. Dropping my arms, I realized I did it! I finally achieved vampire speed!

"Whooo!" I shouted with glee, throwing my arms up to the sky and letting out a holler. I jumped up and scissor-kicked the air before putting my hands on my knees to catch my breath. Now that I stopped moving, I was suddenly extremely tired. It was well past the hour for breakfast.

The smell of the scrambled eggs filled the entire area downstairs with the aroma of garlic and cayenne pepper. Dancing between the counters, I shook out dashes of hot sauce into the pan while moving my hips in time with the music. I was so absorbed in cooking that I almost failed to notice the sound and sight of my phone vibrating on the counter.

I stretched over to glance at it with one hand still over the stove, mixing the pepper into my eggs; but when I saw the name on the phone screen, I dropped the spatula and grabbed the phone as fast as I could.

"Karen!" my voice was high and tight, "where have you been?"

"Where have I been? Where have you been? We've been really worried about you, Vanessa, you didn't talk to us for ages!" Karen snapped into the phone. There was no trace of her usual, cheerful voice.

"I know and I'm sorry about that, but the police thought it would be best if I kept a low profile for a while."

"But we're your best friends! Didn't you think you could trust us?" her voice started to sound like her familiar pout.

"Of course, I know I can trust you. But Detective Hache was really adamant about me not telling anyone where I was. I promised him I would take his advice seriously."

"Well, I can understand that, I suppose; I just hated not knowing what was going on with you. I've had to deal with

Mr. Mooney all by myself, and you know that's never any fun. You owe me big time for that."

"Look who's talking about being out of the loop. I hear someone has a secret boyfriend."

There was a long silence on the line. "What do you mean?" she asked flatly.

"Oh, nothing. Sophia was just telling me that you're seeing some new guy..." I waited expectantly, but she didn't say anything. "Some new guy who's name is..." I tried again.

"There's no new guy," Karen finally said, "I've just been busy, that's all. Sophia got it wrong."

"Oh, okay. Sorry. She just seemed really sure."

"Well, she was *wrong*," Karen curtly finished.

I was silent for a moment, thinking it over. Karen was acting so strange, and I couldn't help thinking she was lying to me, but I couldn't figure out why she would feel the need to.

"Did you get the message I left you?" I asked, thinking it was best to change the subject. After all, there were much more important things to worry about than her potential phantom boyfriend.

"You mean the one about leaving town? Yes, I got it; and no, I'm not going."

"But Karen—"

"Don't bother, Vanessa, it's not going to work, okay? I'm not going anywhere. Look, I've got work to do, I just wanted to call you back. I'll talk to you later, okay?"

I started to argue with her, but she already hung up.

Something was definitely wrong with her; it wasn't like Karen to be so short-tempered and evasive.

I turned the stove off and removed the pan from the heat. The eggs looked delicious, but after that conversation, I completely lost my appetite.

"That was fast," I said as I sipped my wine and looked over at William when he came in the door, back from feeding. He was only gone for about an hour, which seemed like a bit of a rush job, if you asked me.

"Would you prefer I go out again and come back later? I'm sure I could find some sort of trouble to get myself into this evening," he joked as he leaned against one of the high-backed dining chairs and smiled at me.

"Well, I'm not trying to kick you out of your home or anything, I just didn't expect you until a bit later. I guess I thought you were going to make a night of it, or something," I replied with a shrug as I stared into my wine glass, swirling the liquid gently.

"I was hungry, I ate, I came home." Pushing away from the chair, he came over and sat on the coffee table in front of me, arranging my legs on either side of him, with my feet on the table by his thighs before resting his hands on my ankles. "But what about you?"

"What?" I barely heard him, being so distracted by the caress of his thumb, which he rubbed gently over the insides of my ankles.

"You haven't fed in a while; aren't you going out tonight?"

"No," I replied before swallowing more wine. I looked at a spot over his shoulder, trying to ignore the figure eights his thumbs were now drawing and added, "I was just going to hang out here. Maybe watch a movie or something."

"Is it wise to go so long without feeding? Wouldn't want you to lose control the next time you got your hands on someone." His voice was a low rumble and my body flushed. I wished that he would either take his hands off me, or put them somewhere useful before I went nuts.

"It hasn't been all that long yet; I've gone longer. I'm still okay."

His hands moved slowly from my ankles up the back of my legs, over my calves and stopped just behind my knees. A light pattern of goose bumps rose on my flesh in the wake of his cool hands.

"It would probably be safer for everyone involved if you fed though, don't you think? You want to make sure you're at the top of your game, right?"

"Of course, I do. I suppose I could go out and find someone..." My eyes darted to the front door, but I didn't move to get up.

"Or..." Sliding forward off the coffee table, he knelt on the floor in front of me and his hands continued their journey, exploring my bare legs, over my outer thighs, stopping at the hem of my shorts. "You could stay in and eat."

"I don't think feeding off you is a good idea," I replied. I shifted in my seat, trying to ease my discomfort, but it didn't help. "Things always seem to get out of hand."

"Is that really such a bad thing?" William leaned forward and took a firm grip on my thighs. He pulled me towards him until he was nestled firmly between my legs.

Gasping, I suddenly found myself pressed up against him. I put my hands on his chest to try to keep some distance between us.

"Not necessarily bad," I stared at his lips. It would have been so easy to lean forward and nibble on them. "I'm just not sure if it's wise."

"Sometimes, wisdom can be highly overrated," he grinned.

"Oh, is that a fact?" I laughed, "Right now, I'm not so sure about that."

"Well, you're going to have to feed eventually, aren't you? Why go through all the work of going out to find someone when you have someone very willing right here?" He must have been reading my mind because the next thing I knew, he was nibbling on my bottom lip.

I had no idea why I fought so hard with him on that. It wasn't as though the idea was not incredibly appealing. He really did have a point. Why put off feeding for longer than I had to? Especially when I had someone so willing right here? It's not as if I was doing myself any favors by postponing it indefinitely.

"Kiss me, Vanessa," he growled against my mouth.

"I don't think—"

"Don't think, just kiss me," he insisted, running his thumb over my bottom lip before kissing me fully on the mouth.

I froze for a moment before I relaxed and wrapped both of my arms around his neck. He moved his hands to my hips and squeezed them, then stood up from the floor, taking me with him.

The hunger kept rising inside me, urging me to take him and I struggled to control it. I didn't want to feed yet; I just wanted to feel William's mouth on mine. It didn't seem to matter what I told myself, as soon as he kissed me, I didn't want him to stop.

He walked us around to the back of the couch and knelt back down on the floor, bending forward and lowering me onto my back before settling on top of me. The smooth, hardwood floor felt cool against my bare skin, and I liked being sandwiched with the chilliness of his skin lying above me.

"Have I told you how beautiful you are?" he asked as he ran a hand up my side.

"Feel free to tell me again," I replied, taking his hand from my side and bringing it to my mouth. I bit his thumb lightly. He closed his eyes and growled deeply in his throat. The sound sent a spike of heat shooting through me.

"You're amazing," his head dipped down and he kissed me fiercely, stealing my breath away.

My control snapped and the hunger overtook me. I dug

my nails into his shoulders and inhaled deeply, pulling his energy inside me. Tearing my mouth away from his, I let my head fall back and rode the pulsing high of raw energy.

I released his shoulders and fell back to the floor, panting as the hunger subsided. "Are you okay?" I asked him.

He dropped his head onto my shoulder and nodded, but didn't say anything.

"Are you sure?" I nudged him in the shoulder, and he grabbed my hand and stretched my arm out above my head. Then he slid his hand down my arm and over my chest, giving my breast a quick squeeze. I laughed and relaxed, "Yeah, you're fine."

William and I lay on the floor, staring up at the ceiling. My head rested on his stomach as he played with my hair. "You know what I could go for right now? Haagen-Dazs cookie dough ice cream," I moaned.

"Sorry, love, you're out of luck. No ice cream here," he laughed.

"Well, I really didn't think there would be." I smacked him on the stomach. "I just really want some."

"Is that your not-so-subtle way of asking me to go out and get you some ice cream?"

"No, actually, it's not." I propped myself up on one elbow and tossed my hair over my shoulder. "I can forage for my own ice cream, thanks. Besides, if I sent you out for it, you would probably just get it wrong anyway." I stuck my tongue out at him and stood up.

"Would you like some company?"

"No, you go ahead and lie there; I've got this one covered." Smiling, I walked around the couch and grabbed my phone before adding, "I'll be back in a few minutes."

CHAPTER TWENTY-TWO

The young guy behind the counter in the gas station smiled at me as I walked in. I gave him a small wave before strolling over to the coolers in the back of the store. I loved this station; they had the best ice cream selection. I couldn't believe it was hidden from me for so long. Wasn't there some law about hiding that much frozen dairy product goodness from a woman?

I grabbed a pint of cookie dough ice cream and stood in front of the open cooler door, taking a moment to enjoy the chill. The air outside was hot and humid, even so long after sundown, and a trail of sweat ran down the back of my neck after my two-block walk to get there.

My phone buzzed in my pocket so I shut the cooler door, and fished it out of my pants.

"Oh, my God," I dropped the ice cream on the scarred linoleum, my hand flying to my mouth while staring down in disbelief at the call display on my phone. A moment later, the buzzing stopped and the screen went blank.

Hands shaking, I closed my eyes and tried to process what I just saw. The phone started buzzing again and I squeezed it tightly before hitting the answer button.

"Colleen?" I whispered, nearly choking on her name.

"Vanessa?" Her voice was tiny and sounded far away, "Vanessa, I'm scared."

"Colleen, you're alive! Oh, my God! Where are you?"

"I don't know," she sniffed and whimpered. My heart clenched and a tear rolled down my cheek.

"Colleen, honey, you have to tell me where you are; what do you see?"

"I don't know, it's dark. They just gave me a phone and made me call you. I don't understand."

"They? Who's they, Colleen? What do they look like?"

"I—" She was cut off as the phone line went dead.

"Colleen? Colleen!" I screamed.

The blood pounded in my ears like a roaring storm and I sprinted for the door, slamming into a man that was on his way into the store.

"Hey!" he yelled.

Ignoring him, I rushed down the street towards the apartment building. The wind was suddenly knocked out of me and something slammed into my chest right before a hand covered my mouth and a pair of strong arms grabbed me. They hauled me into the alley.

"Gag her," someone barked, and a dirty rag was shoved into my mouth before a bag came down over my head.

I kicked out at them and tried to extricate myself from their tenacious grips, but there were too many of them. Someone grabbed my legs and held them together. I could feel my ankles being pressed tightly against someone's side.

This isn't happening! This cannot be happening! I fought and struggled against my captors, but could not shake them off. A sharp, sudden pinching in my arm made me hiss in pain behind the gag.

"Get her inside!" I heard the sound of the vehicle doors being opened before I was suddenly airborne. Slamming down hard on a metal floor, the pain seemed strangely far away. It almost felt as if it were happening to someone else. My brain was swimming inside my skull. *What had those fuckers done to me?* I tried to sit up, but my mind wasn't ready and I fell back down, knocking my head hard against the metal floor.

The muffled voices buzzed in my ear as I pushed myself up through the black tar of unconsciousness. I tried to move my hands and feet, but they refused to cooperate, lying so still, they may as well have belonged to someone else.

"Is the bitch still out?"

"Yeah, she should be out for a while longer from the dose we gave her."

"Who would have thought that one little slut could end up causing us so much trouble? I don't see why we can't just kill her now and get it over with. I have better things to do tonight than babysit her ass!"

"We all do; okay? But he wants her alive so we keep her alive. And no snacking."

"Did I say anything about snacking?"

"You didn't have to, I saw it in your eyes. Don't kill her, and don't eat her. I'm going to check on things upstairs. You cool here?"

"Yeah, just don't leave me down here too long. I may get bored and forget a couple of the rules."

"Ha! Well, if you do, you're dead. So unless you aspire to become a pile of ash, I suggest you write them down on your hand or something, whatever it takes to make sure that you *don't* forget. Otherwise, you'll have one hell of a time explaining your way out of that one."

"Yeah, yeah, I know the score; get out of here already."

"Cool, I'll see you in a couple of hours."

The voices faded away as whatever drug they injected into me started to take its effect and drag me back under.

"Vanessa!" A rough, cracked voice hissed my name. "Vanessa, wake up! Damn it! Vanessa!"

My head felt like it was more than three times its normal size and six times as heavy. I struggled to lift my chin from my chest. My captors removed the gag from my mouth, but my eyes were still blindfolded.

"Vanessa, are you awake?" came the voice from the

darkness again.

"Who's there?" My words were strangely slurred, and my tongue felt thick in my mouth. I could barely recognize my own voice.

"It's John, Detective Hache," he coughed, before going silent.

"John? Are you okay? John?"

I could hear the faint sound of his ragged breathing and dry, raking cough across the room from me. "Oh, crap! John! Please say something."

"I'm okay," he said before taking a few labored breaths, "and glad to see you alive."

"What are you doing here? How did they find you? Bull told me you were safe."

"I was, but—" the sound of a door unlocking cut John's answer off and he fell silent again.

I could hear footsteps crossing the floor, but they didn't seem to be coming closer to me.

"Who's there?" I turned my head back and forth, trying to pick up any other sounds or movements. "Where the hell are we?"

The burning hot pain on my cheek surprised me as a sharp slap across my face knocked my head to the side.

"Shut up, unless you want another one. I'm not here for you," a male voice replied.

A few seconds later, I heard scuffling and whimpering on the other side of the room. "Leave him alone!" I yelled, "what do you want with him? Let him go!"

There was no reply as the man forcibly took John from the room and closed the door behind him. A moment later, their departure was followed by the sound of the door locking.

My hands were bound behind my back and my arms were wrapped around a wide column. I strained against my bonds, but they secured my wrists with metal bands. As I moved my hands, I could hear the clanging of chain links between the wrist cuffs. There was no way I could break the chains. I could barely muster enough strength to hold my head up straight. If they hadn't bound me in a sitting position on the floor, I would have already collapsed.

A woman's screams cut through the silence. A bit muffled, due to the distance between us, they were swiftly cut off. With my heart racing, I used the ensuing burst of energy from my fear to again struggle against my chains, rocking ineffectually back and forth, and kicking out my feet. Unfortunately, all I succeeded in doing was exhausting myself once again.

Shit! I refuse to die in what I can only imagine must be a dank, dirty hell hole, out in the middle of nowhere. It reminded me of every lost-in-the-woods horror movie I'd ever watched. Of course, according to horror story rules, everyone knows only the virgins make it out alive. *Shit! Shit! Shit!* I was so beyond screwed.

I can't panic. If I panic, I'm dead. Okay, who am I kidding? I could reach nirvana in this basement and they could still come down here and snap my neck for me. If I panic, I will have no shot at all of saving my ass. All right, so the big question is: why am I not dead yet?

Taking a few deep breaths, I rested my head back on the column that was propping me up. *I'm tied up in what is probably the basement, if this ice cold cement floor is any indication, but they haven't killed me yet. Why not?*

The more I calmed down, the better I could hear what was happening on the floor above me. I heard multiple sets of footsteps shuffling around upstairs. Focusing my efforts on listening harder for any sound that could be John's voice, I strained my ears, but failed to hear anything.

How did they even know where to find me? William's place must not have been as secret as we both assumed. They probably were biding their time, waiting for my guard to be down, or for me to be distracted. Well, they sure took advantage of my distraction.

The memory of Colleen's phone call at the gas station flashed in my mind. She was alive this whole time? They had bitten her, taken her away, and then strung up the body of someone that looked like her for me to find? Obviously, they wanted me to think she was dead all this time. Why? Just so they could use her as bait in order to catch me later?

"Damn it!" I spat out, "why do they keep playing these goddamn mind games!" They kept toying with me, but never killing me. I didn't know if Colleen were better off being alive, especially if it meant she was trapped with these psychos for all this time. *Even if I find some way for us to get out of here, will they have hurt her beyond repair?*

My butt was starting to go numb from sitting in the same position for so long. I wiggled uncomfortably in my efforts to get some circulation going. There was no way I could tell how long I'd been down here. Hopefully, William will have realized something was wrong by now. At least, there was a good chance the guys would be out looking for me soon.

God, I can't believe I'm even thinking this, but I kind of wished William had fed off me again. At least that way, their chances of finding me would have increased substantially by having my blood in his system right now, But oh no! I insisted on being a bite-free zone, didn't I? Stupid! I mean, you'd think one of us would have seen the possibility of this coming. Like, hey, Vanessa, maybe I should feed off you just in case you're ever kidnapped by a group of raging, homicidal, psychopathic vampires and I need to find you before they suck you dry and snap your neck! Talk about hindsight being twenty/twenty.

CHAPTER TWENTY-THREE

Hearing the door unlocking pulled me from my thoughts and I waited anxiously for it to open, praying they brought John back in one piece.

"Well, look at you! All tied up with nowhere to go?" Merrick's voice mocked me.

"What's the matter, Merrick? Afraid that if you untie me, I'll kick your ass again?"

"That's seriously unlikely. I just enjoy the sight of you down there. So lost, so helpless. I just can't help but smile."

"Why don't you bring that smile over here so I can kick out a few teeth for you? It might be a good look on you, and a serious improvement," I offered sweetly.

The blindfold was ripped off my eyes and Merrick shoved his ugly face into mine, his fangs extending as he looked me over.

"I would watch my mouth if I were you, lest you find your current state of alive-and-kicking abruptly cut short.

That is, of course, unless you have a death wish. Is that it? Because if you do, I am more than happy to oblige," he said as he leaned into my neck and inhaled deeply.

"Get. The fuck. Away from me," I growled.

"Or what?" he replied as he moved back slightly and smirked at me.

Shifting slightly to give myself a little more space, I tilted my head back before snapping it forward as hard as I could, and headbutting him squarely in the forehead.

"Ow! Shit, bitch!" he swore with one hand holding his head.

"Or that," I laughed, swaying slightly. My vision was blurry and I also managed to give myself a splitting headache, but it was completely worth it to see the look on his face.

Standing up, he backed away from me and spat on the floor. "You keep misbehaving like that, and you're going to get punished. I suggest you start cooperating; otherwise, you won't like what happens next," he warned me as he walked to the door.

"How about taking that ugly face of yours and shoving it right up your—" I replied, but he slammed the door shut before I could finish.

I let my head drop to my chest and squeezed my eyes shut, trying to ignore the pounding in my forehead. "Ow, my head," I groaned. *I am never ever headbutting anyone again. Why do they make it look so cool in movies? I'm totally going to get a concussion.*

My stomach growled loudly and I couldn't help remembering the ice cream I dropped on the floor when I answered the phone. Oh, God! This was so not my day.

I couldn't tell how much time passed in the dimly lit basement before I heard shuffling feet outside the door again. When it opened, a vampire came in, hauling a very limp John behind him.

John's eyes were closed and his breathing sounded labored as they dragged him into the room and tied him up to a metal bar on the other side of it. The vampire didn't even bother to spare me a glance as he walked out of the room again without saying a word.

"John?" There was no answer as John lay lifelessly on the cement floor with his eyes closed and his mouth partially open. He was wearing a torn, dirty, white t-shirt, and equally dirty jeans.

My eyes widened in horror as I looked at his arms. Dozens of bite marks covered his exposed flesh, and the skin was bruised and torn. They were feeding off him!

I remembered what the young vampire said in the hospital. Something about having humans brought to them and sharing them amongst themselves. Except John was still alive. There was no way eight blood-starved vampires could have been feeding off him at once, unless they were getting stronger and more disciplined.

"John! Please wake up," I whispered again, but still received no reply.

I sat there quietly, willing him to be all right while

listening to the shallow, ragged sound of his breathing. At least, he was alive, for now.

John suddenly coughed and moaned, "Vanessa?"

"John? Oh, thank God. I thought you were done for!" I sighed with relief at the sound of his voice.

"I'm alive," he answered, and his breathing sounded short and tight when he rolled slowly onto his back.

"They've been feeding off you?" I asked him, not bothering to mask my horrified tone.

"Yeah, ever since I got here. They come in pairs and take turns. Then they give me a little time to rest before the next pair starts feeding. But I won't be able to keep it up much longer. It gets harder and harder not to black out when they're feeding. The only thing that keeps me conscious is my fear that if I do pass out, I may never wake up again. Or worse, I'll wake up as one of them."

"That's not going to happen! Do you hear me? I will not let them turn you. We are going to get out of here somehow."

"Promise me. Promise me that if they turn me, you will put a stake in me."

I shook my head fiercely. "That's never going to happen. I won't let it."

"Promise me," he insisted, "that if they turn me, you will kill me before I can hurt anyone else like this. I don't want to become one of those monsters."

"I promise. I promise I'll do it. But it's not going to come to that."

"There's something else that you have to know."

"What is it?"

"It's about how I got here. How they found me. I'm so sorry."

"It's not your fault; none of this is your fault. You have nothing to be sorry for."

"No, I'm sorry I have to tell you this, but you need to know. You were betrayed by someone on your team. Someone was working with the renegade vampires the whole time," he said before stopping to catch his breath and closing his eyes.

An icy chill ran through me as I waited for him to finish. I wanted to free myself and go over there and shake the person's name out of him, if I had to, but after all he'd been through and since we were already captured, I could spare him a moment to catch his breath.

"Who was it, John?"

He was silent before he rolled over and looked at me. "Bull," he said finally, "it was Bull."

My heart stopped. *It was Bull*. Bull, who saved me from becoming vamp chow on our first mission out. Who shielded me from the explosion at our apartment. Who was an all-around lovable teddy bear... Bull was working against us this whole time? I couldn't wrap my mind around what I was hearing.

"Are you sure?" I asked. There had to be some kind of a mistake, some kind of misunderstanding.

"I'm sorry, Vanessa, I know he was your friend. But it

was him, I promise you. He brought me here himself. It was after they bombed your apartment. He said he was taking me to a safe house, somewhere they would never find me, and he brought me here. And they've been feeding off me every day since."

My mind was swirling.

"He has probably been giving them information about the task force since day one. That must be why it was so hard to hunt them down, even as a team. If they always knew where we would be looking for them, they could make sure they weren't there."

"Right," John nodded stiffly, his body so weak and tender, "but they couldn't avoid you completely; otherwise it would start to look really suspicious. You had to feel like you were making progress, getting somewhere. And the rave? That was all a trap." Everything was starting to fall in line now.

"Bull was in the position to make sure it all went off without a hitch. Getting you there, convincing you to come with us, making sure we didn't die in the bombing, all of it. Being on the inside, he could move us around like chess pieces, making sure we were exactly where we needed to be, whenever we had to be there. And none of us ever saw it coming."

He was even able to fool Elizabeth, who hand-picked him for the task force, thinking that he was among her most loyal coven members. What about the rest of the team though? Was anyone else in on it? Was there anyone on the task force that I could trust? Maybe none of them are out looking for me right now because they all know exactly where I am!

"What I still can't figure out though is why we're here. If we caused them so much trouble, why not just take us out? Merrick came in here earlier to gloat. Just to rub my face in having been captured and tell me he could snuff my life out whenever he wanted, but he didn't. I'm still here, I'm still alive. This isn't about Bull, and it isn't about Merrick. There has to be someone else behind this, and for some reason, whoever it is doesn't want me dead. I just don't know who, or why."

"As long as you're alive, you have a fighting chance."

"*We* have a fighting chance," I corrected him. "You and I are going to get out of this together, all right? You just have to hold on and stay strong. I promise I'll find a way out of this. I will kill each and every single one of them if I have to, if that's what it takes to get us out of this place. Do you understand?"

Getting no answer, I looked over at him. His body lay still on the cement, totally unmoving. "Oh, God! John?"

"All right," he finally replied, his voice sounding very weak.

I sighed with relief and closed my eyes while sending up a silent prayer to whoever might be listening. *Please don't let us die here.*

John fell into a deep sleep and I watched over him, slightly worried that he might not wake up again. Judging by the amount of bite marks on his arms, it was no less than amazing that he lasted this long, especially if they were feeding off him for the last few days.

There was no way that he could have been their only source of food, however, which meant, somewhere around here were probably other people locked up and being fed on too. If I got free, there was no way I could leave the other people behind. I had to find a way to get us all out of here together.

I was beyond exhausted from stress, and the lack of food was starting to become an issue. I was nearly nauseated from hunger. I hated feeling weak and helpless, but there was nothing that I could do now, but sit here in the dark, watching over John and waiting until someone came and got me. They obviously had plans for me; otherwise I wouldn't be here. There was nothing more for me to do, but try to conserve my energy. Perhaps someone would eventually decide to tell me about their plan for me.

CHAPTER TWENTY-FOUR

Time passed unchecked as I faded in and out of consciousness. I didn't know if I were tied up there for hours or days. It became impossible to tell with nothing to do but sleep.

I was awakened roughly by someone tugging my hair and shaking me rudely.

"Wake up! I have a gift for you," Merrick said as he grinned down at me and forced my face towards the door.

He let me go and walked back to the entrance of the room, reaching out before pulling someone back in with him.

"Colleen!" I thrashed against my bindings, trying to break free. "Oh, my God! Colleen! Get your fucking hands off her!"

Merrick shoved her brusquely into the room and she sprawled on the floor in front of me. Crawling on her hands and knees, she dragged herself over to me while

Merrick strolled casually behind her, a self-satisfied smirk on his face.

Colleen pulled herself up with her hands on my shoulders and wrapped her arms around me. Her loud, racking sobs shook her body as her tears soaked my shoulder. I desperately wanted to wrap my arms around her and comfort her, but all I could do was lean my head against hers and pray she could take some comfort from my close proximity.

"Shhh, Colleen, shhh, it will be okay. You're all right now." I was so happy to see her, it was hard to contain my joy. "I thought you were dead."

Her shoulders shook with hiccupping tears, and I burned with guilt. After a moment, the crying stopped, but her shoulders continued to shake. She loosened her grip on my shoulders and moved backwards, her sobs becoming giggles, which turned into loud, unfettered laughter. I stared at her as she tossed her head back and laughed in my face.

"Colleen, what the hell is wrong with you?" Did they completely crack her mind?

"Wrong with me? Absolutely nothing, I've never felt better. But you were right about one thing," she smirked at me as two razor sharp fangs descended, "I *am* dead."

"Oh shit! Leen, I'm so sorry," I replied as I stared at her in horror.

"What are you sorry about?" she giggled before standing up. Dusting the dirt from her knees, she rested her hands on her hips and added, "This is the best thing that ever happened to me."

Merrick walked up behind her and wrapped his arms around her waist, pulling her back to him. She smiled and snuggled in his embrace, tilting her head back to look at him. Merrick put a hand on her cheek and kissed her passionately before they wrapped their arms around one another and turned and looked at me.

"Oh, God, I think I'm going to be sick," I said as bile rose up into my throat at the sight of them in each other's arms.

"I don't think she's very happy for us," Colleen pouted. "Come on, Vanessa, you know how hard it is to find a good man these days?"

"Colleen, if your definition of a good man is someone who kidnaps you, feeds off you, and turns you into a monster, then we seriously need to talk."

She stormed over to me and jabbed a finger into my shoulder before pointing it in my face. "Don't be mean," she snapped.

"Colleen, please."

"Colleen, please," she mocked me.

"What have they done to you?"

"Why is it so hard for you to understand?" she yelled, throwing up her hands. "Maybe I'm just not making myself clear enough. Shall I show you just how happy I am now?"

Colleen sashayed over to John and knelt down beside him, saying, "You know what, John? You really are cute."

Grabbing him by the front of his shirt, she hauled him up and licked the side of his face. Turning to look at me, she winked before tearing into his throat.

"No!" I screamed, "No! No! No! Let him go!"

She tilted her head back with her mouth open wide and his blood covering her face before diving back in for more. Tearing her head away viciously, she spat a chunk of his throat on the floor. John gurgled and choked as the blood rushed from his throat in spurts and spewed out of his mouth.

I was blinded by my tears as I sat helplessly watching John die, his blood pooling on the floor around him. Colleen pressed her finger to his lips, then licked the blood from his mouth off her finger. Rising to her feet, she tilted her head to the side, watching him take his last breath.

"Well, there you go," she sang, wiping the back of her hand across her mouth. "Convinced now?"

I choked on my tears as my eyes darted back and forth between John's body on the floor and the vicious stranger now inhabiting the body of one of my best friends. I couldn't get a handle on my breath and started to hyperventilate. It was too much; it was all just too much.

"Come on, Colleen, we have things to do. Say goodbye to your little friend," Merrick said. He was grinning from ear-to-ear as he watched the scene play out.

"Well, I just wanted to stop by and say hi, so I guess we'll be going now," she said as she put her arm around Merrick and wiggled her fingers at me. The two of them kept laughing on the way out of the room.

My hyperventilating breath turned into a high-pitched whining that came in short bursts. I rocked back and forth with my mouth open wide. My whining became a throat-tearing scream as I continued to rock. I screamed in one long breath, which echoed around the room. My vision turned a hazy red as I threw my head back and continued to scream in the dark. With every scream, my heart shattered into smaller and smaller pieces. It felt like there was nothing left in my chest, but an empty, howling void.

A gentle hand slipped beneath my head and lifted it slowly off the floor. A cup was pressed to my lips and a splash of cool water soothed my dry, chapped lips. The moment I felt the water on my throat, I desperately needed more. Gripping the edge of the cup with my teeth, I tilted the cup higher so the water would run into my mouth faster.

"Easy there, easy," a voice soothed, "you'll make yourself sick."

I kept gulping the water down, coughing when it went down the wrong way, but unable to stop on my own. The cup was removed from my mouth after my second coughing fit.

"Thank you," I rasped, coughing up the last bit of water, "thank you so much."

"I heard your screams. I couldn't let you suffer down

here." He ran a finger down the side of my face and brushed back my hair, adding, "it broke my heart."

I shivered at his touch and a cold chill ran down my spine. "Who are you?"

Opening my eyes, I was taken aback at how beautiful he was. His long, black hair fell over his bright, green eyes in thick locks. He stared at me with familiarity and visible hunger in his emerald-green eyes.

"Don't you know me?" he asked with a hint of hurt in his voice.

"I'm sorry," I shook my head, "I don't remember you." Moving gingerly, I sat up straighter to look at him more fully in the face.

"Well, we haven't properly met yet," he said as he set down the cup and put a hand on my knee, "but I know you. I know you very well."

I froze, and a thick, oily feeling slid down my spine as his thumb caressed my knee. "How... how do you know me?" I whispered.

"I've watched you. Have been for a while now. When I first saw you, I knew you were different, special, and oh-so-beautiful." His unabashed gaze raked over my body and I felt my skin crawl.

"Thank you," I said, pressing my back against the beam and trying to subtly put some distance between us.

"You were so perfect," he went on, putting his hand up to the side of my face as if to caress it, but stopping just short of touching me. Instead, he made his hand into a fist and pulled it back. "But you were beyond me. I thought, if I could only show you, and prove to you that I loved you, you would understand, if I just showed you that I was worthy of you..." he trailed off.

"It was you," I breathed, trying to keep the horror out of my voice. "You were the one leaving me all of the..."

"Gifts? Yes!" he admitted excitedly as he clapped his hands together. "You *do* know me; I knew you would. Those were my gifts."

"You left me dead bodies." I was starting to lose control of my anger. "You wanted me to find dead bodies. And you thought that was romantic... *how*?

"You didn't like them?" he looked confused.

"No. No, I really didn't," I snapped.

"But I did it all for you!" he yelled, "Everything, all of it, was just for you!" He grabbed me by my shoulders and shook me roughly until my teeth rattled. "You're just like the rest of them."

"Get off me," I yelled, "what the hell is wrong with you?"

"What's wrong with me? What's wrong with you?" His eyes were dark with fury as he shoved me away from him before rapidly pacing back and forth across the room. "I love you, I worship you."

"You don't even know me; you couldn't possibly love me," I said as I shook my head.

"You think you're so special, don't you? Just because you're a succubus, you think that you're better than me!" He slammed his fist into the wall, causing part of it to crumble away.

God, I was so stupid. Why couldn't I have just played along? This could have been my one chance to get out of here and I blew it, just like that. Now I was trapped, tied up in a locked room with my psychotic vampire stalker who seemed ready to tear my head off.

"I was all that you had here. I was going to take care of you. I was all you had! And now you blew it!" He shoved his face into mine and screamed at me, "You blew it! And now you have no one to protect you from them. I would never have let them hurt you. And they want you. Oh, yes! They want to hurt you so badly." He shook his head and slammed his fist into the column directly above my head, making me jump.

"Why? Why are they doing this to me? Why are *you* doing this to me? Haven't you bastards destroyed my life long enough? Either let me go, or let me die. I'm finished with you people."

"Oh, you're finished all right," he replied as he shoved away from me and stormed over to the door. "You're going to be sorry that you didn't love me back."

The door slammed at his exit and I collapsed on myself. All my former fight rushed out of me and my mind started racing with fear and confusion. I stared at the blank wall across from me and only then realized John's body was gone. The floor was still stained dark where his blood had poured out all over it. I, like an idiot, almost added my own blood onto the floor with his.

The door banged open and Merrick came in. "What the hell are you doing down here? Even locked up, you manage to find a way to piss people off. You want to know what we're doing here? All right then, why don't I show you?

CHAPTER TWENTY-FIVE

Merrick unchained me from the post and hauled me onto my feet. I wanted to shove him off me and make a break for it, but after they starved me, I was barely strong enough to walk across the room.

We made our way up the stairs and out of the basement. The wooden stairs creaked beneath our feet as he shoved me in front of him. I kept one hand pressed against the wall to help me stand upright, and the old, dry paint cracked and fell away beneath my fingers as my palm slid across it, catching the edges of the peelings as we went.

From the basement, we entered a large kitchen on what I assumed was the main level of the house. The huge window above the sink revealed that it was already dark outside, but there was no way for me get a bearing on where I was. Beyond the window stood a great, thick forest, and the trees seemed to go on forever. They also revealed nothing, but unending blackness.

Merrick shoved me towards the dining room table and pressed me down onto one of the hard, wooden, dining room chairs. Once seated, he grabbed my hands and pressed them together in front of me before securing my wrists with a short length of coarse rope.

After spending so much time locked in the dark basement, the bright lights of the kitchen burned my eyes and I had to close them and tilt my face away from the glare just to ease the pain.

"There now," Merrick said with mock compassion, "isn't that better? Aren't you grateful for a little bit of fresh air?"

I said nothing, but sneered at him and looked away, refusing to play his little mind games. If he thought I would grovel and act thankful to him, he must have lost his damn mind.

"You're quite the ungrateful, little bitch, aren't you? And here I was, all set to let you have something to eat too. You must be quite hungry by now. You haven't had a thing to eat in days."

"Thanks, but I'm really not that hungry," I sneered. Just then, my traitorous stomach let out a large grumble, and Merrick barked with laughter.

"Looks like your stomach just made a liar out of you. Lucky for you, Lachlan touched my heart with his pleas for you. You see, the guy is so painfully smitten with you that he couldn't bear to see you in pain down there for a moment longer." Merrick leaned against the table and crossed his legs at the ankles. "He was furious with me when he came storming upstairs just now. He's convinced that I've driven you out of your mind with hunger. Is that it? Is that why you can't love him, succu-slut? Are you just too hungry to see straight?"

A swift movement at the corner of my eye made me glance quickly over toward one of the kitchen doorways. The familiar, oil slick feeling settled in the pit of my stomach, and the back of my neck started to burn. He was there! And still mad at me. But I might have gotten a chance to turn this mess around.

"Lachlan is probably right," I said slowly, "I'm really not my best when I haven't eaten in days. I'm sorry I was so rude to him. I wish I could apologize."

A shadow fell over the table and I sensed a thick, oily presence behind me. I held my breath, waiting to feel the weight of his touch, but it never came.

"I knew you weren't being yourself," his soft breathy voice came from above me. "I knew you could never be so cruel. Not to me. Not when I love you so much."

"I… I'm glad you understand," I said as I clenched my hands together and tried to resist the urge to swing my fists into his face. "Thank you for accepting my apology."

"You can't be serious," Merrick said as he looked at me and then at Lachlan, his face twisting into a disgusted sneer. "Lachlan don't you dare let her get into your head. You're such and idiot. The scheming, little bitch loves you about as much as she loves me."

Lachlan roared and launched himself at Merrick,

knocking him off balance and dragging him to the ground. They rolled around on the kitchen floor, and Merrick tried to fend off Lachlan's wild, uncoordinated punches.

"She doesn't love you!" Lachlan screamed, "She'll never love you. She's mine! She's mine!"

Merrick threw Lachlan off him and got to his feet just as Lachlan launched himself again with spittle flying from his mouth and a demented look in his eye.

"Enough!" Merrick roared as he swung a fist into Lachlan's face, taking advantage of the momentum of his own attack. I watched wide-eyed as Lachlan flew backwards across the kitchen and crashed into the counter before landing in a crumpled heap on the floor.

"You crazy bastard," Merrick said as he wiped his hand across his mouth, smearing the blood from his split lip.

"She's... mine," Lachlan panted, pulling himself up off the floor.

"Yeah, yeah. No one's trying to get between you and your little playmate here. But don't forget that we need her alive. So if she makes you mad, try not to bust her up too badly, all right?"

Merrick looked at me with a satisfied grin as he walked towards the doorway. With one last glance back at us, he gave me a smirk and walked out of the room.

I sat frozen in the chair as Lachlan stood panting in the corner, staring at me. The crazed hunger in his eyes set the back of my neck on fire. I desperately wanted to run screaming from the room, taking my chances in the endless expanse of forest outside and whatever cougars or bears might be lurking in them, rather than spending one more second trapped with this man.

With both hands, he dragged the hair off his face and over his head. Then he tugged on the bottom of his button-down shirt, straightening it out before walking to the table and taking a seat across from me.

"You must be starving," he said.

Unable to speak, I simply nodded and watched him warily as he went to the fridge. It was strange how he moved around the kitchen so casually, making dinner for me as if nothing were out of the ordinary.

"Do you want mustard on your sandwich?" he asked over his shoulder.

I started to nod, but then realized that he couldn't see me with his back turned, and answered, "Yes... please."

"I used to like mustard too. I knew we had things in common," he said as he presented the sandwich on the table in front of me with a flourish and a smile. He seemed like a proud child presenting his homework, after getting top marks on it, to his mother.

"Thank you," I replied as graciously as I could.

Eating the sandwich was an incredibly awkward task with my hands tied, but the moment I tasted food, I didn't care. I took my time to chew carefully before swallowing to avoid choking to death.

Lachlan sat still, watching my every move eagerly and expectantly. I was sure he was waiting for me to say something.

"It's delicious," I said, trying to put a smile on my face that felt more like a pained grimace. Lachlan didn't seem to care though and lit up visibly at my praise.

"I'll make you another one," he said as he grabbed my plate and hurried back to the counter while I slumped in my seat.

When he placed the second sandwich in front of me, I made sure to finish every bite of that one as well. I had no clue when I would get another chance to eat. Not to mention being terrified of running the risk of insulting him by not finishing the meal he made for me. I had no idea what might send him off into another blind rage, and I wasn't willing to risk any misstep.

As he cleared away my plate, I racked my brain desperately for something to say. I wasn't ready to be dragged back to the basement.

"When did you first see me?" I blurted out. Hey, it was as good a question as any, and probably more likely to get an answer than if I asked him to spill his guts about their master plan.

"It was months ago," he smiled, getting a faraway look in his eye. "I was out hunting and I felt you. You were hunting too. I could smell you. You were different, I sensed it."

"Did you know what I was?"

"No, I never met anyone like you before. But you glowed! Everything about you was shiny and bright and beautiful. I knew you weren't like me, but you weren't like them either. Those dirty humans, running everywhere like wild cattle."

"But you never approached me? Why is that?"

He looked away from me, then down at the floor. "I suppose you could say that I was shy. You were strange and wonderful. And I didn't know what to do."

"And so you started leaving me... presents," I swallowed loudly, disgusted by his description of the horror he left on my doorstep.

"I wanted you to be a part of our family," he grinned, "but I didn't know where to start, so I told Merrick about you."

"What, exactly, did you tell Merrick about me?"

He blushed and looked away, shaking his head.

"Come on, Lachlan, you can tell me," I coaxed. "What did you tell Merrick about me?"

"I told him that I found the most beautiful woman in the world, but I didn't think you were a vampire. I said you were something new."

"And what did he think about that?"

Lachlan frowned and looked at me suspiciously. "Why do you care about what he thought? Why does it matter? I'm the one that loves you, not him," he said angrily.

"I know, I know you are. You're the one here with me," I said quickly, "feeding me and taking care of me. I'm just curious about how it all happened, you know? How you came to find me. How Merrick was such a good friend to you in helping you get over your shyness." I smiled so hard,

I thought my face would crack.

"Of course," Lachlan smiled back at me, "Merrick was a good friend with that. He wanted to see you for himself. To understand what made you so special, and why I loved you so much."

I nodded, but stayed quiet to encourage him to go on. If I could just keep him talking, I might be able to find out what the hell was going on around here.

"We found you at a club, the Roxy, and we watched you dancing. You're a beautiful dancer. Did you take lessons?" Shaking his head, he promptly waved away the question and continued. "Merrick saw right away how special you were. He said he wasn't surprised that I was so in love with you. He said I had to work really hard to make you love me too. He told me I would have a lot of competition."

"You were both there at the Roxy a few months ago?" A feeling of dread came over me. "Was it the night that...?"

Lachlan nodded, knowing exactly what I was talking about. "He had his filthy hands all over you. I saw him grab you, and he wouldn't let you go. He should never have treated you like that. Couldn't he tell how special you were? He had to be taught a lesson. To pay for his disrespect," he pounded his hand down on the table and ran his hands through his hair again, calming himself down.

"So you saw him hurt me and you wanted to protect me. That was very caring of you."

"I knew you would understand. I did it for you. So you wouldn't have to be afraid of him hurting you anymore. I didn't want you to feel afraid."

Well, wasn't that just the irony of all ironies? "And the lady you left in my hallway? What about her?"

Lachlan snorted and flipped his hair out of his eye. "I overheard her talking to the cops. She was saying bad things about you, and I didn't like hearing them. She was a stupid, lying, little cow. You deserve better than to have people spreading nasty gossip about you. She got what was coming to her. I know that if you heard her, you would have wanted her to shut up, so I shut her up for you."

"Wow," I couldn't think of a single other thing to say. The months of hiding, running, and fighting all because this twisted sicko thought he was in love with me. And protecting me. And if he stacked enough dead bodies at my feet, he believed I would be compelled to love him back.

The sandwiches that I had just eaten threatened to come back up on me. The guilt of those lives cut short just because I existed, nearly overwhelmed me with grief.

"I... I'm sorry," I said, almost choking on my apology.

"Worried, he hurried around the table and knelt at my side, "What? Why? What could you possibly have to be sorry about? You're here with me now. Everything will be all right now. We'll be happy."

A shudder of revulsion ran up and down my arms. My fingers itched for my gun. I wanted nothing more than to put a bullet between his eyes.

"I'm sorry that I didn't understand your gifts at the time. There was so much going on, I got confused. I thought you were mad at me." I pressed down my rage and tried to fill my voice with sadness.

"How could I ever be mad at you? Why would you think such a thing?"

He obviously forgot about his own rage in the basement just a little while ago. Was he this insane before someone turned him? Had he always been a stalker? Or out of his mind? Or was becoming a vampire the reason? Could that do this to him?

"I thought, well, I thought it might have had something to do with all the other killings going on. So many bodies were found. And the boy in the Roxy, after you took his head too, well, I thought..." I trailed off, looking at him from the corner of my eye.

"I knew it! I knew it! I knew Merrick was wrong," he said as he grabbed my knee. The back of my neck exploded in pain. I bit down on my lip, trying not to whimper out loud.

"Wrong? About what?" I gasped.

"He said that you were hunting me, and you wanted to hurt me. Of course, you were confused, of course, you were." He held his hand up as if to cup my cheek, but kept it a few inches away from me. "How could you have known it was me when it looked like one of theirs?"

"I'm sorry, I still don't understand. I want to. I really do, but there is just so much that I still don't know," I explained to him. "I know now what you did was for me. I understand that now. But what about all the others? Why was there so much killing? The Silverlake Coven isn't supposed to kill humans. No one will tell me why Merrick and your group have started to kill humans. I only hunted you because it was my job. I didn't understand why you were doing it. But I'm listening now. If you want to tell me, and you want me to understand, I promise to listen."

"Right, right, you don't know. How could you know? You're not one of us. They filled you with their lies, didn't they? To turn you against us? To turn you against me?"

"I don't want their lies. I don't want anyone's lies. I want the truth." I looked deeply into his eyes, adding, "and you'll tell me the truth now, won't you, Lachlan? Because you won't lie to the person you love, right? You'll tell me what they won't. I know you will."

"The Silverlake Coven is a bunch of liars. You can't trust a thing they say. That's why we left. We couldn't live with their lies anymore."

"What kind of lies?" I found myself truly becoming curious. All I knew about the Silverlake Coven was what I was told by Elizabeth and William.

"The lies about who we are, who we're supposed to be, and how we're supposed to act. It's all fake, unnatural. It's all that bitch, Elizabeth's fault. She defanged an entire coven with her lies. Making us no better than the humans. We aren't supposed to live in the shadows, hiding from them. We should be ruling over them. What other predator hides from its prey? We became the laughingstock of the entire vampire community. It had to end. It was time to go back to the old ways."

"So you broke away from the main coven in order to live more naturally?"

"I knew you would understand. You see it too, don't you? How wrong it is? How backwards the rules are?"

"But how..." I stopped myself.

"How what?"

"Aren't you worried about what might happen if the humans discover you? If they discover you're real, and you've been killing them this whole time? They'll fight back. And there are more of them than there are of you. Isn't that why vampires went underground in the first place?"

Lachlan waved away my worries. "Times have changed. Merrick says that it's time for a revolution. And the world is ready for a revolution. There might be more of them now, but there won't be for long. Soon, there will be enough of us that they won't dare try to stand against us."

"You're turning people," I whispered, "aren't you? Lots and lots of people?"

"There are going to be more of us now than ever before. And we can finally be our true selves. We can live the way we are supposed to. No more lurking in shadows and stealing our meals. The humans will finally be aware of their true place in this world too. Everything will be as it should be. And you'll be there with us. With me."

CHAPTER TWENTY-SIX

If anyone had told me two hours ago that being chained in the basement was better than being upstairs, I would have locked them up before they could blink. Yet, I felt nothing less than an overwhelming sense of relief when Merrick came back to the kitchen to tell us that my little field trip upstairs was finally over.

Lachlan started to argue with him, but stayed quiet in the end, allowing Merrick to walk me back downstairs to the solitude of utter darkness. I was grateful for the time to myself, especially now that Lachlan had given me a lot to think about.

It all made sense now. I was still alive because Lachlan wanted me to be his succubus queen. Oh, God! Oh, God! What if he decided that wasn't enough and tried to turn me? I had to get out of here before that idea crossed his mind.

Merrick had to know there was no chance I would go

along quietly. Not after what they did to Colleen and John. He would surely try to find some way to get rid of me without arousing Lachlan's suspicions. Either turned, or dead and buried in the woods somewhere, it didn't matter, the days of my life as I knew it were numbered. Merrick must have known that I would put an end to him the first chance I got.

I closed my eyes and tried to picture everything that Lachlan told me, after moving past the initial shock. I mentally laid it all out in front of me like puzzle pieces, trying to fit them all together. One thing was certain, this was so much bigger than just the Silverlake Coven. If they believed they could turn enough people to gain control of the vampire population, it meant there were renegade factions in cities everywhere. And besides them were those groups of vampires that never stopped killing humans. Would the renegades rally them to their cause as well? Or convince them to take their feedings out of the shadows? If William was right, and there were more vampires that preferred to kill their prey than those that mercifully kept them alive, we didn't stand a chance.

I thought of the months spent, night after night, trying to hunt these bastards down and wipe them out before they could do any more damage, or take any more innocent lives, and none of it meant anything, did it? Here we were, trying to stomp out one stupid ant hill, never even realizing we were standing in the middle of a whole field of them.

This went beyond Elizabeth. She might have been head

of this one coven, but how much pull could she have in the vampire community at large? Would she have any influence over the other coven leaders? Enough to move them into action against the oncoming tide?

There wasn't a goddamn thing I could do about it. There was no way for me to get out of here. I would just have to try to stay alive long enough for William to find me. So long as I stayed on Lachlan's good side, I might have a slim chance of surviving for a while longer. When push came to shove, Merrick was the one in charge, and whom I had to watch out for the most.

Colleen would provide no help at all, and that was for damn sure. The sweet Colleen that I once knew was completely lost to me after her change. Witnessing what she did to John was enough for me to admit she was totally gone. There was no saving her now.

It almost seemed like she died twice. Once in the street, in front of my apartment, and again, in this basement. They kept using my friends, dangling them in front of me, only to tear them away from me over and over again. I would burn this hell hole to the ground. The house and every single, dirty, murderous vampire inside it when I lit the match. And if Bull just happened to be here when it all happened, so much the better. That betrayal would never be forgiven.

I looked up at the ceiling and released my anger. In my mind, I pictured every moment of pain, confusion and fear I had to endure since that first night at the Roxy. From finding the body in the stall at the club, to being dragged off the street and brought to this place. I formed every single moment in my mind, allowing all the emotions to come back again and fill every corner of me.

My emotions pounded inside me, a heavy, rhythmic tattoo, centered at my very core. My body shook with it, barely managing to contain it all, and I thought I would shake myself apart. Nevertheless, I continued to hold onto my memories, letting them consume me.

The hunger raged over me, and I allowed it to run rampant for a moment before receding again. Letting go of the memories, one by one, I fell back against the column. I was panting and covered in sweat. When the time came, I would be oh-so-ready.

I stayed very still with my eyes closed and tried to regulate my breathing as best I could to avoid giving myself away. Someone was in the room with me. A new presence had awakened me from my very light sleep and I could hear their soft footsteps inching closer.

As a hand closed around my throat, I couldn't pretend anymore; it was now or never. I prayed with all my heart that Lachlan was still somewhere upstairs.

"Who the hell are you?" I slurred, keeping my eyes closed so as to look as weak and vulnerable.

"Oh, now, don't mind me darlin.' I was just told we had a sweet, little, ol' houseguest, so I thought I'd just come down here and make your acquaintance, that's all. Thought you and me might get to know each other a little better."

"Nice to meet you. Now please piss off," I moaned, rolling my head to the side.

"Well, now, that ain't very friendly, is it? I know you can be friendlier than that," he crooned, leaning in closer and sliding his hand inside the collar of my shirt before squeezing my breast.

"What? Not even a kiss first?" I sneered.

"Aha! Now see? I knew a little slut like you would be askin' for it," he said. Grabbing my face, he shoved his slimy tongue down my throat and continued to fondle my breast.

Unleashing my anger, I let my hunger flare up before I sucked the energy from him as quickly as I could without taking so much as to kill him. He knelt there, looking at me with a dazed expression and one hand still inside my shirt. *Perfect.*

I looked deeply into his eyes, focusing my will on him. "Now bite me. Gently, but draw blood," I tilted my head to expose my neck, wincing with pain when his fangs pierced my skin, and then screaming at the top of my lungs.

Shrieking with each breath for as loud and long as I could, thankfully I didn't have to wait very long. The door to my room flew open with a crash before it slammed back against the wall. The sound of splintering wood cracked through the air just as Lachlan flew into the room, snarling like a feral creature. His eyes landed on us, and I stared up at him with terror and pleading in my eyes.

"Help!" I screamed before bursting into tears and screaming again.

Lachlan was before me in a blink on an eye, ripping the vampire off me. The swift action made his fangs tear my skin as he yanked him off, and I cried out in earnest. *Shit!* Bleeding to death was never a part of my plan.

Lachlan descended upon the other vampire and planted a foot in his chest, then grabbed his head, and with a sharp, wrenching torque, tore his head from his shoulders and threw it across the room. Upon hitting the wall, it exploded into a puff of ash.

I whimpered as he came over to me and tugged on the metal chains that bound me, but they still wouldn't break.

"I'll be right back; hold on," he said before becoming a blur and vanishing from the room. Back in seconds, he was carrying the key for the lock.

I could feel hot blood flowing down my neck as I slumped against him. He lifted me off the floor and took me upstairs.

"Lachlan, what the hell are you doing?" Merrick stood in front of us at the base of the stairs on the main level, blocking our ascent to the upper level of the house.

"Get out of my way! There's no time," Lachlan yelled at him.

"What the hell happened here?" Merrick asked as he moved to the side and followed us up the stairs.

Lachlan gently lay me on a bed. The scratchy quilt

smelled of stale mothballs, but it might as well have been one hundred percent Egyptian cotton spritzed with rose oil, after my discomfort over the last few days.

"He fed on her, he was touching her, and he fed off her again!" Lachlan roared. "We have to help her, she's lost too much blood."

When I opened my eyes again, my blurry vision could barely make out Lachlan tearing his shirt off and putting it up to my neck. He wiped away the blood and examined the wound.

"It's not torn too badly. I should be able to heal it with my saliva," he said as he spat in his hands repeatedly. He rubbed them together, coating his palms.

My revulsion was hard to hide. It was like a thick oil that I had to swallow. I squeezed my eyes shut when he pressed his saliva-covered hands on my neck, putting pressure on the wound and coating it with his vampire spit. I didn't care how effective it might have been as a healing agent; sharing such intimacy with him made my skin crawl.

Finally, he pulled his hand away and I could feel his fingertips pressing gently around the sore area. "It's closing up; she should be okay."

I lifted a shaky hand, holding it out to him and watched how he looked at it coming towards him, his eyes wide in shock and anticipation. *Excellent*. Right before I reached him, I let my arm fall in a dead drop and slammed my eyes shut, rolling my head to the side.

"How the hell could you let this happen, Merrick? Why

was no one watching her? You let that newly turned, trailer trash, redneck get his hands all over her. He could have killed her." There was a thudding impact, but I didn't dare open my eyes.

"Lachlan you need to calm down. You got to her in time. She'll be fine, look at her. She just needs to sleep it off."

"That's not the point. This never should have happened. I never wanted her chained up down there. Treating her like we do the humans. But I let you talk me into it because you promised me that she would be safest down there. Out of reach from the others. You said it would be better if they didn't know she was here, so they wouldn't try to hurt her; and now, look what's happened."

"Having her down there was for the best, Lachlan," Merrick replied, trying to calm him down. That's what happened if you turned a psychopath. You couldn't always manage to keep a handle on them.

"It wasn't for the best," Lachlan hissed. "Does this look like it was for the best? Look at her! She's staying up here from now on. I'll guard her. No one else."

"And how are you going to watch her during the day? Have you stopped to think about that?"

"I'll figure something out. Look at her, she needs me. She would never hurt me by trying to leave."

"All right, Lachlan, all right. You watch her. We'll figure something out."

CHAPTER TWENTY-SEVEN

Blinking my eyes open, I looked around the room once I was sure they were both gone. It was small, and only contained the double bed that I was lying on, a bedside table and a dresser. The floral patterned wallpaper was peeling in sections, and every surface in the room was in dire need of a good dusting. These guys obviously weren't big on domestic skills.

I closed my eyes again and snuggled under the musty bedspread, savoring the feeling of a soft pillow under my head. I was one step closer to escape. It would be much easier to figure something out from up here than being chained in the basement. In the meantime, I needed to gather some of my strength back after so much blood loss. My injuries weren't nearly as bad as I made them look, thanks to feeding right before I was bitten, but I still lost more blood than I planned on, and that would slow me down a bit.

A shadow passed by the crack under my bedroom door, but there was no sound. It didn't matter. I knew Lachlan was out there standing guard, making sure no one could get to me. It disgusted me to play into his delusions this way, but he would never agree to let me go, no matter what I said, or how I pretended to return his feelings. I had to try to get him to at least lower his guard. Not all the showers in the world were enough to wash clean the stain of what I might have to do in order to get myself out of the mess I was in.

The door opened a crack and Lachlan stuck his head inside. I froze when he saw me awake. He came over to the bed slowly and looked at my neck.

"How do you feel?"

"Sore, tired," I stifled my disgust until I could finally say, "grateful."

He dipped his head in acknowledgement, and his hair fell into his face. "You won't be going back downstairs again. You'll be up here from now on."

"I will?"

"It's not safe for you down there. I knew it wasn't. I never should have allowed that to happen. So you'll be up here, where I can protect you properly."

"Thank you. Thank you for getting to me so quickly. He would have killed me, or worse."

"Never! That will never happen to you, so don't even say it," he snarled.

"I just wish that you could protect me from Merrick. He

scares me. I believe he would hurt me if he could."

"Why do you say that?" he asked.

"I can see it in his eyes. He likes seeing me in pain."

"No, he wouldn't dare. He knows how special you are. He knows I love you." He shook his head, but I could hear the doubt in his voice.

"I don't know," my voice hitched, "I just know that I'm scared." I put my face in the pillow and shook my shoulders gently as if I were crying, then sniffed. "I'm sorry, I'm just so tired...," I let my voice drift off before lying quietly and not moving.

A few moments later, I heard him leave the room as I smirked into the pillow.

The next morning, I woke up to find a woman sitting in the corner, staring at me. She looked to be about my age, but it was hard to tell beneath the layers of dirt and bruises that covered her. Her eyes looked vacant and far away as she watched me.

"Who are you?"

She continued to sit there, staring at me, but didn't say a word. I couldn't tell if her mind was broken after all the time she, no doubt, spent trapped here, of if they glamoured her. If that were the case, it must've been within an inch of her life to make sure she didn't run away while serving guard duty.

I was surprised they chose a woman instead of a man. It

wouldn't have taken much for me to overpower her, not that a man would have proven more of a challenge. Of course, they thought I was still weak from blood loss. And they were right. I was nowhere near the top of my game, and there was no way I could live with myself if I drained one of their captives purely to save my own skin.

I climbed off the bed and inched closer to her, standing on the balls of my feet, poised and ready to dive out of the way in case it was an act and she took a swing at me. She must have had some sort of trigger. Something surely to set her off, otherwise, what good could she be as my guard?

I avoided looking anywhere near the bedroom door just in case she took that as a sign I was trying to escape. I stopped a few feet away from her, and stayed just out of arm's reach.

"Do you have a name?" I asked again, but she still didn't answer.

I stretched out my hand towards the window and put it on the glass. The moment I connected, the woman jumped out of the chair and flew at me in a rage.

I leapt back and held up my hands to fend off her attack while trying to catch her by her wrists. My energy was starting to fail me, but at last, I managed to get a grip on her and tug her toward me. Our faces collided, and the hunger flared up inside me, urging me to feed from her.

I had to be careful not to take it all, just enough to gain my strength and break through the glamour they cast on her, if that were even possible. Sending up a quick prayer, I pressed my mouth on hers and pulled her energy into me. After a moment, she slumped against me, all the fight gone from her and I closed my eyes to enjoy the head rush.

"Hey, hey! Can you hear me?" I smacked her on the cheek gently, trying to get her to open her eyes. She gazed up at me, looking just as vacant as before, but this time, she nodded her head. *Well, that's progress at least*. I breathed a sigh of relief.

I stared deeply into her eyes and focused on wrapping my energy around her, bringing her inside me and pushing my will through. "Do you understand me?"

Again she nodded, but didn't say anything. Blowing out a breath, I brushed my tangled hair away from my face and simply held her.

"Okay. I need you to do exactly as I say. Sit here. Stay quiet, and don't move until I come back. All right?" Again, she nodded and I crossed my fingers, hoping that would be good enough until I got back.

I walked over to the door quickly and placed my hand on the doorknob. I waited to see if she reacted, but she stayed exactly where I left her, staring off into space. Breathing a sigh of relief, I cracked the door to the bedroom open as quietly as possible and slowly stuck my head out the door.

The moment I did, a young boy lunged at me. He couldn't have been anymore than sixteen years old, but I didn't hesitate. I grabbed him and sucked the energy from him as well, leaving him standing, but very docile in the hallway before I crept quietly down the stairs.

At the bottom of the landing, I stopped to see if the coast was clear. It didn't look like there were any more glamour slaves ready to take my head off if they saw me. Those charming little minions had to have been Merrick's idea. They were way too vicious.

I poked my head into the kitchen and almost squealed in delight. There, on the counter, was a cordless phone. Rushing to it, I snatched it up and slapped a hand over my mouth when I heard a dial tone. Punching in William's phone number, each ring seemed to take ages. I stood there, exposed, but finally, his voicemail kicked in.

"William, it's Vanessa," I hissed, "the renegades grabbed me. I don't know where I am, but it's definitely the place we've been looking for. You've got to get me out of here. I'll send someone to you tonight. They'll be downstairs. Please, please! Come get me."

I hung up the phone and pulled open all the kitchen drawers until I found a small paring knife and an old dishcloth; then I ran upstairs as quietly as possible.

I sat in my room, staring out the window until the sun passed the highest point in the sky and began its descent. I couldn't risk leaving it any later than that.

Kneeling in front of the woman in my room, I took both of her hands in mine and stared into her vacant eyes, focusing as much of my energy on her as possible.

"Can you hear me?" Again, she nodded silently and waited for my instructions.

I pulled out the paring knife and tea cloth that were hidden beneath the mattress and undid my pants. I counted to three and sliced a shallow cut across the top of my thigh. I pressed the tea cloth against it to soak up the blood. It wasn't much, but hopefully enough for what I intended.

"Take this cloth and guard it with your life. You must never lose it, and no one can take it from you, but William. Do you understand? Leave this house and go to the address I tell you. Wait downstairs for William. Wait as long as it takes. He will find you. Let nothing stop you." Leaning forward, I whispered William's address in her ear before releasing her hands.

Quickly, she rose before rushing quietly to the door. I watched her go down the stairs and held my breath as I heard a door down below open up and close.

I licked my blood off the edge of the paring knife to mask the scent, and shoved the knife between my mattress and box spring before climbing back into bed. All I could do now was wait.

CHAPTER TWENTY-EIGHT

I was awakened to the sound of frustrated voices, arguing outside my door. There seemed to be some confusion over which guard was on duty outside my room. The door to the bedroom slammed open, and I sat up quickly, surprised when Merrick stormed in.

"Where the hell is she?" he demanded, pointing to the empty spot in the corner where my guard was standing only hours before.

"I don't know, I've been sleeping."

"She should be here watching you! Why the hell isn't she here?"

"How the hell should I know? Maybe she decided she'd much rather be in Mexico? If your treatment of me is anything to go by, your hospitality is seriously lacking."

"What did you do to her? Tell me now, or I will break every finger in your pretty, little hand."

"You really are unbelievably stupid, aren't you? If I could

have figured out a way to do something to her, don't you think I would have used that time a little more wisely? Like to, oh, I don't know, escape maybe?" I sneered at him and leaned against the headboard. "But as I'm so obviously still your hapless prisoner, whatever is wrong is very much a product of your own glaring incompetence."

Merrick crossed the room and slapped me so hard, a light exploded behind my eyes. "Don't think that you can hide behind your little admirer forever. I'm happy to play his little game for now. But don't you ever forget that I'm the one who decides if you come out of this in one piece or in seven. And don't, not even for a moment, doubt that I can break you into seven pieces and still keep you alive."

"Will you ever actually tell me why you're keeping me alive? Or shall we continue to play charades?"

He slapped me again, this time, splitting my lip open. I spat the blood out onto the quilt where it splattered like a Rorschach test.

Merrick stormed out of the room, but not before slamming the door behind him. As soon as he was gone, I grabbed the knife from under the mattress and reopened the wound on my thigh, adding more blood to the bedspread. Since Merrick already knew I was bleeding, hopefully he wouldn't notice the scent of a little more blood. And if William didn't pick up my scent like a homing beacon as soon as he got close enough, I was pretty much flat out of ideas.

Sitting in the middle of the bed with my legs crossed, I kept trying to make my mind completely clear. The energy that I absorbed from the two guards earlier still coursed through my veins. I tried to steady myself. Freedom was so close, I could almost taste it, and my anticipation soon had me twitching like a hopped-up junkie looking for her next fix.

Some shouting came from the lower levels of the house, and someone sent up an alarm. I could hear screams that were coming from the trees outside, being carried back towards the house on the night breeze. It looked like the cavalry was finally here, and they weren't coming quietly.

I walked over to the window and looked up at the moon, so full and round in the sky, as wisps of glowing clouds floated across it. It would provide plenty of light for our escape.

I looked down and saw shadows moving quickly towards the edge of the tree line. William was down there, and I could almost feel him. If he were here, there was no doubt in my mind he could feel me too. I wasn't sure if the washcloth with my blood on it was enough for him to taste and be able to sense me, but it looked like he didn't need all that much.

I turned at the sound of steps thundering up the stairs and down the hallway, holding the paring knife tightly in my hand. It wouldn't do much against a vampire, but I could cut Merrick's head clean off with it even if I had to sit there and saw away at it for the next half hour. I would too, if it meant getting out of this room.

"You little bitch!" Merrick screamed as he crashed into the room and flew at me in a blind rage.

In my moment of fear, I couldn't grasp my energy, and my power just slipped away from me like so many silken threads.

We tumbled to the floor with him on top of me, snapping his fangs at my face like a savage animal intent on tearing it clean off.

"You've ruined everything!" he screamed. "Everything!"

I grabbed him by his ears, trying to hold his face away from me as he stared down at me, his eyes burning with fury.

All of a sudden, the pressure of his weight was removed in a rush and he flew over the bed. I was instantly looking up into William's smirking face. Damn! I'd never been so happy to see his smug expression before in my life.

"Look out!" I barely got the words out before Merrick tackled William and the two of them crashed through the bedroom window in a hail of splintered wood and shattered glass shards.

"Oh, my God!" I shrieked as I scrambled off the floor to shove my head out the window. The two of them were down below, still tearing into one another.

I had no time to waste. Grabbing my paring knife from where it dropped, I ran out of the room and clattered down the stairs to the main floor where all hell had broken loose. Everywhere I looked, vampires were clawing at one another, all of them trying to get the upper hand.

I slammed backwards into a wall as a vampire rushed passed me, Anastasia was not far behind, swinging an axe at his head. She stopped and held the axe high before heaving it and letting it fly. The blade buried itself deeply into her quarry's skull. Sashaying up to the fallen body, she pulled the axe free before swinging it down across the vampire's neck, thereby cleaving its head from his shoulders. A few moments later, the slain vampire was no more than a large pile of ash.

"Holy shit, Ana!" I gushed, amazed at the sight.

"Vanessa!" she looked up at me and grinned.

"Behind you!" I yelled, pointing at the vampire I spotted there.

Swinging around in one fluid motion, she deftly decapitated the vampire in a single, smooth stroke, and he fell headless onto his knees in front of her. Planting a heeled boot in the body's chest, she kicked it over backwards away from her.

The back of my neck began to burn and an arm wrapped around it. Gripping the wrist and forearm, I bent over forward, allowing my assailant's momentum to whip him over my shoulder where he landed with a crash on the floor, flat on his back. Straddling him, I dropped to my knees on his chest and bent over him. I took his face into my hands, digging my nails into the sides of it.

I let the hunger sweep over me again before sucking every bit of energy from him in one long pull. The room swayed and my head rushed as I stood up again. He began to shake and foam at the mouth before the black veins crawled all over his skin and he finally lay still.

A vampire rushed at me from the side and I shot my hand out, grabbing him by the throat. His eyes widened in fear and I grinned before our mouths came together in a crash of teeth. I barely registered the feeling of his fangs piercing my lip, and had sucked all the energy from him before being mildly annoyed that he cut me.

Releasing my grip on his throat, I let his body fall to my feet. Euphoria ran through me and I had to giggle before bursting into laughter. My vision blazed red as I took in the mayhem around me.

"Ana, I need to find any surviving humans. Lend me your axe?"

"Sure," Anastasia tossed her axe at me and I caught it by the long handle before racing for the basement stairs.

At the bottom of the stairs, I turned and ran down the long hallway, passing the room where I was held for days.

Naked lightbulbs hung from the ceiling all the way down the length of the corridor. They must have built this hidden extension after the house. From up above, no one would guess this was down here. Not only did it serve as perfect holding cells for the newly turned vampires, and their prey, but it also ensured the vampires' safety by providing a well-concealed sanctuary out of the sun during the daylight hours.

I held the axe with both hands at the ready as I ran, but there were no more doorways, just a long expanse of concrete walls. There were no vampires down below to challenge me, or guarding the humans, They must have all gone up above to battle with Elizabeth's task force.

The rank smell of blood, rotting flesh, and soiled clothes grew stronger the further down the corridor I went until I finally came upon a large metal door. It was slightly ajar. Adjusting the grip of the axe in both hands, I used my foot to push the door open wider, fully prepared for an ambush or attack.

"Oh, God!" I brought my hand up to my nose to mask the smell as I bent over, gagging.

The room reeked of sick, unwashed people, and human waste. From the doorway, there seemed to be ten lifeless bodies piled up on the floor, and every one of them was dead. No wonder there was no one down here to stop us from trying to free them. They were probably all killed as soon as the alarm was sounded. Sadly, there was nothing I could do for them now.

Turning my back on the putrid scene, I ran down the hall to the staircase, my lungs burning with rage. So much human life being destroyed and wiped out without a single care or thought. That was what lay in store for the human race if the renegades had their way. Doomed to living half lives in chained, abusive servitude, and being fed on constantly. To be passed around with no more consideration than one would show to a basket of fries.

The kitchen was empty when I got back upstairs, but I could hear yelling outside. The majority of the fighting must have spilled outside the house, so I headed for the front door. I really hoped the guys left a few asses for me to kick.

William, Thatcher and Anastasia had Merrick on his knees, surrounded. I ran forward, only then finally starting to feel safe.

"William," I called to him, but a movement by the tree line caught my eye.

"I think that's the last of them," Bull said as he came forward.

"You!" I screamed as my vision blazed, blinding me with rage.

In my rushed message to William, I completely forgot to warn him about Bull. Now, here he was, standing casually as if he never handed me over to our enemies. He practically wrapped me up with a satin bow and put an apple in my mouth.

I flew at him, shrieking, with my axe held high. I was so ready to claim his head, along with his lying tongue. Thatcher moved to intercept me, but I slammed my axe into his shoulder with the flat of the blade, knocking him flying. Nothing could get between me and my prey.

Understanding flashed in Bull's eyes as he watched me rushing at him. I was happy, so happy that he knew exactly why he was about to die.

He jumped back, dodging the swing of my axe, and said, "Think you're going to be the hero to take me down, little one?"

"And gladly, you traitorous piece of shit!" I swung again, this time, slicing his arm, but inflicting no real damage.

"What the hell is going on?" Thatcher demanded.

"He gave them John!" I screamed, blinded by hunger and outrage, "and he gave them me!"

William was past me in a flash, knocking him backwards and into a tree, "How could you betray us like that?" he demanded.

"Because the way we have been forced to live is unnatural," Bull hissed. His normally soft tone, was now the voice of a stranger.

"Guys, Merrick is getting away," Anastasia hollered to us from the ground where Merrick had tossed her. She was pointing to the trees. I suddenly saw a flash of bright blonde hair and knew that Colleen wasn't far behind him.

William pulled a stake out of his pocket, and instantly jammed it as far as it would go into Bull's chest before pulling it out again.

Bull mouthed soundless words before crumbling into ash. I was a little disappointed that I wasn't the one to do it, but at least, he got what he deserved.

"We have to catch Merrick and Colleen," I said, tugging on William's arm.

He started towards the woods before stopping and turning back to me. Grabbing me in a bone-crushing embrace, he kissed me fiercely before pressing his forehead on mine for a moment. He released me just as quickly.

Thatcher, Anastasia, William and I ran at full speed and headed for the trees to catch Merrick. He had too much to answer for and we would not let him slip through our fingers. If we lost him now, we might never find him again.

"Aaah!" I screamed as I slapped a hand to the back of my neck. It felt as if the flesh were being peeled from it with a blazing, iron, fire poker. Lachlan was here.

"Vanessa!" His wild scream ricocheted off the trees, surrounding me and stopping me dead in my tracks. An icy-cold fear took hold of my heart as I stood there, too afraid to turn around.

Finally, I heard pounding and turned and looked up, only to see him standing on the roof of the house. He was staring down at me with madness and betrayal in his eyes. And at that moment, I knew he must've seen William kissing me, and would probably tear my heart out for it.

I turned and ran blindly into the trees, my fear overtaking my grip on my powers. I crashed wildly through the branches, stumbling over sticks and loose rocks, and the underbrush tangled around my ankles. My legs burned with the effort to push myself ever faster, to get as far away from him as possible without stopping. If I stopped, I was dead.

I didn't have a stake, or my guns, only the axe. An axe that was feeling heavier and heavier with every step I took. I could hear branches whipping behind me as Lachlan gained on me faster. I kept pushing myself forward, while trying to squeeze out every single spare inch of my lead.

I was completely lost, with nothing to guide me. The only light came from the full moon overhead.

I broke through the trees into a wide clearing and sped into the center of it. The sound of tree branches breaking and parting behind me made my heart beat so fast and hard, it felt as though it would explode any moment.

Screaming in desperation, rage, and fear, I turned to face him. His beautiful, pale face glowed in the moonlight, and his hair shone like smooth obsidian. Desolation had an angelic face, but I refused to let this night be my last. I fought too hard and held on too long to let him claim me now.

"Vanessa," he said, and the sound of his voice burned my skin. I wanted to just lie down in the field and weep until death took me.

My ragged breathing was loud in my ears as I took one step backwards, and then another, wielding the axe high in front of me with shaking hands.

"Get away from me!" My voice came out in a broken whisper, but I knew he could hear every word.

Rage and pain flashed across his face as he took another slow step towards me.

"How could you do this to me, Vanessa, to us? I love you, and you betrayed me. So many of my brothers and sisters are dead."

"What about the dead on your hands?" I screamed,

taking another slow step back. "All of the people you and your so-called family have killed over these past months. The people you kept locked up and tortured in your cellar. The bodies that I found down there tonight. All of them dead in the blink of an eye, and for what?"

"What good would they be to anyone if we let them free? They knew their place. And understood what they really were. None of them wanted freedom."

"And where have you been this whole time, huh? Hiding like the coward you are while the rest of them died? I didn't see you in there trying to stop any of it."

"You challenge my loyalty?" Outrage fuelled his booming voice.

"No," I said, my voice shaking as I tried to pull myself up straighter and look him in the eyes. "I'm challenging your manhood."

He was across the field and upon me in a flash, the breadth of him taking up my vision. He seemed to be twice his former size; either that, or I somehow shrank to half of mine. The creature in front of me was the true face of vampire, a savage killer, a bloodthirsty monster. Blood, hunger and insanity, his honest face. He and his kind would sweep across the world and drink us dry, leaving nothing in their wakes but the empty husks of our former humanity.

"You would have been my queen," he whispered, trailing one finger down the side of my face.

Fury overtook me when I heard his audacity. How dare

he lay a hand on me after the hell he put me through! How dare he even stand in front of me now and try to call his feelings for me *love!* To bastardize and taint everything that was simple and pure and true with his sick, twisted obsession!

I spat in his face, and let the power roll over me, pounding like trapped thunder. "I would never be your queen," I replied.

Dropping the axe, I brought both of my hands up and smashed the flat of my palms into his chest. The impact knocked him onto his back and sent him sliding across the ground, leaving a trail of compressed grass.

"You think I could ever, in a million years, deign to lower myself to be with you? You murderous, delusional, psychotic piece of shit?"

I advanced on him as he scrambled to his feet, and watched him from deep inside myself, cocooned in warmth and certainty. I rode the hunger like a wild bronco between my thighs. I gave it free rein to do as it chose. There was no need to hold back here, in this silent place where the moon looked down and kept all secrets.

I felt like I was floating above the grass, standing there in front of him before the intention was even fully formed in my mind. Our eyes locked and I smiled softly, no doubt left in my mind that he was completely mine.

"On. Your. Knees," I commanded with a hand on his shoulder I rested it there as he sank to the ground, his eyes unblinking, but still boring into mine.

"Now tilt your head back," I whispered.

Fully enthralled, he obliged me, tilting his head up to the sky. His beautiful green eyes glittered like the finest emeralds, and I saw the reflection of the moon in his irises.

A flock of bats was startled out of the trees and danced across the night sky, disappearing over the forest. I brushed the hair off Lachlan's face, my fingertips just barely grazing his tresses.

Their were so many ways I could do this. So many ways that he deserved to die. I could take his head. Or walk into the trees and find the perfect branch to shove into his cold, unbeating heart. But there was only one way that seemed right. A fitting end to the nightmare. I buried my hands in his hair and leaned down, gently pressing my mouth on his.

"I hope you burn in hell," I whispered.

I drew the energy from him slowly, stretching it out even though every part of me screamed to inhale it as quickly as possible. I wanted it to be slow and painful. I wanted him to feel every last bit of his life leaving him. Along with the fear and helplessness that he so cavalierly inflicted upon his victims. He knelt there, unable to move or free himself. I didn't care whether or not it was true justice. It was surely vengeance, and that was mine.

I let go of him and took a step back, watching him in the throes of final death. I wanted to memorize every moment of it. The black veins began to creep over his skin. At last, he just knelt there, a delicate statue of ash, staring blindly up at me.

I took my hands and opened them wide on either side of his head. Inhaling deeply, I let it out in a solid stream before slapping my hands together as hard as possible.

His head exploded between my fingertips in a rain of ash just before I closed my eyes and collapsed.

CHAPTER TWENTY-NINE

Rolling over, I pressed my nose more deeply into the tea rose-scented cloud. My whole body was bathed in warmth, and I feared opening my eyes, lest I awaken from whatever dream of heaven I was having. Every inch of my body felt as if it were being caressed by nirvana and I dreaded having the wonderful moment end.

Moving my hand up to cradle the cloud under my head, I heard a soft crinkling. Then it suddenly dawned on me that heaven was beginning to feel a whole lot like very soft sheets. I brought my hand to my stomach and felt the area. Nirvana was rapidly starting to take on the form of a short, satin nightgown.

I opened a single eye very quickly before shutting it again. *Oh, please, God, let this be real.* Opening my eyes again, I scanned the room around me. The sheets on the bed were a beautiful robin's egg blue and unbelievably soft to the touch, and my head was cradled in a small mountain of down pillows. Easing the sheets back, I took in the short, black satin nightgown I was wearing, adjusting one of the thin straps that slipped off my shoulder during the night.

The nightgown ended above my thigh, revealing pure, unblemished skin with no sign of the cuts that I previously inflicted. I was back in my bed in William's apartment, surrounded by sweet-scented comfort, and not a hint of dirt or blood on my body. It almost seemed as if the whole ordeal was one terrible, long, unbelievably bad dream. Someone even took the trouble of combing out my hair for me. It swished over my shoulders in a heavy, mahogany curtain.

I tried to take in my surroundings, but still couldn't believe I was safe at home. The bright summer sun poured into my bedroom, promising a gorgeous day, and I burst into uncontrollable sobs.

The tears racked my body as I buried my face in my hands. All of my fright and loss swarmed back to me, mingled with some relief to be alive and guilt for the lives I was unable to save.

They came for me in the end, William and the others. They came for me and brought me home. I never felt more grateful.

When the tears finally subsided, I wiped my eyes and got out of bed. It was a gorgeous day outside, and I was determined to feel the sun on my face. I skipped down the stairs to the living room and rushed to the balcony doors, throwing them open and running outside. The sounds of the city floated up to greet me. An indistinguishable chatter of the people down below, mixed with the honking traffic and the few birds that flew past, all calling to one another. I never heard anything so beautiful as boring, everyday, human life. I clenched the railing, letting the warmth of it heat the palms of my hands as I closed my eyes and soaked up the rays.

A wave of exhaustion overtook me and I swayed against the rail, tightening my grip on it to stay upright. It was such a gorgeous day, but whether I wanted to admit it or not, I couldn't keep my eyes open for much longer to enjoy it at this rate.

I slipped back inside and closed the sliding glass door behind me. The cool, crisp breeze of the air conditioner chilled my face as I slipped silently back upstairs. I walked down the hall until I came to stand in front of the closed door to William's room.

I pressed my hand against the door and paused for a moment, simply feeling the smooth wood beneath my palm before grasping the doorknob and turning it as quietly as I could. My feet sank into the plush carpet of his bedroom, which muffled the sound of my crossing the room to climb into his inviting king-sized bed.

The room was pitch-black inside, but I didn't need the light. I could sense him as my eyes slowly adjusted from the brightness outside. I knew exactly where he was.

When I reached the bed, I pulled the covers back and climbed in beside him. Curling my body around his side, I rested my head on his still chest and closed my eyes, sighing in contentment.

A firm arm wrapped around me, pressing me into a solid chest, and the feeling of fingers dancing up and down my back sent a flutter of shivers down my spine. I kept my eyes closed and enjoyed the sensation as I tightened my grip on William and pressed a kiss on his bare chest.

"I thought I lost you, love," he whispered over the top of my head.

"Only misplaced me for a minute, but I'm back now."

"When you didn't return that night, I tore the city apart, looking everywhere for you, but I couldn't find you anywhere. Your blood had already left my system and I couldn't sense you any longer."

"Well, it's nice to see that you left at least one or two buildings standing in your quest to find me."

He pressed a kiss to my forehead and sighed in frustration. "I'm serious, pet. I can't remember the last time I felt so helpless. I can't even imagine what you must have gone through."

I shuddered and snuggled more tightly against him. "I don't want to talk about it right now. I can't, not yet."

"It's all right, I'm not asking you to."

"I'm so glad that you did find me. I don't even know how long I was gone. But don't, don't tell me. I don't want to know yet. I just want to lie here with you where we're safe."

My breath caught as William rolled us over so he was stretched out on top of me. My eyes finally adjusted to the darkness, and the tender expression on his face was the most beautiful thing I ever saw. Reaching up, I brushed the pads of my fingers across his lips and along his jaw, exploring the lines of his face.

I sighed as his lips pressed against mine. That feeling had become as familiar to me as my own skin during the time we were together, and I welcomed it with open arms.

His arms wrapped around me and he pulled me up toward him, tilting my head back so he could gain deeper access to my mouth. His kisses turned more demanding as he thrust his tongue into my mouth, demanding that I meet every one with a parry of my own. My need for him grew, but not so much for his energy, as for the man in my arms, every solid inch of him.

I buried my nose in his neck and inhaled his scent, fresh earth and spiciness, as it hit the back of my throat and heightened my need. His hands roamed over my body, exploring every inch of me. I flushed when his hand landed between my legs for the briefest of moments before moving on.

He gathered the bottom of my nightgown and slid it up over my waist, the fabric sending sparks along my skin as it moved higher. With his other hand, he slipped the thin straps down off my shoulders, and I pulled my arms free, letting the black satin gather around my waist. I lay back, completely exposed to him.

I emitted a sharp gasp when he grabbed me by my ankles and pulled me abruptly closer, until my breasts were right in line with his mouth. A position that he obviously intended to take every advantage of. He suckled one, then the other before taking my mouth with his quickly, one more time.

"Never scare me like that again," he stated. His voice was rough and tight as he stared into my eyes.

"I won't," I promised.

He rolled me over onto my stomach and trailed kisses down my back to the base of my spine. Then, taking my hips in his hands, he flipped me onto my back again.

"Promise me again," he demanded, taking a firm hold of my thighs and spreading my legs.

"I promise."

The first swipe of his tongue had me arching up off the bed. He pressed down more firmly on my thighs to keep me in place before covering me with his whole mouth. He ran his tongue up and down my core in rhythmic undulations, refusing to release me as I grasped the bedspread, and the sound of my heavy breathing filled the room.

He pressed a kiss to my inner thigh before nipping at it gently, then slid his body back up alongside mine. He replaced his tongue with two fingers, slipping them inside me, and moving them in and out. Shuddering, I clamped down on them and bit his shoulder while he stroked me.

"God, you're so wet," he growled.

I was unable to reply, too blissful with what his fingers were doing to me.

He spread my legs open wider, and I felt his rigid length pressing against my entrance. Every muscle in my body was wound tight in anticipation as I looked up into his eyes. He thrust his hips forward and entered me, stretching me to accommodate him before taking in his entire length.

My body arched right up off the bed to meet his as he thrust in and out of me. I wrapped my legs around his waist to keep him tightly next to me.

The hunger inside me flared up and started to overtake me, so I rolled us over and straddled him from above. I let my head fall back as I continued to ride him, rocking back and forth. He grasped my hips and matched me for every thrust.

I cried out as my completion overtook me, my body shaking so hard, I was sure it would fall apart. Shortly afterwards, William's cries matched my own, and we collapsed onto the bed, panting.

He tilted my head back and kissed me softly before tucking my head under his chin. I sighed contentedly and then surrendered to a peaceful sleep.

I sat with the rest of the task force in Elizabeth's manor, feeling grateful for the few days of down time Elizabeth gave me in order to recover from what happened. Now, I had to get back to work.

There seemed to be a gaping hole in the room where Bull used to be, and we all still felt the sting of his betrayal. The fact that he was even assigned to the task force in the first place was a huge wakeup call. We had no way of knowing when he turned against the coven, before or after he was recruited to the team.

Elizabeth sat behind her giant, oak desk. She was looking troubled, and her brows were furrowed on her perfect face. It was the first time I ever saw anything even remotely close to what I could call a wrinkle in her flawless skin. A blemish on the face of perfection frozen in time long ago.

"So you're telling me," she began in a deathly quiet tone, "that Merrick got away?" She stood up from her desk and leaned forward, her head poised like a snake about to strike. It took everything I had not to take a few steps back to establish some distance between us. If she completely lost it, I really didn't want to be directly in her line of fire.

"Yes," William took a step towards the desk and looked her straight into her eyes. "Merrick and Colleen escaped into the woods. When we couldn't find them, we doubled back and found Vanessa, who had already killed her stalker. This, Lachlan."

Elizabeth's eye twitched as she put a hand up to her face with a sigh. "I am, of course, pleased that you retrieved Vanessa before it was too late. But we still have the leader of the renegades running around, and he's still on the loose out there," she yelled.

"No, actually, we don't," my eyes opened wide as the words came out. Oh crap! Was that me? Right. Like I hadn't already learned my lesson about contradicting pissed off vampires.

"Oh? What do you mean? Have you got him hidden somewhere? Tied up with a little bow for me?" She smiled at me, but it didn't reach her eyes.

"I mean, Merrick isn't the leader of the Renegades. A general maybe, but there's no way he's running the whole thing. It is much, much bigger than that."

I looked at everyone in the room and took a deep breath before resting my hip against Elizabeth's desk. It was time they all knew.

"Merrick told me they were working on something much larger. It wasn't about a couple dozen vampires in Silverlake that wanted to feed off people and make kills as they saw fit. It's about *all vampires*, *everywhere*, getting sick of living in the shadows, and wanting to put humans in their rightful place. Housing them like animals to be harvested as food. Breed, feed, slaughter, and repeat. This faction was just one small piece of a widespread movement. They intend to out you guys. All of you. To show the world you're not only here, but you're taking over."

"But that's complete madness," said Anastasia. "Powerful or not, the humans far outnumber us."

"I know. And that's why they intend to turn as many new vampires as possible, so that the numbers will also be on their side."

I looked at Elizabeth, who took her seat again as I spoke, and complete disbelief clouded her features.

"And there's more," I looked at William with worry in my eyes. "They were keeping me alive for a reason, and it wasn't just because of Lachlan. Merrick was the one that initially told Lachlan that he should try, despite his twisted mind, to woo me. Then, after they had me, Merrick made threats about hurting me, and breaking me, but still keeping me alive. He wanted me dead. He hated me. But someone... someone else above him needs me alive for something. I just wasn't able to find out who and what."

William reached out and pulled me into his arms. "It doesn't matter. Whatever they want you for, they aren't going to get it, love. Do you hear me?"

I nodded and untangled myself from him. Now wasn't the time to lean on him, we didn't have the luxury.

"If that's not enough, we still have to figure out how they managed to shield themselves from being sensed by other vampires. I don't know how we're going to stop this, but we have no choice. If we let them expose you, it's all over. The whole world will go to war; and it will be the most brutal slaughtering of humanity the human race has ever seen. We can't let that happen. I don't know how far this plan has spread yet, but maybe if we're lucky, we can stop it before it goes too far."

Elizabeth looked at each of us in turn before nodding. "We have to fix this. Find Merrick, weed out the other

Renegades in Silverlake, and make them talk. Do whatever you have to do in order to keep this from spreading; do you hear me?"

We left her office with renewed determination. I intended to do whatever it took to protect my new family and the humans I loved. Smiling, I climbed into the passenger seat of William's car as the hunger began to rise inside me.

Time to get to work.

COMING SOON

BOOK 2 OF

THE VANESSA KENSLEY SERIES

SANGUINE MOON

(TURN PAGE FOR PREVIEW)

CHAPTER ONE

Either this guy was a friggin' track star when he was alive or I'm out of shape from indulging all of those chocolate chip cookie ice-cream sandwich cravings I've been having lately. The crisp air burned my lungs as my feet hammered down the rain-soaked grass. The rich, mineral scent of damp earth and green foliage assaulted my nose as I sprinted across the park grass, steadily closing the distance between the quarry and myself. Slipping on the grass, I skidded to a halt as he lunged over a cement park table without missing a beat. *Oh! To hell with this!*

The smooth, rosewood butt of my gun felt comforting and familiar in my hand as I raised my sig sauer and aimed for my target. Exhaling, I planted my feet and pulled the trigger in two quick successions. I winced at the sound of gunshots echoing through the park. That's what I deserved for not using a silencer, but it was too late to worry about it now, so taking aim again, I fired off two more shots.

The vampire stumbled and fell on one knee as the bullets struck his body. I really didn't care that the shots weren't fatal. There was something oh-so satisfying about knowing the liquid silver that spread quickly inside him was, no doubt, burning like hell. I held my gun down before running again, using his injuries as an opportunity to catch up. *Please, God, don't make me give up the ice-cream cookie sandwiches!*

"Well, that was fun," I said while exhaling heavily and trying to catch my breath. I pointed my gun at his head and added, "but why don't we just cut the shit, yeah? Where the hell is Merrick?"

A sneer flashed across his face and he spat on my boot. The thick glob stuck to the tip of my steel-toed combats in a solid clump. Bad move on his part; you just don't disrespect the shoes.

"Merrick? Sorry, never heard of him," he groaned.

"Right! Of course, you haven't," I nodded while keeping my gun pointed on him as I scanned the park. Swiftly grabbing my knife from my thigh, I plunged it into his shoulder right where it connected to his neck.

He screamed in pain as the silver-edged blade burned into him. Tendrils of smoke rose from his wound and the telltale odor of roasting flesh started to fill the air.

"Let's try that once again, shall we? Where... the hell... is Merrick?"

"I don't know," he hissed as he tried to pull away, but I kept a firm grip on the knife handle. "You think we all get together with him for tea parties and shit? He lit outta here, and I don't know where to."

I pulled the knife from his neck and backhanded him across the face with my gun, sending him sprawling into the wet grass.

"Well, then I guess I have no further use for you."

The soft sound of a snapping branch drew my attention and I scanned the trees behind us again, but the leaves were too dense to see anyone there.

"Oof!" The air came whooshing out of me as the vampire planted his foot in my stomach, taking advantage of my distraction long enough to knock me off balance.

I pointed the gun at him, but he kicked it out of my hand and continued to come at me, his tightly clenched fists swinging for my face.

I jumped back from the first swing and ducked under the second before coming up inside his arms and burying my fist in his stomach. The moment he doubled over, I brought my elbow down hard onto his back, sending him onto his knees before bringing my knee up into his face and knocking him over backwards.

"If you see Merrick, give him a message for me? Tell him to burn in hell!" I whipped out my stake and plunged it deeply into the vampire's heart.

Slowly standing up, I realized I was panting as the vampire briefly hardened before dissolving into ash.

"Never mind; I'll tell him myself!"

The rain started again and I wiped the fat raindrops out of my eyes and ran my hand over my head. Strands of hair came loose from my ponytail and were plastered on my face. I tilted my head back and let the rain wash my face clean of the sweat and frustration, just as it washed away the ashen body at my feet as if it never existed. But it had existed. And before it was ash, it was a vampire; and before becoming a vampire, he was a man. Maybe even a good man. But I couldn't dwell on that. It wasn't his life that mattered to me, only his afterlife, and his choices after his heart stopped beating while he continued to walk the earth. They were very bad choices.

I sniffed and frowned, then sniffed again. Lowering my face, I listened closely as the faint scent of marijuana reached my nostrils. *Shit. Someone is definitely watching me.* I walked over to where my gun lay as casually as possible, then meandered over to the trees where I heard the branch snapping earlier.

The bushes shook violently before a young man exploded from them, blind panic filling his eyes as they met mine. He hastily took off across the grass towards the parking lot. *Seriously? More running?*

I ran after him and tackled him from behind, dragging him to the ground.

"Get off me!" he yelled. "Help! Help!" He bucked wildly while clawing at the grass and desperately trying to extricate himself from my grasp.

I grabbed his belt and pulled myself up his body before flipping him over and covering his mouth with my hands. He swung at me and connected with my face, his punch catching me right below the eye.

"Ow! Fuck!" I removed one of my hands from his mouth and grabbed his wrist while keeping the other hand firmly on his face.

"Shut up, just shut up!" I snapped at him. "Everything will be okay, I swear, but you really need to stop yelling, seriously."

I couldn't help but feel sorry for him as the hot air inside him came out in bursts on the side of my hand and his eyes darted frantically back and forth. If I were he, the sight of what just happened here probably would have scared me witless too. But I couldn't just let him go. I had to make sure he forgot what he saw here tonight; and I couldn't do that until I got him to stop freaking out.

"Look, I want to let you up, okay? And I want to take my hand off your mouth, but I can't do either of those things until I'm sure that you won't scream your head off, or try to run, or do anything stupid like that, okay?"

He nodded his head really fast as his chest continued to rapidly rise up and down.

"I'm having a bit of a tough time believing you, so why don't you just take a few deep breaths for me, okay? Nice and easy, slowly in and out." I watched him carefully as he breathed deeply through his nose a few times and his heaving chest started to slow down.

"Okay, all right, there we go. Nice and easy. Now I'm going to take my hand away from your mouth. You just keep your eyes on me, okay? Just keep looking at me. Are you ready?"

He nodded slowly this time, and I smiled. What a complete shit show the night turned out to be! Another dead-end and a terrified witness. All I wanted now was to get out of the stupid rain and into my nice, warm bathtub. Was a cozy night at home really so much to ask for?

I kept a firm grip on his wrist (in case he got it into his head to try and take another swing at me) before slowly removing my hand from his mouth. When he didn't start yelling, I allowed myself to relax a little. Maybe everything would be okay after all.

"Hi," I said, but he didn't reply. Oh, well, silence was infinitely better than screaming. "I'm sure you're very scared and have lots of questions, but I promise you everything is going to be much better in a moment."

I let the energy flow over me as I opened myself up to the hunger and leaned in towards him, all the while keeping his gaze riveted on mine. One little kiss and I could easily put this mess of a night behind me.

"Hey! What's going on over there?" A homeless man was walking towards us, pushing a grocery cart heaped high with his treasured possessions.

The man beneath me shoved me off him with an unexpected burst of energy, the connection between us hopelessly lost by the vagrant's unwelcome arrival.

"Damn it!" I swore as I started to run after him.

He fled through the parking lot and across the busy street, dodging the traffic, and I followed after him through the four-car lanes. Hearing a double blast of a horn, I managed to jump back just in time to avoid being hit by an SUV. When the vehicle passed, I made the final dash to the other side of the street, but I couldn't see the witness anywhere.

"Shit!" I yelled as I looked up and down the street, trying to find him amongst the few people still hanging around. "Shit!" Elizabeth would have my ass when she found out about this.

I fished my cell phone out of my pocket and punched in William's phone number, continuing to silently curse myself as I waited for him to pick up.

"Hello, love, get anything useful?" His English accent

washed over me and I couldn't help smiling at the sound of it. Cocky, arrogant and a serious pain in my ass, but none of that prevented me from wanting to jump him the moment he got within ten feet. I was amazed that I managed to keep my hunger under control at all when he was around.

"We've got a problem," I closed my eyes and pinched the bridge of my nose. I could already feel the start of a tension headache coming on.

"What happened?" All humour vanished from his voice. A muffled sound came from his end of the line, followed by a thump and a sickening crunch.

"William? What the hell is going on over there?"

"Nothing to worry about, love, it's all under control. Hold on a moment, will you?" I leaned against the wall of the instant cash loan business and watched the cars speeding by, their windshield wipers swishing frantically back and forth as the rainfall increased .

I could hear lots of puffing and cursing over the line as William ostensibly dealt with his own problems. Looked like everyone was having an interesting night.

"Sorry about that, pet; you were saying?"

"Everything all right over there?"

"Oh, yeah, he was just young and stupid."

"And now dust?"

"Very much so. Now stop stalling and tell me what's wrong."

"Someone got away from me. A human someone. A, umm... human witness someone," I held my breath and anxiously waited for the news to sink in.

"Vanessa, love," William said sweetly, "a witness to what,

exactly?"

"He saw me dust my lead. I caught him hiding in the bushes and was about to glamour the memory away when we were suddenly interrupted and he used that moment to bolt. I lost him in traffic."

William was silent and I started to grow impatient. It wasn't like I didn't know how badly I screwed up, I really didn't need for him to emphasize the point with a dramatically-timed silence. This wasn't a goddamn spy movie after all.

"Will you please say something?" I snapped testily.

"Have fun telling Elizabeth," he laughed.

"You're a real asshole, you know that? I think I'll tell her from the safety of my own home."

"Aren't you coming over tonight?" His laughter was tempered by unmasked disappointment.

"No, I think I'm just going home and calling it a night. If Elizabeth doesn't have me killed, I'll call you tomorrow, all right?

"Sweet dreams, love," he whispered.

"Watch your back," I answered before hanging up the phone.